The Case of the
Sulky Girl

Erle Stanley Gardner

BALLANTINE BOOKS • NEW YORK

Copyright © 1933 by Erle Stanley Gardner
Copyright renewed 1961 by Erle Stanley Gardner

All rights reserved under International and Pan-American Copyright Conventions. Published in the United States by Ballantine Books, a division of Random House, Inc., New York, and simultaneously in Canada by Random House of Canada Limited, Toronto.

ISBN 0-345-37145-3

This edition published by arrangement with William Morrow and Company, Inc.

Printed in Canada

First Ballantine Books Edition: February 1992

10 9 8 7 6 5

Chapter 1

The girl walked past the secretary who held the door open, and surveyed the law office with eyes that showed just a trace of panic.

The secretary gently closed the door and the girl selected an old fashioned, high-backed, black leather chair. She sat down in it, crossed her legs, pulled her skirt down over her knees, and sat facing the door. After a moment, she pulled the skirt up for an inch or two, taking some pains to get just the effect she wanted. Then she leaned back so that her spun-gold hair showed to advantage against the shiny black leather of the big chair.

She looked pathetic and helpless as she sat in the big office, dwarfed by the huge proportions of the leather chair. And yet there was something about her which gave the impression of having deliberately brought about that effect. There was a hint of feline efficiency in the care with which she had placed herself, in the very perfection of her helplessness.

Judged by any standard, she was beautiful. Her hair was silken, her eyes large and dark, the cheekbones high, lips full and well formed. She was small, yet perfectly proportioned, and well groomed. Yet there was a studied immobility of expression; an effect of complete detachment as though she had surrounded herself with a protective wall.

The door from an inner office opened and Perry Mason walked into the room. He paused when he had advanced two steps from the door, surveying the girl with patient eyes that seemed to take in every detail of her appearance. She bore the scrutiny without change of position or expression.

"You're Mr. Mason?" she asked.

Mason didn't answer until he had walked around behind the flat-top desk and dropped into the swivel chair.

Perry Mason gave the impression of bigness; not the bigness of fat, but the bigness of strength. He was broad-shouldered and rugged-faced, and his eyes were steady and patient. Frequently those eyes changed expression, but the face never changed its expression of rugged patience. Yet there was nothing meek about the man. He was a fighter; a fighter who could, perhaps, patiently bide his time for delivering a knock-out blow, but who would, when the time came, remorselessly deliver that blow with the force of a mental battering ram.

"Yes," he said, "I'm Perry Mason. What can I do for you?"

The dark eyes studied him warily.

"I," said the girl, "am Fran Celane."

"Fran?" he asked, raising his voice.

"Short for Frances," she said.

"All right," said Perry Mason, "what can I do for you, Miss Celane?"

The dark eyes remained fastened on his face, but the girl's forefinger went exploring around the arm of the chair, picking at irregularities in the leather. There was something in the probing gesture which seemed an unconscious reflection of her mental attitude.

"I wanted to find out about a will," she said.

There was no change of expression in Perry Mason's steady, patient eyes.

"I don't go in much for wills," he told her. "I'm a trial lawyer. I specialize in the trial of cases, preferably before juries. Twelve men in a box—that's my specialty. I'm afraid I can't help you much on wills."

"But," she told him, "this will probably be a trial."

He continued to watch her with the emotionless scrutiny of his calm eyes.

"A will contest?" he asked.

"No," she said, "not exactly a contest. I want to know something about a trust provision."

2

"Well," he said with gentle insistence, "suppose you tell me exactly what it is you want to know."

"A party dies," she said, "and leaves a will containing a clause by which a beneficiary under the will . . ."

"That'll do," said Perry Mason, "don't try that line. This is a matter that you're interested in?"

"Yes."

"Very well then," he said, "give me the facts, and quit beating about the bush."

"It's my father's will," she said. "His name was Carl Celane: I'm an only child."

"That's better," he told her.

"There's a lot of money coming to me under that will, something over a million dollars."

Perry Mason showed interest.

"And you think there'll be a trial over it?" he asked.

"I don't know," she said. "I hope not."

"Well, go ahead," said the lawyer.

"He didn't leave the money to me outright," she said. "He left it in a trust."

"Who's the trustee?" asked Mason.

"My uncle, Edward Norton."

"All right," he said, "go on."

"There's a provision in the will that if I should marry before I'm twenty-five, my uncle has the right, at his option, to give me five thousand dollars from the trust fund, and to turn the balance over to charitable institutions."

"How old are you now?" asked Mason.

"Twenty-three."

"When did your father die?"

"Two years ago."

"The will's been probated then, and the property distributed?"

"Yes," she said.

"All right," he told her, speaking rapidly now, "if the provision in regard to the trust was carried through in the decree of distribution, and there was no appeal from that decree, there can be no collateral attack, except under exceptional circumstances."

3

Her restless finger picked at the arm of the chair, and the nail made little noises as it dug into the leather.

"That's what I wanted to ask you about," she said.

"All right," said Mason, "go ahead and ask me."

"Under the will," she said, "my uncle controls the trust moneys. He can invest them any way he wants, and he can give me whatever money he thinks I should have. When I'm twenty-seven he's to give me the principal if he thinks that the possession of such a large sum of money won't spoil my life. Otherwise, he's to buy me an annuity of five hundred dollars a month for life, and give the balance to charity."

"Rather an unusual trust provision," said Perry Mason, tonelessly.

"My father," she said, "was rather an unusual man, and I was just a little bit wild."

"All right," said Mason. "What's the trouble?"

"I want to get married," she said, and, for the first time her eyes dropped from his.

"Have you spoken to your uncle about it?"

"No."

"Does he know that you want to get married?"

"I don't think so."

"Why not wait until you're twenty-five?"

"No," she said, raising her eyes again, "I want to get married now."

"As I understand your interpretation of the will," ventured Perry Mason cautiously, "there's complete discretion vested in your uncle?"

"That's right."

"Well, don't you think that the first thing to do would be to sound him out and see how he would feel about your marriage?"

"No," she said shortly, clipping the word out explosively.

"Bad blood between you and your uncle?" he asked.

"No," she said.

"You see him frequently?"

"Every day."

"Do you talk with him about the will?"

"Never."

4

"You go to see him on other business then?"

"No. I live in the house with him."

"I see," said Perry Mason, speaking in that calm expressionless voice. "Your uncle is intrusted with a whole lot of money, and given a discretion which is rather unusual. I take it that he's under bond?"

"Oh yes," she said, "he's under bond. As far as that's concerned, the trust fund is perfectly safe. My uncle is meticulously careful—too careful. That is, he's too methodical in *everything* he does."

"Does he have money of his own?" asked the lawyer.

"Lots of it," she said.

"Well," said Mason, with just a trace of impatience, "what do you want me to do?"

"I want you," she said, "to fix it so I can get married."

He stared at her for several seconds in silent, meditative appraisal.

"Have you got a copy of the will or of the decree of distribution?" he asked at length.

She shook her head.

"Do I need one?" she asked.

The lawyer nodded.

"I can't very well give you an interpretation of a legal document until I've seen the document."

"But I told you exactly what it said."

"You gave me your version of what it said. There may be a great deal of difference."

She spoke swiftly, impatiently. "I understand that conditions in a will which prevent a person from marrying can be set aside."

"That's not correct," he told her. "Generally speaking, a condition by which a party is prevented from marrying is considered against public policy and void. But that's subject to certain qualifications, particularly in the case of trusts of the type which are known as 'spendthrift' trusts. Apparently the trust which was created under your father's will was one of this nature.

"Moreover, you note that there is no restriction upon marriage after you have reached the age of twenty-five. As a

5

matter of fact, your uncle seems to be given a wide discretion in the matter, and the provisions of the will as you have given them to me merely indicate the circumstances under which he is to exercise his discretion.''

She seemed suddenly to have lost her protective poise. Her voice rose. ''Well, I've heard a lot about you,'' she said. ''They say that some lawyers tell people what they can do and what they can't do, but that *you* always fix things so a person can do what he wants to.''

Mason smiled, the smile of wisdom garnered from bitter experience, of knowledge amassed from the confidences of thousands of clients.

''Perhaps,'' he said, ''that's partially true. A man can nearly always think his way out of any situation in which he finds himself. It's merely a paraphrase of the old saying that where there's a will there's a way.''

''Well,'' she told him, ''there's a will in this case. I want the way.''

''Whom do you want to marry?'' he asked abruptly.

The eyes did not waver, but stared steadily at him in dark appraisal.

''Rob Gleason,'' she said.

''Does your uncle know him?''

''Yes.''

''Does he approve of him?''

''No.''

''You love him?''

''Yes.''

''He knows of this provision in the will?''

Her eyes lowered.

''I think perhaps he does now. But he didn't,'' she said.

''What do you mean he didn't?'' asked the lawyer.

There could be no question now that the eyes were avoiding his.

''Just an expression,'' she said, ''I didn't mean anything by it.''

Perry Mason studied her intently for a few minutes.

''And I take it you want to marry him very much.''

She looked at him then, and said in a voice that was vibrant

6

with feeling: "Mr. Mason, don't make any mistake about it. I am *going* to marry Rob Gleason. You can take that as being final. You have got to find some way by which I can do it. That's all! I'm leaving that end of it up to you. I'm putting myself in your hands. I am going to get married."

He started to say something, then paused to study her carefully before he spoke.

"Well," he said, "you seem to know pretty much what you want."

"I do," she flared.

"Suppose then, you come back at this time to-morrow morning. In the meantime I will have looked up the court records."

She shook her head.

"To-morrow morning," she protested, "is too long. Can't you do it this afternoon?"

Perry Mason's patient eyes dwelt steadily on her face.

"Perhaps," he said. "Will four o'clock suit you?"

She nodded.

"Very well," he told her, getting to his feet. "Come back then. You can leave your name and address with my secretary in the outer office."

"I've already done that," she told him, arising from the chair and smoothing the line of her skirt. "I'll be back at four."

She didn't look back as she walked across the office, opened the door and swept out into the outer room.

Perry Mason sat at his desk, narrowing his eyes in thoughtful appraisal, as he watched the door through which the young woman had gone.

After a moment he extended a sturdy forefinger, and jabbed a button on the side of his desk.

A young man with unruly hair, and a face that seemed pathetically eager, popped his head through the doorway leading from a law library, then entered the room.

"Frank," said Perry Mason, "go up to the court house and find the papers in the Celane Estate. A Frances Celane was given property amounting to more than a million dollars in trust. The name of the trustee is Edward Norton. Check

7

the decree of distribution, and also the will. Make copies of the trust provisions, then get back here as soon as you can.''

The boy blinked his eyes swiftly, twice.

"Celane?" he asked.

"Yes," said Mason. "Carl Celane."

"And Norton?"

"Yes, Edward Norton," said Mason.

"Thank you," said the boy. He turned abruptly, crossed the office with nervous, self conscious haste, as though painfully aware of the gaze of Perry Mason, and plunged into the outer office.

Perry Mason rang for his secretary.

Della Street, his secretary, was about twenty-seven years old. Her manner radiated assurance and efficiency. She pushed open the door from the outer office.

"You rang?" she asked.

"Yes," he told her, "come in."

She stepped into the office and closed the door gently behind her.

"Let's check our impressions," he said, "about that girl."

"How do you mean?" she asked.

He stared at her moodily.

"I think," he said, "that I put the words in your mouth. You said she looked trapped or sulky. Now I am wondering which it was."

"Does it make a lot of difference?" asked Della Street.

"I think it does," he told her. "In your impressions you are usually right and you had a chance to see her when she wasn't posing. She started to pose as soon as she came into my office."

"Yes," said Della Street, "she's the type that would be good at posing."

"She sat down in the chair," he told her, "and figured just how to hold her head, just how to cross her knees and arrange her skirt, just what kind of an expression to put on her face."

"Did she tell you the truth?" asked Della Street.

"None of them tell the truth the first time," he told her, "at least the women don't. That's why I want to know just what kind of an impression she made on you. Did she look trapped, or did she look sulky?"

Della Street spoke thoughtfully, as though weighing her words carefully.

"She looked both trapped and sulky," she said, "as though she got caught in some kind of a trap and had turned sulky."

"Are you sure," he asked, "that it wasn't panic?"

"How do you mean?" she wanted to know.

"Lots of people," he said, "try to put on a poker face when they are in a panic and when they try to put on a poker face they look sulky."

"And you think she was in a panic?" asked Della Street.

"Yes," he said, slowly. "I think she was in a panic. I think she's a self-willed little devil who nearly always gets her own way and who has an ungovernable temper. I think she's caught in some sort of a trap and is trying to get out. When we know her better we'll find out more about her temper."

"A hell-cat?" asked Della Street.

He twisted his lips in a smile.

"Let's call her a hell-kitten," he said.

Chapter 2

Della Street pushed open the door of Perry Mason's private office. There was something almost surreptitious in her demeanor as she slipped through the door and carefully closed it behind her.

Perry Mason was seated at his desk. His eyes squinted carefully.

"Why the secrecy?" he asked.

She advanced a step or two into the room and looked at him, then turned to glance at the door and make certain that it was closed.

"There's a man in the outer office who gives his name as Robert Gleason."

"What does he want?" asked Perry Mason.

"He wants information about Miss Celane."

"The one who has just been here?"

"Yes."

"You didn't tell him she had just been here?"

"Certainly not."

"What did he say?"

"He said that he wanted to see you. I asked him what the nature of his business was and he said it was about a client of yours. I told him that he would have to give me the name of the client and tell me something of the nature of the business. He said that it was about Miss Celane and he was very anxious to see you about her."

"All right," Mason said, "what did you tell him?"

"I told him that I wasn't familiar with the names of your clients; that he would have to be more specific concerning his business. He's frightfully excited."

"What's he excited about?" asked Mason. "The girl, his business, or what?"

"I don't know. He's excited and nervous."

Mason squared his shoulders as though reaching a sudden decision.

"Send him in," he said, "I want to talk with him."

She nodded and turned, holding the door open.

"You may come in," she said.

There was the rustle of motion. A man came into the room who radiated restlessness. He was a thin man with a very pointed nose and large ears. He walked with nervous jerky steps. He was in the late twenties or early thirties.

"You're Mason, the lawyer?" he asked, his voice quick with impatience.

Perry Mason surveyed him with patient eyes peering out from under heavy eyebrows.

"Sit down," he said.

His visitor hesitated, then sat down on the edge of one of the straight-backed chairs.

"Now, what did you want?" asked Perry Mason.

"I want to find out whether Frances Celane called on you to-day."

Perry Mason's face was patiently appraising.

"This is a law office and not an information bureau, Mr. Gleason," he said.

Gleason jumped nervously to his feet, made three swift strides to the window, stood against the light for a moment, then whirled to stare at the lawyer.

His eyes were dark and smouldering. He seemed to be fighting some overpowering emotion.

"Never mind the wisecracks," he said. "I've *got* to know whether or not Fran Celane was here talking with you."

Perry Mason's voice did not change its expression in the least. The other man's impatience dropped from his calm manner as easily as butter slips from a hot knife.

"Let's not have any misunderstanding about this," said Perry Mason. "You're talking about a Miss Frances Celane?"

"Yes."

"Do you know Miss Celane personally?"

"Of course I do."

Perry Mason made a frank, disarming gesture with his right hand as though the entire matter were dismissed as of no importance.

"That simplifies it," he said.

"What does?" asked Gleason, suspiciously.

"The fact that you know Miss Celane," said Perry Mason. "Under the circumstances, all you have to do is to ask her if she has consulted me. If she has not, there will be no necessity for you to return. If she has and doesn't want you to know it, she will doubtless find some way of concealing the fact. If she has consulted me and doesn't care if you know the fact, she will tell you."

He got to his feet and smiled at his visitor as though the interview were terminated.

Robert Gleason remained standing by the window. His face showed that he was laboring under a great strain.

"You can't talk that way to me," he said.

"But," explained Mason, patiently, "I have already talked that way to you."

"But you can't do it."

"Why not?"

"It would be all right to talk that way to a stranger," he said, "but I'm not a stranger. I'm close to Fran Celane. I've got a right to know. She's being blackmailed, and I want to know what you propose to do about it."

Perry Mason raised his eyebrows in polite interrogation.

"Who is being blackmailed?" he asked. "And by whom?"

Gleason made an impatient gesture.

"What's the use of all that hooey?" he asked. "I know she was here, and you know she was here. You know she's being blackmailed, and I want to know what you propose to do about it."

"I think," said Mason, "that under the circumstances I'm going to ask you to step out of the office. You see, when I asked you to come in, I thought that you had some matter of legal business to take up with me. As it happens, I am rather

12

busy to-day, and I really haven't time to discuss with you the only matter which seems to interest you."

Gleason kept his position.

"At least," he said, "you can tell me *who* is doing the blackmailing. That's all I want to know. If you'll give me that information I'll arrange to take care of it myself."

The lawyer walked to the door, standing there very efficient and gravely dignified.

"Good-by, Mr. Gleason," he said. "I'm sorry that I can be of no assistance to you."

"That's final?" asked Gleason, his lips twisting with emotion, until he seemed to be snarling.

"That's all," said Perry Mason, in a tone of finality.

"Very well," said Gleason, and strode across the room and through the door without another word.

Perry Mason closed the door gently, hooked his thumbs in the armholes of his vest, dropped his head forward and started pacing the floor.

After a few moments, he went to his desk, and took out the typewritten paper containing the copy of the clause in the will of Carl Celane, setting forth the terms of the trust to Frances Celane.

He was still studying this typewritten document when Della Street opened the door once more.

"Miss Celane," she said.

Mason looked at her speculatively for a moment, then beckoned to her.

She interpreted the gesture, and stepped fully into the room, pulling the door closed behind her.

"Did Gleason go out of the office as soon as he left here?" he asked.

"Yes," she said, "in just about nothing flat. He acted as though he was trying to win a walking race."

"And Miss Celane just came in?"

"Yes."

"You don't think they met in the elevator?"

Della Street pursed her lips thoughtfully.

"They might have, Chief," she said, "but I don't think they did."

"How does Miss Celane seem?" he asked. "Excited?"

"No," she said, "cool as a cucumber, and she's trying to look her best when she comes in. She took out her compact and is making her face all pretty. She's got her hair arranged just so."

"All right," said Mason, "send her in."

The secretary opened the door. "Come in, Miss Celane," she said.

As Frances Celane walked into the room, the secretary slipped out through the door, and noiselessly closed it behind her.

"Sit down," said Perry Mason.

Frances Celane walked over to the same leather chair which she had occupied earlier in the day, sat down, crossed her knees and regarded the attorney from limpid black eyes in wordless interrogation.

"A Robert Gleason called on me a few minutes ago," said Mason, "and insisted on my telling him whether or not you had been here."

"Bob's so impulsive," she said.

"You know him then?"

"Yes, of course."

"Did you tell him you were going here?" he asked.

"I mentioned your name to him," she said. "Did you tell him that I had been here?"

"Certainly not. I told him to get in touch with you if he wanted to ask any questions about your affairs."

She smiled faintly.

"Bob Gleason wouldn't appreciate your talking to him like that," she said.

"He didn't," Mason told her.

"I'll see him," she said, "and tell him."

"Gleason," went on the attorney, "said that you were being blackmailed."

For just a fraction of a second there was a look of startled terror in the eyes of the young woman. Then she regarded the attorney with a placid and impassive face.

"Rob is *so* impulsive," she said, for the second time.

Mason waited for her to tell him more if she wished to take advantage of the opportunity, but she sat calmly placid, waiting.

Mason turned to the papers on his desk.

"I have copies of the trust provisions of the will, and the decree of distribution," he said. "I also find that there have been annual accounts submitted by the trustee. I'm afraid that I can't give you very much hope, Miss Celane, as far as the decree of distribution itself is concerned. The administration of the trust seems to be largely discretionary.

"You see, even if I should be able to get the provision in regard to marriage set aside, as being in violation of public policy, we would still be confronted with the fact that the distribution of the trust estate remains largely in the discretion of the trustee. I am afraid that your uncle would consider our attack upon the will in the light of an interference with the wishes of your father, and with his authority as trustee. Even if we should win our point in court, he would have it in his discretion to nullify our victory."

She took the blow without flinching, and said, after a moment: "That's what I was afraid of."

"There is another peculiar provision in the trust," said Mason, "to the effect that the discretion vested in the trustee is a personal discretion, due to the confidence which your father had in his judgment. The will and decree of distribution provide that in the event the trust should terminate because of the death, inability or refusal on the part of the trustee to continue to act, that then and in such event, the entire trust fund is to be vested in you unconditionally."

"Yes," she said, "I know that."

"There is therefore," said Mason, "some possibility that your uncle *might* be placed in a position where he could no longer act to advantage. In other words, we might make some legal attack upon his capacity to act as trustee—perhaps show a commingling of trust funds with his own accounts, or something of that sort. It's rather sketchy, and I'm mentioning it to you simply because it seems to be the only possible plan of campaign open to us."

15

She smiled at him and said: "You don't know my uncle."

"Just what do you mean by that?" asked Mason.

"I mean," she said, "that my uncle is meticulously careful, and is so obstinate that no power on earth can swerve him from anything he wants to do, or decides that he doesn't want to do. He is entirely self-sufficient."

For the first time during the interview, there was some feeling in her voice—a certain bitterness which colored her tone, though her eyes remained calm.

"Have you any suggestions?" asked Mason, watching her closely.

"Yes," she said, "I think that something might be done through Arthur Crinston."

"And who," asked Perry Mason, "is Arthur Crinston?"

"Arthur Crinston," she said, "is my uncle's partner. They are engaged in business together, buying, selling and mortgaging real estate, and buying and selling stocks and bonds. Arthur Crinston has more influence with Uncle than any other living person."

"And how does he feel toward you?" asked Mason.

"Very kindly," she said, and smiled as she said it.

"Would there be any chance," asked Mason, slowly, "that Crinston could persuade your uncle to give up the administration of the trust and let you have the entire trust fund?"

"There's always a chance of anything," she said, abruptly, getting to her feet. "I'm going to have Mr. Crinston come in and see you."

"Sometime to-morrow?" asked Mason.

"Sometime this afternoon," she said.

He regarded his watch. "It's twenty minutes past four. I close the office at five. Of course I could wait a few minutes."

"He'll be here at quarter of five," she said.

"Do you want to telephone from here?" he asked.

"No, it won't be necessary."

"What," asked Perry Mason, snapping the question at her without warning, as she stood in the doorway of the office, "did Rob Gleason mean when he said that you were being blackmailed?"

16

She regarded him with wide, tranquil eyes.

"I'm sure," she said, "I haven't the faintest idea,"—and closed the door.

Chapter 3

Arthur Crinston was forty-five, broad shouldered, and affable. He strode across Mason's private office, with his hand outstretched, and said in a booming voice of ready cordiality:

"Mighty glad to meet you, Mr. Mason. Fran told me that I must come in right away, so I dropped everything to run up."

Perry Mason shook hands and surveyed Crinston with his steady, appraising stare.

"Sit down," he said.

Arthur Crinston dropped into the same black leather chair which Frances Celane had occupied, fished a cigar from his pocket, scraped a match across the sole of his shoe, lit the cigar and grinned through the smoke at the lawyer.

"Wants to get married pretty badly, doesn't she?" he said.

"You know about that?" asked Perry Mason.

"Sure," said Crinston heartily, "I know everything about Fran. In fact, she's nearer being my niece than Edward's niece. That is, we get along together and understand each other."

"Do you think," asked Mason, "that anything could be done by a talk with Edward Norton?"

"Talk by whom?" asked Crinston.

"By you," Mason suggested.

Crinston shook his head.

"By Miss Celane then?" ventured Mason.

Again Crinston shook his head.

"No," he said, "there's only one person who could talk with Norton and do any good."

"And who is that?" asked Mason.

"You," said Crinston emphatically.

The lawyer's face did not change expression, only his eyes

betrayed surprise. "From all I can hear of Mr. Norton's character," he said, "I would think my interference would be exactly the thing that he would resent."

"No it wouldn't," said Crinston. "Edward Norton is a peculiar chap. He doesn't want any sentiment to influence his business judgment. He's perfectly cold-blooded. He'd be far more apt to listen to you making him a purely business and legal proposition, than to either Fran or myself, who would have to talk with him on the ground of sentiment."

"You'll pardon me," said Perry Mason, "but that hardly seems logical."

"It doesn't make any difference how it seems," said Crinston, grinning, "and I don't know as it makes any difference whether it's logical or not. It's a fact. It's just the character of the man. You'd have to see Norton and talk with him in order to appreciate it."

Della Street opened the door from the outer office. "The young lady who was here this afternoon is on the telephone and would like to speak with you," she said.

Mason nodded and picked up the French telephone on his desk.

"Hello," he said.

He heard Miss Celane's voice speaking rapidly.

"Did Mr. Crinston come there?"

"Yes. He's here now."

"What does he say?"

"He suggests that I should interview your uncle."

"Well, will you please do so then?"

"You think I should?"

"If Arthur Crinston thinks so, yes."

"Very well. Sometime to-morrow?"

"No. Please do it to-night."

Mason frowned. "On a matter of this importance," he said, "I'd prefer to take some time to figure out the best method of approach."

"Oh that's all right," said the girl. "Arthur Crinston will tell you just what to say. I'll make an appointment with my uncle for eight thirty this evening. I'll pick you up at your

19

office and drive you out there. I'll meet you at eight o'clock. Will that be all right?"

"Hold the line a moment please," Mason said, and turned to Arthur Crinston.

"Miss Celane is on the line and thinks I should see her uncle this evening. She says she'll make an appointment."

"That's fine," boomed Crinston, "a splendid idea. I don't know of anything that could be better."

Mason said into the receiver: "Very well, Miss Celane, I'll meet you at my office at eight o'clock, and you can drive me out."

He hung up the telephone and stared thoughtfully at Crinston.

"There's something strange about this affair," he commented. "There seems to be a frantic haste on the part of everyone concerned."

Arthur Crinston laughed.

"You don't know Fran Celane very well," he said.

"She seems to be a very calm and very poised young lady," Mason remarked tonelessly.

Crinston took the cigar out of his mouth to laugh explosively.

"You should be enough of a judge of human nature, Mason," he boomed, "to know that you can't tell a damned thing about these modern young ladies from the way they appear. Don't ever let her get her temper up. When she gets mad she's a hell-cat."

Mason regarded his visitor unsmilingly.

"Indeed," he said, in that same toneless voice.

"I didn't mean any offense," Crinston said, "but you certainly have missed it on Fran Celane. That girl is just plain dynamite.

"Now, I'll tell you what I'll do. If you're going to see Norton to-night, I'll run out a little bit in advance of your appointment, and try and soften him up a trifle. He's a peculiar chap. You'll understand when you see him. He's all cold-blooded business efficiency."

"Will Miss Celane have any difficulty making an appointment for this evening?'' asked Mason, watching Crinston shrewdly.

"Oh no," said Crinston, "he's one of these fellows who likes to work nights. He has a regular office fixed up in the house, and he likes to do a lot of night work. He makes most of his appointments for afternoons and evenings."

He pulled himself to his feet, strode across to the attorney, and extended his hand.

"Mighty glad I met you," he said, "and I'll see if I can soften up Edward Norton a bit before you talk to him."

"Have you any suggestions," asked Mason, "as to the line of argument I should use with him?"

"None at all," said Crinston, "except that I would advise you not to make *any* particular plan of approach. You'll find that Edward Norton is very much of a law unto himself."

When Crinston had left, Mason paced back and forth for a few moments, then opened the door of his office, and stepped out into the outer room.

His private office was in the corner of a suite of offices which included two reception rooms, a law library, a stenographic room, and two private offices.

Perry Mason employed a typist, Della Street, combination stenographer and secretary, and Frank Everly, a young lawyer who was getting practical experience in Mason's office.

Perry Mason strode across the office to the law library, opened the door and nodded to Frank Everly.

"Frank," he said, "I want you to do something for me, and do it quickly."

Everly pushed back a calf-skin book which he had been reading, and got to his feet.

"Yes sir," he said.

"I think," said Perry Mason, "that a certain Robert Gleason has married a certain Frances Celane. I don't know just when the marriage took place, but probably it was several weeks ago. They've tried to cover it up. You've got to chase through the licenses to find what you want. Ring up some clerk in the license bureau, arrange to have him wait over after hours. They'll be closing in a few minutes, and you've got to work quickly."

"Yes, Chief," said Everly, "when I get the information where do I reach you?"

"When you get the information," said Mason, "write out whatever you find, seal it in an envelope, mark it personal and confidential, and put it under the blotter on the desk in my private office."

"Okay, Chief," said Everly, and started for the telephone.

Mason walked back to his private office, hooked his thumbs through the armholes of his vest, and started slowly and rhythmically pacing the floor.

Chapter 4

Fran Celane drove the big Packard roadster with a deft touch on the wheel, and skilled foot on the throttle.

When she had sat in the huge leather chair at the lawyer's office, she had seemed small, frail and helpless. Now that suggestion of helplessness had gone from her. The hint of the feline power in her nature was more pronounced. Her handling of the car was swiftly savage as she sent it hurtling through openings in traffic, coming to abrupt stops when the traffic lights were against her, leaping into almost instant speed as she got clear signals. Her face still held a pouting, sulky expression.

Seated at her side, Perry Mason studied her with eyes that were intent in watchful speculation.

The girl topped a hill, turned to a winding driveway in a scenic subdivision, and nodded her head in a gesture of indication.

"There's the place," she said, "down at the foot of the hill."

Mason looked down the winding road to the big house which showed as a blaze of light.

"Regular mansion," he said.

"Yes," she answered curtly.

"Many servants?" he asked.

"Quite a few: gardener, housekeeper, butler, chauffeur, and secretary."

"Would you call the secretary a servant?" asked Mason, watching her profile with mild amusement.

"*I* would," she snapped.

"Evidently you don't like him," Mason remarked.

She paid no attention to the comment, but swung the car

around a curve at sufficient speed to bring a scream of protest from the tires.

"Incidentally," went on Perry Mason, "if you're feeling particularly savage about something, and want to take it out on the car, I'd prefer you let me get out. I have to move around in order to make my living. I couldn't gesture very emphatically to a jury with an arm in a sling."

She said: "That's all right. You might have both legs gone," and screamed the car into the next turn with an increased speed.

Mason reached over and shut off the ignition.

"We won't have any more of that," he said.

She slammed a foot on the brake, turned to him with eyes that were blazing with wrath.

"Don't you *dare* to touch this car when I'm driving it!" she stormed. "Do you hear me, don't you *dare*!"

Perry Mason's tone was almost casual.

"Don't try to show off to me," he said, "by risking both of our lives. It isn't at all necessary."

"I'm not showing off to you," she blazed. "I don't give a damn what *you* think. I don't want to be late for our appointment. If we're as much as five minutes late, we're all through. He won't see us at all."

"*I* can do you a great deal more good," said Mason, "if I get there in one piece."

She had braked the car from high speed to a dead stop. Now she took her hands from the wheel as she turned to the lawyer with blazing eyes.

"I'm driving this car," she said, "and I don't want you to interfere with me!"

Suddenly she smiled. "Forgive me," she said impulsively, "I was wrong and I'm acting like a spoiled child. I guess I was in a hurry, that's all."

Mason remarked complacently: "That's all right, but you *have* got a temper, haven't you?"

"Of course I have," she said. "I thought you knew that."

"I didn't," he said, "until Crinston told me."

"Did he tell you?"

"Yes."

24

"He shouldn't have."

"And my secretary," he went on, calmly, "told me you were sulky. I thought at first she might have been right. But she wasn't. You're not sulky, you're just in a panic, that's all. You look sulky when you're frightened."

She whirled to face him with half parted lips and startled eyes. Then, wordlessly, she turned back to the road and started the car. Her lips were pressed into a thin line of determined silence.

Neither of them said anything more until she swept the car up the driveway and braked it to a swift stop.

"Well," she said, "let's go get it over with."

Mason got out.

"You don't intend to be present at the interview?" he asked.

She whipped the car door open and jumped to the driveway with a flash of legs, a flounce of skirt.

"Just long enough to introduce you," she said. "Come on. Let's go."

He followed her to the front door, which she opened with a latchkey.

"Right up the stairs," she said.

They walked up the stairs and turned to the left. A man was just coming out of a doorway, and he paused to stare at them. He held a stiff-backed stenographic notebook in his hand, and some papers under his arm.

"Mr. Graves," said Frances Celane, "my uncle's secretary. Don, this is Mr. Perry Mason, the lawyer."

Mason bowed and noticed as he did so, that Don Graves stared at him with a curiosity which he made no attempt to conceal.

The secretary was slender, well dressed, yellow haired and brown eyed. There was about him a certain alertness, as though he were just about to break into conversation, or just about to start running. Both his physical pose and his manner indicated physical and mental tension.

The secretary said, with a rapidity of utterance which made the words seem to tread each on the heel of the other:

"I'm very pleased to meet you. Mr. Norton is expecting you. If you'll go in, he'll receive you."

Perry Mason said nothing. His bow sufficed for an acknowledgment of the introduction.

The girl pushed on past the secretary. The lawyer followed her. Fran Celane led the way across an outer office which contained a stenographer's desk, a safe, a battery of filing cases, two telephone instruments, typewriters, an adding machine, a file of card indexes.

She pushed open the door of an inner office without knocking and Perry Mason found himself facing a tall man of fifty-five, who stared at them with a bland, expressionless countenance.

"You are late," he said.

"Not over a minute, Uncle Edward," said the girl.

"A minute," he said, "is sixty seconds."

She made no answer, but turned to the lawyer.

"This is my attorney, Perry Mason, Uncle Edward," she said.

The man said in those precise, expressionless tones: "I am very glad that you have consulted counsel. I think now it will be easier for me to explain certain things to you. You never would accept my word for them. Mr. Mason, I am very glad to meet you and very glad that you have called upon me."

He extended his hand.

Perry Mason nodded his head, shook hands, and sat down.

"Well," Fran Celane said, "I'll be running along and leave my future in your hands."

She smiled at them and left the room. As she closed the door of the private office, Mason heard her voice rattling in swift conversation with Don Graves, the secretary.

Edward Norton did not waste a single second in idle talk.

"Undoubtedly you have looked up the terms of the decree of distribution and the trust," he said.

"I have," Mason told him.

"You are familiar with them?"

"I am."

"Then, you understand, a great deal is left to my discretion."

"I would say a very great deal," said Mason cautiously.

"And I take it my niece has asked you to secure some specific modification of the provisions of the trust?"

"Not necessarily," said Mason, choosing his words cautiously. "She would like, I think, to have a certain amount of latitude, and would like to know your possible reactions in the event she should do certain things."

"In the event she should marry, eh?" said Norton.

"Well, we might consider that as one of the possibilities," Mason admitted.

"Yes," said Norton drily, "we do so consider it. Her father considered it, and I consider it. You probably don't realize it yet, Mr. Mason, but my niece has one of the most ungovernable tempers in the world. She is a veritable tigress when she is aroused. She is also impulsive, headstrong, selfish, and yet thoroughly lovable.

"Her father realized that she had to be protected from herself. He also realized that leaving her any large sum of money might turn out to be the worst thing he could do for her. He knew that I shared his views, and that was the reason this trust was created.

"I want you to understand that in the event I exercise the discretion given to me under that trust, and disburse the money elsewhere than to my niece, I shall do it only because I consider it would be very much to her disadvantage to give her the money. Great riches, with a temperament such as hers, frequently lead to great suffering."

"Don't you think," said Mason diplomatically, "that it would be much better, however, all around, to accustom her to the handling of larger sums of money by gradually increasing the amount which she receives? And don't you think, perhaps, that marriage might exert a steadying influence?"

"I am familiar with all those arguments," said Norton. "I have heard them until I am tired of them. You will pardon me. I mean nothing personal. I say simply what I have in mind.

"I am the trustee of this estate. I have administered it

27

wisely. In fact, despite the economic readjustment of values which has taken place in the last few years, I am glad to report that the trust funds have shown a steady increase, until now the amount of the trust is far in excess of what it was at the time it was created. Recently I have entirely cut off my niece's allowance. She is not receiving a penny."

Mason's face showed surprise.

"I see," said Norton, "that she has not confided to you the exact situation."

"I didn't know that you had cut off her income entirely," said Mason. "May I ask what is the reason for such a step?"

"Certainly," said Norton, "I have every reason to believe that my niece is being blackmailed. I have asked her about it, and she refuses to tell me who is blackmailing her, or what specific indiscretion she has committed which gives a blackmailer an opportunity to collect money from her.

"Therefore I have determined to place it out of her power to make *any* cash donations to *any* blackmailer. Under those circumstances, I am satisfied that another few days will force the situation to a head."

Norton stared at Mason with cold eyes which contained no trace of cordiality, yet no trace of hostility.

"You understand my position in the matter?" asked Mason.

"Certainly," said Norton. "I'm glad that my niece has consulted an attorney. I don't know if she has made arrangements for your compensation. In the event she has not, I propose to see that a sufficient amount is forthcoming from the trust fund to furnish you a reasonable fee. But I want you to impress upon her mind that she is legally powerless to do anything."

"No," said Perry Mason, "I'll take my fee from her and I'm not binding myself to give any particular advice. Let's talk about the *way* you're going to use your discretion, instead of whether you've got the right to use it."

"No," said Norton, "that is one matter which is not open to discussion."

"Well," Mason remarked, smiling affably and keeping his temper, "that is primarily what I came here to discuss."

"No," Edward Norton said coldly, "that phase of the discussion is entirely out of order. You will confine yourself to a discussion of the legal rights of your client under the trust."

Mason's eyes were cold and appraising.

"I've always found," he said, "that a legal matter has a lot of angles. If you'll just look at this thing from the human viewpoint and consider . . ."

"I will allow you to be heard," Norton interrupted, in cold, level tones, "upon no matter other than the question of the legality of the trust and the interpretation thereof."

Mason pushed back his chair, and got to his feet.

His voice was as cold as that of the other. "I'm not accustomed to having people tell me what I will talk about and what I won't talk about. I'm here representing the rights of Frances Celane, your niece, and my client. I'll say anything I damned please concerning those rights!"

Edward Norton reached out to a button and pressed it with his bony forefinger. The gesture was utterly devoid of emotion.

"I am ringing," he said, "for the butler, who will show you to the door. So far as I am concerned, the discussion is terminated."

Perry Mason planted his feet wide apart, standing spread-legged, he said: "You'd better ring for two butlers, and the secretary too. It'll take all of them to put me out of here before I say what I've got to say!

"You're making a mistake, treating this niece of yours as though she were a chattel or a lump of clay. She's a high-spirited, high-strung girl. I don't know where you get the idea that she's being blackmailed, but if you have any such idea . . ."

The door of the private office opened, and a broad-shouldered, burly man, with a wooden face, bowed from the hips.

"You rang sir?" he asked.

"Yes," said Edward Norton, "show this gentleman out."

The butler put a firm hand on Perry Mason's arm. The lawyer shook him off, savagely, continued to face Norton.

29

"Nobody," he said, "is going to show me out, or is going to throw me out until I have had an opportunity to say what I want to say. If that girl is being blackmailed, you'd better act like a human being instead of a cash register, and give her a break . . ."

There was a rustle of motion, and Frances Celane rushed into the room.

She looked at Mason with black eyes, which gave the effect of being expressionless, with a face that seemed pouting.

"You've done all you can do, Mr. Mason," she said.

Mason continued to glower at the man behind the desk.

"You're more than a treasurer," he said, "or should be. She should be able to look to you for . . ."

The girl tugged at his arm.

"Please, Mr. Mason," she said, "please. I know you're trying to do me a favor, but it's going to have just the opposite effect. Please don't."

Mason took a deep breath, turned, and stalked rigidly from the room. The butler slammed the door shut behind him. Mason turned to Frances Celane and said: "Of all the obstinate, cold-blooded, unsympathetic icebergs I have ever met, that man is the worst!"

She looked up at him and laughed.

"I knew," she said, "that if I tried to explain to you how utterly obstinate my uncle was, you would never believe me. So I welcomed the opportunity to let you find out first-hand. Now you understand the necessity for taking legal steps."

"All right," said Mason, grimly, "we'll take them."

Chapter 5

Perry Mason let himself into the office with his key, walked to his desk and picked up the blotter. There was an envelope under it, marked "Confidential." He ripped it open and saw a notation in Frank Everly's handwriting:

"ROBERT GLEASON AND FRANCES CELANE TOOK OUT A MARRIAGE LICENSE ON THE FOURTH OF LAST MONTH. THEY WERE MARRIED IN CLOVERDALE ON THE EIGHTH."

The message was signed with the initials of the law clerk.

Perry Mason stared at it for several minutes, then hooked his thumbs in his vest and started pacing the floor of the office.

After a while he swung into the law library, took down a volume of "*Cyc.*" dealing with wills, started reading.

He interrupted his reading to go to the book case and get a volume of the Pacific Reporter. He read the reported cases for some little time, then started taking other case books from the shelves.

He worked in cold, silent concentration, moving efficiently and tirelessly, his eyes hard and steady, his face without expression.

Somewhere a clock struck midnight, but Perry Mason kept on working. The pile of law books on the table grew larger and larger. He prowled around through the library, pulling down various books, turning to cases, studying intently. Once in a while he made a brief note. Frequently he book-marked cases, and placed them to one side.

About fifteen minutes past one o'clock in the morning the telephone rang.

31

Mason frowned and paid no attention to it.

The telephone continued to ring insistently, imperatively.

Mason uttered an exclamation, turned to the telephone and picked up the receiver.

"Hello," he said, "you've got the wrong number."

A voice said: "I beg your pardon, sir, but is this Mr. Mason, the lawyer?"

"Yes," said Perry Mason, irritably.

"Just a minute," said the voice.

Mason held the telephone, and heard a swift whisper, then the voice of Frances Celane: "Mr. Mason?"

"Yes."

"You must come at once," she said.

"Come where, and why?" he asked. "What's the trouble?"

"Come out to the house," she told him. "My uncle has just been murdered!"

"Has just what?"

"Has just been murdered!" she said.

"Do they know who did it?" he asked.

"They *think* they do," she said, in a low, almost surreptitious voice. "Come at once!" and the line went dead as the receiver slipped into place on the other end of the wire.

Perry Mason left the office without pausing to switch out the lights. The night watchman brought up the elevator and Mason pushed his way into it as soon as the door was open.

"Been working rather late, haven't you?" said the watchman.

Mason smiled mechanically.

"No rest for the wicked," he said.

He left the elevator, crossed the lobby of the office building, ran diagonally across the street to a hotel where there was a taxicab stand. He called the address of Norton's residence to the taxi driver. "Keep the throttle down to the floorboards," he said.

"Okay, buddy," said the driver, and slammed the door.

Mason was slammed back in the cushions, as the car lurched forward. His face was unchanging, though his eyes were squinted in thought. Never once did he glance at the scenery which whizzed past.

Only when the taxi swung off to the driveway which sloped down the hill, did Mason lose his air of abstraction, and begin to take an interest in the surroundings.

The big house was illuminated, every window was a blaze of light. The grounds in front were also illuminated, and more than a dozen automobiles were parked in front of the place.

Mason discharged the taxicab, walked to the house, and saw the bulky form of Arthur Crinston silhouetted against the lights on the porch.

Crinston ran down the three steps to the cement. "Mason," he said, "I'm glad you came. I want to see you before anybody else does."

He took the lawyer's arm and led him across the cement driveway, over a strip of lawn, and into the shadows of a hedge.

"Listen," he said, "this is a serious business. We don't know yet exactly how serious it is. I want you to promise me that you will stand by Fran. No matter what happens, see that she doesn't get mixed into this thing."

"Is she going to get mixed in it?" asked Mason.

"Not if you stand by her."

"Do you mean she's implicated in any way?" Mason demanded.

"No, no, not at all," Crinston hastened to assure him, "but she's a peculiar individual, and she's got the devil's own temper. She's mixed up in it somehow, and I don't know just how. Shortly before his death, Edward Norton telephoned the police station and wanted his niece arrested, or that's what the police claim."

"Arrested?" exclaimed Mason.

"Well, not exactly that," said Crinston, "but he wanted her disciplined in some way. I can't just get the straight of it. You see, she had his Buick sedan out driving it. According to the police, Norton telephoned in that the sedan had been stolen and wanted the police to pick up the car and put the

33

driver in jail. He said it didn't make any difference *who* was driving it.''

"Then that must have been after I left here, and before Norton's death," Mason said.

Crinston shrugged his shoulders.

"According to the police," he said, "it was at eleven fifteen. Personally I think it's all a lot of hooey. The police must have made a mistake. Norton had his faults, and there were plenty of them, but he loved his niece in his own peculiar fashion. I can't believe he wanted her arrested."

"Well," said Mason, "forget that. How about the murder? Do they know who did it?"

"Apparently," said Crinston, "that's all taken care of. Pete Devoe, the chauffeur, got drunk and killed him in order to get some money. He tried to make it appear that burglars had broken in from the outside, but he bungled the job."

"How was Norton killed?" asked Mason.

"Devoe beat his head in with a club. It was a messy job. He hit him a frightful lick."

"Did they find the club?" the lawyer asked.

"Yes," said Crinston, "that's where Devoe slipped up. He took the club and hid it in a closet in his room. He didn't think the police would search the place, because he tried to make it appear burglars had broken in from the outside. You see, the police discovered the crime a lot sooner than anyone thought they would. It's quite a story, and I'll have to tell it to you when we've got more time. Don Graves actually saw the crime being committed."

"Give me a quick outline," said Mason. "Spill it fast."

Crinston took a deep breath, then hurried into speech. "You know Norton is a night owl. He frequently keeps his office open until midnight. To-night he had an appointment with me, and I had an appointment with Municipal Judge Purley. I was late getting things cleaned up with Purley, so I persuaded Purley to drive me out here in his car, and wait for me. I only had to see Norton for a few minutes.

"I ran in and had my conference with Norton and then came out and started away with Judge Purley. Just as we started to drive away, Norton opened the window on the upper floor and called down to ask me if I would mind taking Don Graves with me. He was sending Graves after some important papers, and wanted him to go with us to save time. You see, they were papers that I had agreed to get for Graves—some documents relating to some of our partnership business.

"I asked Judge Purley if he had any objections, and Purley said it would be all right. So I called up to Norton to send Graves down, but Graves, anticipating it would be all right, by that time was at the door, and he ran right out and into the automobile.

"We started up the road toward the boulevard. You know how it curves and twists around. There's one place where you can look back and see into Norton's study. Graves happened to be looking back. He let out a yell. He said he had seen the figure of a man standing in Norton's study; that this man had a club, and had swung it down on Norton's head.

"Judge Purley ran the car to a place where he could turn around. He thought Graves might have been mistaken, but Graves insisted he couldn't have been mistaken. It was something he'd seen plainly. He insisted he was right. So Judge Purley drove back to the house, going pretty rapidly.

"When we got there, the three of us rushed into the house and up the stairs to the study.

"Norton was lying across his desk with the top of his head smashed in. His pockets were turned inside out. His wallet lay empty on the floor.

"We notified the police right away.

"There was a window in the dining room which had been jimmied open, and there were footprints outside in the loam. The prints were of very large feet, and the police think now that Devoe probably put a large pair of shoes on over his other shoes, in order to leave those prints and fool the police. You'll get the facts of the case when you go in."

Perry Mason stared thoughtfully into the half-darkness of the shadowed hedge.

"Why," he asked, "should Norton have accused his niece of stealing an automobile?"

"Probably a misunderstanding," said Crinston, "I don't

think Norton had any idea his niece was the one who had the car. He just knew the car was missing, and telephoned the police. They were working on that when they were advised of the murder. So they're making inquiries, figuring the car business may have had something to do with it."

"Do they know that his niece had the car?" asked Mason.

"Yes. She's admitted having taken it out," said Crinston.

"It seems strange Norton would have wanted her arrested," persisted Mason.

"Well, he did," Crinston said, "unless the police got the wrong name, and that isn't likely, because they got the right car numbers. But Fran is a peculiar girl. You can't tell what she will do. For heaven's sake, talk with her, and don't let her get mixed up in this thing."

"You certainly don't think that she has anything to do with the murder?" asked Mason.

"I don't know," said Crinston, then hastily added: "No, no, of course not, she couldn't have She's got a temper and they had quite a fight after you left. But she wouldn't have had the physical strength to strike such a blow anyway. And if she had had an accomplice . . . Oh well, there's no use speculating about that anyway, because it's all foolishness. Devoe is the one that's guilty all right. But you know how a murder is. It's going to bring out a lot of complications. I want you to get in touch with Fran and keep her out of the complications."

"Very well," said Mason, starting once more for the house. "But either you think she's mixed up in it, or else you're keeping something from me."

Crinston grabbed Mason's arm.

"As far as compensation is concerned," he said, "there's going to be a big difference now that Norton is out of the way. The partnership that Norton and I had has some assets, and then there's quite a bit of money in the trust fund which will go to the girl without any question, as I understand it.

"I've got confidence in you and I want you to step right in the saddle as attorney for everything. Act as attorney for the estate, as well as for the girl, and stand between her and too much police questioning."

Mason stopped still and turned to face Crinston.

"You might just as well be frank with me," he said. "You seem to think that the girl can't stand too much questioning."

Crinston's jaw snapped forward and his eyes met those of the attorney in a gaze that was every bit as steady as the gaze of the steely eyes which stared into his.

"*Of course*, she won't stand too much questioning," he snapped. "Have I been talking to you all this time without giving you any idea at all of what I'm driving at?"

"Why," asked Mason insistently, "won't she stand too much questioning? Do you think she's mixed up in the murder?"

"I'm just telling you," said Crinston obstinately, "that she won't stand too much questioning. She hasn't got the temperament for it, in the first place, and she's a spitfire when she loses her temper. It isn't the murder, it's the incidental things that may come out in connection with the investigation. Now you get to her and keep the police from asking her questions."

Mason said: "All right, I just didn't want to misunderstand you, that's all. I wanted to know if you felt there was danger of her getting into trouble."

"Of course there is!" Crinston snapped.

"You mean about her private affairs?" asked Mason.

"I mean about everything," Crinston said. "Come on. Let's get in the house."

An officer stood at the front porch and questioned Mason.

"He's all right," said Crinston. "He's my attorney, the attorney for the estate, and also the personal attorney for Frances Celane."

"All right," said the officer, "you folks that live here can go in and out, but you understand that you're not to touch anything, or interfere with the evidence at all."

"Of course," said Crinston, and pushed on ahead of him into the house.

Chapter 6

Frances Celane wore a short sport outfit, with a blue and gold sweater which set off to advantage the spun-gold effect of her silken hair.

She sat in her bedroom on an overstuffed chair, with her knees crossed, her dark eyes staring at the face of her lawyer. There was that about her which indicated she was warily watchful. She seemed to be listening, waiting for something to happen.

All about them the big house echoed with sounds; creaked with a suggestion of packed occupancy. Feet were constantly pounding the boards of floors, hallways and stairs in an endless procession. Doors made noise as they opened and shut. The drone of voices sounded as a distant rumble.

Perry Mason stared down at Fran Celane. "Go ahead," he said, "and tell me exactly what happened."

She spoke in a voice that was a low monotone, expressionless and thoughtful, as though she might be reciting a part that had been learned by rote.

"I don't know very much about it. I had a fight with Uncle Edward after you left. He was impossible. He was trying to make a chattel of me and break my spirit. I told him that that wasn't what father wanted, and that he was being false to his trust."

"What did you mean by being false to his trust?" asked Mason.

"I meant that Father had created that trust only because he wanted to see that the money didn't go to my head too much, and make me too wild. He didn't intend that Uncle Edward should grind me down so I became just an automaton."

"All right," said Mason. "Did anyone know of the quarrel?"

38

"I guess so," she said dispiritedly. "Don Graves knew about it. And I think some of the other servants heard it. I got mad."

"What do you do when you get mad?" he asked.

"Everything," she said.

"Did you raise your voice?" he inquired.

"As high as I could."

"Did you do anything unladylike? That is, did you curse?"

She said, still in the same toneless voice: "Of course I cursed. I was angry, I tell you."

"All right," he said, "then what happened?"

"Then," she said, "I came downstairs and decided that I would run away and leave Edward Norton and his money and everything. I just wanted to get away."

"That was when you took the car?" asked Mason.

"No," she said, "I'm coming to that. I got things packed up as though I was going away, and then decided not to do it. I commenced to cool off a little bit. I've got a bad temper, but after I get over it, I can realize when I've made a mistake. So I knew that I'd make a mistake if I ran away. But I did want to get some air. I didn't want to go out and walk. I wanted to drive a car. I wanted to drive a car fast."

Perry Mason made a dry comment: "Yes, I can understand how you could keep your mind off your troubles by driving fast."

"Well," she said, "you have to do something to get your mind off your troubles."

"All right," he told her, "go on. What happened?"

"Well," she said, "I went to the garage. My Packard was in behind the Buick and I was going to have to move the Buick anyway, so I moved the Buick, and didn't see any reason why I should go back for my Packard."

"The Buick was your uncle's machine?" he asked.

"Yes," she said.

"He didn't allow you to use it?"

"He's never forbidden me to use it," she said, "but I've never used it much. He babies it along a lot, keeps records of the mileage and the oil and gas, and all of that, and has it greased every so many miles, and the oil changed every so

39

often. I don't bother with my Packard that way. I run it until something gets to sounding funny, and then I have it repaired.''

"So you took the Buick without your uncle's consent?''

"Yes, if you want to put it that way.''

"And where did you drive it?''

"I don't know. I just drove it around, taking curves as fast as I could take them.''

"That was pretty fast?'' he asked.

"Of course that was pretty fast,'' she told him.

"How long were you gone?''

"I don't know. I came back to the house a little while before the police arrived here. I must have returned ten or fifteen minutes after the murder.''

"And while you were gone your uncle discovered the loss of the car—that is, he discovered that the car was missing. Is that right?''

"I think that Devoe must have told him,'' she said.

"How did Devoe know?''

"I don't know. Perhaps he heard me drive away, and went out to the garage to see what car I'd taken. I never did like Devoe. He's one of those big, cumbersome fellows who can't think a thought of his own, but goes through life making motions.''

"Never mind that,'' he told her, "what makes you think that Devoe told your uncle?''

"I don't know,'' she said. "It was the time of uncle's telephone call, I guess, and then I always had him figured for a snitcher.''

"What time was the telephone call?''

"Uncle called the police to report the car theft at about a quarter past eleven. I think the police records show that it was exactly eleven fourteen.''

"When did you leave with the car?'' he asked.

"About ten forty-five, I think it was,'' she said.

"Then you'd had the car for half an hour before your uncle reported the theft?''

"Yes, about that long I guess.''

"And when did you return?''

"Somewhere around quarter past twelve. I was out about an hour and a half."

"What time did the police arrive here?"

"About an hour and a half ago."

"No, I mean how long before you returned the car."

"Ten or fifteen minutes, I guess."

"All right," he said, "what did your uncle tell the police?"

"All I know," she said, "is what they told me. One of the detectives talked with me and asked me if I knew any reason why my uncle should have reported the car as stolen."

"All right," he said, "what did your uncle tell them?"

"Well," she said, "according to what this detective told me, my uncle telephoned the police and said that it was Edward Norton talking, and that he had a criminal matter to report. Then there was a delay. I think he was cut off or something, and the police officer, I guess they call him a desk sergeant, held the telephone for a minute until Uncle Edward got another connection, and said that he wanted to report a crime—the theft of an automobile. And he described it, a Buick sedan, 6754093, with license number 12M1834."

"You seem to remember those figures pretty well," said Mason.

"Yes," she said, "they're likely to be important."

"Why?" he asked.

"I don't know," she said. "I just feel that they may be important."

"Did you tell the detective that you had the car?" he asked.

"Yes," she said, "I told him exactly what happened. That I took the car out about quarter to eleven, and brought it back about twelve fifteen, but that I hadn't asked my uncle's permission."

"The police seemed to take that explanation all right?" he asked.

"Oh yes," she said. "They have discontinued working on that end of the case. At first they thought that perhaps the burglars might have stolen the Buick for a get-away."

41

"They've about concluded now, I understand, that there weren't any burglars," said Mason.

"That's right," she said.

Mason paced up and down the floor.

Suddenly he whirled, and stared at the girl.

"You're not telling me the whole truth about this thing," he said.

She showed no resentment whatever in her manner, but stared at him with eyes that were coldly speculative.

"What is there in my story that doesn't hang together?" she asked, and her tone was impersonally thoughtful.

"It isn't that," he said, "it's something in your manner. You haven't told me the truth. You didn't tell me the truth when you first came to my office."

"What do you mean by that?" she wanted to know.

"About wanting to get married and all that," he said.

"Why what do you mean by that?"

"You know what I mean. You had been married already."

Every bit of color drained from her face, and she stared at him with eyes that were wide and round.

"Who told you that? Have you been talking with some of the servants?"

He countered her question with another.

"Do the servants know about it?" he asked.

"No," she said.

"Why then did you think that I had been talking with the servants?"

"I don't know," she said.

"You were married?" he asked her.

"That's none of your business," she said.

"Of course it's my business," he told her. "You came to me with a problem. You can't gain anything by lying to me, any more than you could by lying to a doctor. You've got to tell your lawyer and your doctor the whole truth. You can trust me. I don't betray communications made by my clients."

She pursed her lips and stared at him.

"What do you want me to tell you?" she asked.

"The truth."

"Well, you know it, so what's the use of my telling you?"

"You are married then?"

"Yes."

"Why didn't you tell me that before?"

"Because we were keeping it secret."

"All right," said Mason, "now somebody knows that secret. There is somebody blackmailing you."

"How do you know that?" she asked.

"Never mind that. Answer me."

She extended her right forefinger and started pushing it along the arm of the chair, squirming it around every irregularity in the cloth.

"Under the will," she said slowly, "now that my uncle is dead, does it make any difference if I am married?"

His eyes regarded her in cold, fixed appraisal.

"As I remember the provisions of the will," he said, "your uncle is given the option of turning the money over to charity in the event you marry before you are twenty-five."

"And on his death," she said, "the trust terminates?"

"On his death the trust terminates."

"Then if he can't exercise that option it doesn't make any difference whether I'm married or not?"

"Offhand," he said, "that would be my interpretation of the will."

She heaved a sigh of relief.

"Then," she said, "it doesn't make any difference whether anyone tries to blackmail me or not?"

Mason's eyes stared at the girl as though they would rip the mask from her face and probe the interior of her soul.

"I wouldn't," he said, "make very many comments about that, young lady."

"Why?" she asked.

"Because," he said in a low steady monotone, "if the police should stumble onto that theory of the case, it would show a most excellent motive for a murder."

"You mean that *I* murdered him?"

"It would mean," he said, stubbornly and steadily, "that you had an excellent motive for murdering him."

"Pete Devoe murdered him," she insisted.

43

"They might say that Pete Devoe was an accomplice," he told her.

"They *might*," she agreed, shrugging her shoulders, and regarding him with enigmatical black eyes.

"All right, all right," Mason said, his voice now showing a trace of impatience, "come down to earth. Suppose you try to be fair with me."

"Listen," she told him, speaking rapidly, "I'm going to come into a large sum of money. I'm going to need some one to protect my rights. I've heard about you, and I know you've got a wonderful mind. You're going to be well paid for everything you do for me—everything. You understand?"

"All right," he said, "what do you want me to do?"

"I want you to represent my interests and *my* interests alone. I am going to pay you a fee of forty thousand dollars, and if you have to do any work about getting the trust fund, that is, work like going to court or anything, I am going to pay you more."

He regarded her for a few moments in silent speculation, then said: "That's a lot of money to pay a person to protect your rights if there's nothing to be done."

"How do you mean?" she asked.

"If," he said, "you simply borrowed your uncle's car without his permission and went out for a ride, returned the car and found him murdered, there is no necessity for paying an attorney forty thousand dollars to protect your rights."

She twisted her fingers together and asked: "Are you going to argue with me about that?"

"No," he said, "I simply made that comment. I wanted you to understand the facts."

"You understand what I mean when I say that I will pay you forty thousand dollars if you protect *my* rights?" she inquired.

"Yes," he said.

She got up and crossed the room with quick, nervous stride, dropped into a wicker chair in front of a writing desk, pulled a piece of paper to her and scribbled out a document in pen and ink, which she signed with a flourish.

"Here you are," she said, "my promissory note to pay to

you the sum of forty thousand dollars as soon as I have received that amount from the inheritance left me by my father. And I also mention that if there is any litigation about the inheritance, I will pay you more.''

Mason folded the note and dropped it into his pocket.

"Have the police questioned you in detail?" he asked.

"No," she said, "they aren't annoying me at all. You see, the fact that I had the car out when the murder was committed gives me an alibi. That is, they know I wouldn't know what took place in the house at the time of the murder."

"What time was the murder?" he asked.

"They can fix that very exactly," she said. "It was about eleven thirty-three or eleven thirty-four. You see, Mr. Crinston had Judge Purley with him in the car, and Judge Purley wanted to get home. He started away from the house promptly at eleven thirty. He remembers because he looked at his wristwatch and I believe some comment was made about the fact that he had been here less than half an hour. I think Mr. Crinston promised Judge Purley that if the judge would drive Mr. Crinston out here, he would be detained less than half an hour in all. Mr. Crinston had an appointment with my uncle for eleven o'clock, and he was seven minutes late.

"I guess you saw enough of my uncle to know how he would feel about that seven minutes. Mr. Crinston kept urging Judge Purley to 'step on it,' all the way out here."

"I still don't see," said Mason, "how that fixes the exact time of the murder."

"Well, you see," she explained, "Don Graves saw the murder committed. Now, if the car started from the house at eleven thirty, it would have taken about three minutes to get to the point in the driveway where Graves could look back and see the persons clubbing my uncle."

"Persons?" he asked.

"Person," she amended quickly.

"I see," said the lawyer dryly.

Chapter 7

Perry Mason encountered Don Graves just after that individual had been released from police questioning.

Graves mopped his forehead and smiled at the attorney.

"Never had such an ordeal in my life," he said. "I certainly am glad that *I* wasn't here."

"What do you mean by that?" asked Mason.

"They might have tried to pin it on me," he said. "They tear you to pieces and doubt everything you say."

"I wonder," said Mason, "if you'd mind giving me an outline of just what you told them?"

Graves sighed wearily.

"I've told the facts so often now," he said, "that I'm hoarse."

Mason took the young man's arm and piloted him unsmilingly through the dining room to a solarium, where there were some chairs grouped around a wicker table.

"Smoke?" he asked, extending a package of cigarettes.

Graves nodded eagerly.

Perry Mason held a match to the cigarette. "Get started," he said.

"Well," said Graves, "there isn't very much that I can tell. That's the trouble with it. The police want me to tell too much. At first, when I saw the murder being committed, Judge Purley thought that I was crazy because he claimed I couldn't have seen all that I said I saw through the window, and now the police are jumping on me because I don't tell them more, and seem to think I'm holding something back."

"You saw the murder?" asked Mason.

"I guess so," said Graves wearily. "I've been hammered around so much now that I don't know what I saw."

Perry Mason made no comment.

46

"Well," said Graves, exhaling twin streams of smoke from his nostrils, "Mr. Crinston had an appointment for eleven o'clock, and was seven minutes late. Mr. Norton was very much exasperated over several things that had happened—one of which was your visit, and then he had some trouble with his niece afterwards. But Mr. Crinston says that I'm not to mention that trouble with Fran Celane unless somebody specifically questions me about it.

"Well, Crinston was late for his appointment, and you know how that would affect Norton. He was in one of those cold rages. He showed it by being cold-blooded, efficient, and exceedingly disagreeable.

"I don't know what Crinston talked about with him. They were having some violent difference of opinion. Frankly, I think Crinston was pretty much exasperated when he decided to leave. He had promised Judge Purley that he would leave not later than eleven thirty, and at just about eleven thirty Crinston came out of the inner office.

"Mr. Norton wanted him to stay. Crinston refused. He said he'd promised Judge Purley to leave at eleven thirty. Then Mr. Norton made some sarcastic remark that Crinston would keep him waiting seven minutes, and think nothing of it, but wouldn't think of detaining a municipal judge for as much as ten seconds. He was mad, all right—good and mad.

"Crinston had only been gone a minute or two when Mr. Norton came out and told me that he wanted me to rush out to Crinston's house and get some papers. They were some agreements that he and Crinston had been discussing, and Crinston had promised to send them to Norton. Norton suddenly decided that he didn't want to wait, but wanted them right away. He told me to wake up Devoe, that's the chauffeur, and get him to drive me out to Crinston's house and pick up the agreements.

"At that time, Crinston and Purley were just about to drive away. They had, I believe, started their car.

"Then Mr. Norton suddenly got the idea that if I should drive out with Mr. Crinston, I could save a little time. He intended to have Devoe, the chauffeur, come in and pick me up. But it was going to take Mr. Crinston a few minutes to get the documents, after I got there, and the chauffeur would take a little time dressing and getting the car out; so Norton thought he could save time by having me go in with Mr. Crinston. There wasn't any sense to it. Devoe could have driven me there just as well, but I mention it to show how excited Norton was. He was simply furious.

"So Mr. Norton raised up the window in his office and called down to Mr. Crinston to wait a minute. I'm not certain, but I think Mr. Crinston got out of the machine and walked back so that he stood under the window to hear what Mr. Norton said. I heard Norton ask if it would be all right for me to ride in with them, and I heard Crinston say that he'd go over and ask Judge Purley if there were any objections.

"I knew right away there wouldn't be any objections, so I started hot-footing down the stairs. The way Norton felt, I didn't want to waste a second.

"Crinston had asked Judge Purley, and was standing beneath the window, talking with Mr. Norton, when I got down. Mr. Crinston said to me: 'Hurry up, Graves, I've promised Judge Purley that he would leave here promptly at eleven thirty, and he's in a rush to get home.' So I ran across and jumped into the machine. I think that I got into the machine before Mr. Crinston did, or maybe we got in together, at any rate, Mr. Crinston got into the machine at just about the same time.

"Judge Purley had the engine running, and just as soon as the door slammed, he started the car. I was in the back seat, and Mr. Crinston was sitting up in front with Judge Purley.

"You know the way the road winds around up the side of the hill. Well, I don't know what prompted me to look back through the window at the house. Maybe it was just curiosity, maybe it was some sense of what was happening.

"Anyway, I was looking back through the rear window of the car, and just as it rounded the curve where I could see into the study, I saw people in the study, and a man swinging a club."

"How many people?" asked Perry Mason.

Don Graves did not answer for a moment. Then he took a deep breath and said slowly: "Only one that I was sure of. That is, I saw one person raise his arm and strike another person."

"That you were *sure* of?" said Mason.

"Yes sir," said Graves, "that I was sure of."

"There *might* have been another person present?" asked Perry Mason.

Don Graves said in a very low voice: "I don't think, if I were you, sir, that I'd go into that."

"Why not?" asked Perry Mason explosively.

"I'd rather not state," said Graves, squirming uncomfortably. "But you might find, if you pressed that line of inquiry too far, that it wasn't of any particular advantage, either to you or your client."

"I think I see," said Perry Mason softly.

Graves sighed his relief.

"You were, of course, some distance away?" asked Mason.

"Yes," said Graves, "I was some distance away."

Mason looked at the young man searchingly, but Don Graves kept his eyes averted.

"How clearly could you see?" Mason pressed.

Graves took a deep breath. "I could see quite clearly that somebody was standing over somebody else, and striking a blow," he blurted.

"And did you see that other person fall?"

"I don't think so. You know, it was quite a distance away, and I only had a flash as the car was swinging around the curve in the road."

"Could you say that there were *only* two people in the room?" asked Mason.

"No, of course not, because I couldn't see the entire room."

"Could you say that you only *saw* two people in the room?" Mason inquired.

"I *did* say that," said Graves, and added after a moment, "to the police."

Perry Mason's voice was low. "Let's not misunderstand

49

each other, Graves. In the event that you saw anything which indicated that there was another person in the room, did you see anything that would identify that person?''

Graves spoke very softly and with obvious reluctance. ''Confidentially, Mr. Mason, one can't trust one's impressions in a momentary glimpse like that. It isn't as though you had a photograph of it. And yet there's something that's etched on my brain that I haven't mentioned—to the police. I might tell *you*, in strict confidence, that, if there was another person in that room, and if I saw such a person, *that person was a woman.*''

Perry Mason stared steadily at Graves, then asked:

''Could you identify that woman?''

''I have not mentioned to anyone that I saw that woman,'' said Graves slowly, ''and I would not care to make any identification.''

''But,'' said Mason, ''have you been absolutely positive and emphatic in saying that you did *not* see such a person?''

Graves met his eyes. ''I have tried to tell the truth, Mr. Mason. So far, whenever the question has been asked me, I have answered in such a way that the inquiry has taken another turn. You understand that I am going to answer questions truthfully when I get on the witness stand, if I get on the witness stand. But you will also understand that everyone of us is exceedingly loyal to your client.''

''Meaning?'' asked Mason.

''Meaning Miss Celane.''

''Do I understand,'' said Mason very softly and almost ominously, ''that such a loyalty would lead you to protect her against a murder charge?''

''No,'' said Graves frankly, ''it would not. But it certainly would be sufficient to lead us to keep her name out of an investigation which could only be abortive at any rate.''

''And what do you mean by that?'' pressed the attorney.

''I mean by that, that inasmuch as Miss Celane was not in the house at the time, it would naturally have been impossible for her to have been in that room.''

''Then you did not see a woman in the room?'' Mason asked.

"I didn't say that either," said Graves. "I said that *if* there had been another person in the room that I had seen, that person would probably have been a woman."

"Why," asked the lawyer, "do you say that?"

"Well," said Graves, "there is in my mind a more or less confused impression of a woman's head and shoulders showing momentarily in one corner of the window. But of course I couldn't be sure of it, because my glance was riveted on the man with his arm upraised."

"One more question," said Mason. "Did the police take down, in shorthand, the answers which you gave to the questions they asked you, when they inquired about what you had seen?"

"Yes," said Graves.

"And you didn't mention anything about a woman at that time?"

"No."

Mason said slowly: "You understand, Graves, that there is something very peculiar about this. Both you and Crinston have intimated to me that my client might be in some danger. Yet, apparently, she was not anywhere near the house at the time."

"That's right," said Graves eagerly, "she wasn't here."

"Then how could she be in any danger?" asked Mason.

"She isn't," said Graves. "That's the point I'm trying to make. And I'm trying to protect her against any insinuations which might be made, because, you understand, there's a motive which might be attached to her."

"Very commendable," said Mason dryly. "I wouldn't want you to commit any perjury, Graves, but you will, of course, understand that *if* you tell your story a few times without mentioning the woman, and that story is recorded in shorthand, or reported in the press, and *then* you should subsequently be placed upon the stand and asked specifically if you saw a woman or had the impression that a woman was there, an answer which tended to change your previous story wouldn't do my client such a great amount of harm. On the other hand, it wouldn't do you such a great amount of good."

51

Graves said with dignity: "I am prepared to make some sacrifices in order to protect the good name of Miss Celane."

"And," went on Perry Mason, ominously, "when you did amplify your story to include a woman, as being present in that room, I'd rip you wide open."

"Sure," said Graves, readily.

"And," Mason told him grimly, "when I say wide open, I mean wide open."

At that moment, a door opened and a detective looked into the room, stared at Mason, then shifted his eyes to Graves, and beckoned.

"Graves," he said, "we want you back upstairs. There are one or two questions we want to ask you. When you gave your statement, you seemed to have evaded answering one of the questions. That is, the chief thinks that you did, now that your statement is being read over."

Graves looked at Mason with eyes that were suddenly apprehensive.

"You won't mind answering these questions?" asked the detective.

"Not at all," said Graves, and walked from the solarium.

When the door closed behind Graves and the detective, Perry Mason pulled a paper from his pocket, unfolded it and examined it with thoughtful appraisal. The paper was Frances Celane's promissory note for forty thousand dollars.

Chapter 8

The woman slipped in through the door of the solarium and stared at Perry Mason, watched him pacing back and forth, following him with her eyes, studying every motion.

There was a keen concentration in the intentness of her gaze; she might have been a motion picture director, studying a new star for the strong, as well as the weak, points. She was short and broad, but not particularly fat. She seemed heavily muscled and big-boned; a woman of immense strength, capable and self reliant, and in her eyes was a glitter of greedy vitality.

Her features were rugged; the chin rounded and heavy, the nose distended at the nostrils. The lips were not thin, but uncurving. The mouth was a straight line, stretching under the nose and calipered at the ends by wrinkles which came from the nostrils. The forehead was rather high, and the eyes black and snapping—highly polished eyes that glittered as though they had been huge, black glass beads.

Perry Mason continued his pacing for several seconds before he sensed her presence. Then, as he turned, the woman's form struck his vision, and he came to an abrupt pause.

Mason looked at her with eyes that were steady in their scrutiny, yet seemed to take in every detail of the woman's appearance from head to foot.

She said: "You're the lawyer."

"Yes," he said, "I'm Perry Mason."

"I want to talk with you," she told him.

"Who are you?"

"I'm Mrs. Mayfield."

"I don't know that that conveys anything to me, Mrs. Mayfield," he said. "Could you be more explicit?"

"I live here," she told him.

53

"Indeed," he said tonelessly.

"Yes, sir," she said, "my husband and myself."

Mason stared at the broad shoulders, the thick arms, the black dress which covered the rugged lines of her body.

"You're the housekeeper?" he asked.

"Yes."

"And your husband?"

"He acts as gardener and general man about the place."

"I see," said Mason, unsmilingly, "and what was it you wanted to talk with me about?"

She took three steps toward him, lowered her voice, and said: "Money."

Something in her tone caused the lawyer to glance over her shoulder to the door of the room. Then he took her arm and led her to the far corner of the room.

"Exactly what," he asked, "was it about money that you wanted to discuss with me?"

The woman said in a low, intense voice: "You're an attorney. You're not in business for your health. You're representing Miss Celane. She's going to get a lot of money, and when she gets it, you're going to get a big slice of it. I want some money. I want some from you, and I want some from her."

"Just why," asked Mason, "should you want money from her and from me?"

"Because," said the woman, slowly, "if I don't get it, you don't get it."

"Exactly what do you mean by that?"

"Just what I say. If you think you can deal me out on this, you've got another think coming."

Mason laughed, a laugh that was utterly mechanical.

"Really, Mrs. Mayfield," he said, "you have got to explain. Things have been happening rather rapidly to-night, and I was called in at the request of Miss Celane. I don't know exactly what my duties will consist of, but I presume it is possible that I may have charge of handling the estate. I don't know whether or not there was a will."

"Never mind that," said the woman, "it isn't Norton's

54

estate that I'm talking about. I'm talking about the trust money.''

Mason simulated surprise, but his eyes were patiently watchful and very hard.

"Why," he said, "that matter is all taken care of by a decree of distribution made months ago. Miss Celane doesn't have to employ an attorney to collect that money for her. It will be distributed to her by an order of the court under the provisions of the trust.''

"You're not fooling me any with all that line of talk," said the woman.

"Exactly what," asked Mason, "do you have reference to?"

"I have reference that if she ain't careful she don't get any of that money at all," said the woman.

"And you are intimating, I take it," said Mason, cautiously, "that you can assist her in being careful?"

"I don't know what you're driving at now," she said, "but I think you've got my idea."

She smirked and put her hands on her broad hips, tilted her chin upward, and stared with unwinking intensity into the attorney's face.

"Suppose," he said, "you should be more explicit."

"The girl's married," she said.

"Indeed," said Mason.

"Yes," she said, "does that mean anything?"

"Not now it doesn't," said Mason. "In the event what you say is true, I understand that Mr. Norton had the right to terminate the trust by delivering a small amount of the principal to Miss Celane, and giving the balance to charitable institutions. But that was something entirely in his discretion. He died without the discretion having been exercised. Therefore, the trust has terminated.''

"Don't be too sure he didn't do anything about that trust," said the housekeeper.

"Did he?" asked Perry Mason.

"Suppose," said the woman, without directly answering his question, "Fran Celane and her uncle had a big fight after you left last night? And suppose that he then and there told her he would give her five thousand dollars of the money, and give all the rest to charity?''

"Did he?" asked the lawyer.

"I'm asking you what would happen if he had."

"Well," said Mason, "there certainly isn't any evidence that he did, is there?"

"There ain't now," she said.

"Exactly what do you mean?" he asked.

"Suppose there should be some evidence like that?"

"We'll cross that bridge when we come to it," said Mason.

"Well," she snapped, "if you don't do business with me, you'll come to it."

"That's hardly possible," said the lawyer. "Come, come, Mrs. Mayfield, if you want to make any insinuations against Miss Celane, you will have to make them in a manner which will be substantiated by the circumstances of the case.

"The evidence in this case shows that Miss Celane left the house before eleven o'clock and didn't return until after the police had arrived."

"Yes," said the woman, "that's what the evidence shows, and you'd better see that it ain't changed."

"I still don't get what you mean," said Perry Mason.

"You will," said the woman, "when you've made Fran Celane come clean and quit pulling the wool over your eyes. I'm not going to stand here and have you high hat me with your lawyer talk. I've told you what I want, and I'm too smart to make any threats."

"In other words," said Mason, "you want money."

"Yes."

"Very good," said Mason. "I take it that everyone wants money."

"You know what I mean," she said, "and if you want to get some more evidence, you might look up what Bob Gleason was doing at the time this murder was committed."

"Gleason?" said Mason, arching his eyebrows. "Why Gleason wasn't even here in the house."

"Oh wasn't he?" said the woman.

"Was he?" asked Mason.

"Ask your Frances," she said.

Mason suddenly turned, planted his feet wide apart, and stared at her.

"Look here, my woman," he said, in his best courtroom manner, "I don't know whether it's ever occurred to you, but you may be guilty of a very serious crime. If you are seeking to frighten me or to frighten Miss Celane into paying you money by making insinuations, you are guilty of a crime known as extortion, and in a case of this kind it might be a very serious crime."

The beady black eyes stared at him snappingly with hostility reflected from their burnished surfaces.

"You're not frightening me a bit," she said.

"And," said Perry Mason, "may I advise you that *you* are not frightening *me* in the least?"

"I ain't trying to frighten you—yet," she said. "I just told you certain things."

"What things?" he asked.

"That I'm going to get some money out of it. Otherwise, nobody gets any money."

"Nobody?" he asked.

"Neither you nor the girl," she agreed.

"That would be unfortunate," said Mason tonelessly.

"Wouldn't it?" she said. "And then again I might find somebody that would pay me, if you didn't see which side of the bread had the butter. Some of these charities for instance."

"Really," said Mason, "I don't get you. You've got to give me more particulars of what you're driving at."

She said: "I'm too smart for you, Mister Lawyer. You go ahead and make your own investigation. Don't think that you're dealing with an ignorant woman, because you ain't. You talk with Frances Celane, and then you can talk some more with me."

"I have talked with Miss Celane," said Mason.

The woman's laugh was harsh and bitter.

"Oh no, you haven't," she said, "you've listened to her. Frances Celane is the best little liar in the world. Don't listen

57

to her. *Talk* to her. Make her mad and *then* see what she says.''

And the woman turned and walked from the room with quick, vigorous strides, a veritable bundle of energy.

Perry Mason stared at her broad back until she had left his field of vision. His eyes were clouded with speculation.

He was standing so, when a man with keen gray eyes and bushy white hair came walking through the room beyond, to the door of the solarium. His manner was grave and dignified, his walk unhurried, his face placidly serene.

Perry Mason bowed to him.

''Judge Purley,'' he said, ''I have practiced before you, Judge.''

The judge fastened his keen eyes upon the attorney, and nodded.

''Perry Mason, I believe. Good evening, Mr. Mason.''

''We can call it morning, I think,'' said Mason. ''It will be daylight pretty soon.''

Judge Purley frowned.

''I was in a hurry to get home too,'' he said. '' I was very, very tired.''

''The police about finished with their investigation?'' asked Mason.

''I think so,'' said Purley. ''They've got the man who did it, beyond any doubt.''

''This chap, Devoe?'' asked Mason.

''That's the chap. He made rather a bungling job of it, too, if you ask me.''

''I didn't get the details,'' said Mason invitingly.

Judge Purley selected one of the reclining chairs, stretched himself in it, gave a sigh of weariness, and took a cigar from his waistcoat pocket.

He carefully clipped off the end of the cigar, smelled the wrapper and muttered: ''Pardon me, Mr. Mason, but this is my last, and I need it.''

''Go right ahead,'' said Mason, ''I only smoke cigarettes anyway.''

''Yes,'' said the judge, speaking gravely and judiciously, in measured tones, ''the thing that confused the murderer, of course, was the fact that our machine turned around and came directly back to the house. He had counted on an interval of half an hour or so during which he could have masked his crime.

"However, when he heard us returning to the house, he knew that the only thing for him to do was to get into bed and pretend he was dead drunk. He managed to get the odor of whisky pretty well on his breath, and put up rather a credible imitation of intoxication.

"In fact, it is possible he imbibed enough so that he was genuinely intoxicated. A man can drink a lot of whisky in a short time."

Perry Mason smiled.

"That is, judge," he said, "if he has it to drink."

The judge saw no humor in the remark. He looked at Perry Mason with judicial appraisal.

"Well," he said, "this man had plenty to drink."

"He's the chauffeur, I believe?" asked Mason.

"Yes, the chauffeur."

"Wasn't he going out some place?" asked Mason. "Didn't Norton telephone for him to take one of the cars and run an errand?"

"If my understanding is correct," said Judge Purley, "that is what happened. Norton wanted his secretary to get some papers at Mr. Crinston's house, and the chauffeur was to go and pick him up."

Perry Mason eyed the judge in shrewd appraisal.

"Well," he said, "let's see if we can figure out what happened. Norton asked you to permit Graves to ride in your car, is that right?"

"That is correct. That is, Norton addressed his comment, I believe, to Mr. Crinston, but I, of course, heard it. He called out the window."

"Okay, then," said Mason. "Let's start from there. Graves went downstairs to join you two. It's reasonable to suppose that Norton then sent for the chauffeur. He probably simply told him to come to his office. Now, it would have taken the chauffeur a minute or two to get there."

"That's right," said Judge Purley wearily. "But if you'll

pardon me, counsellor, I don't see as there's anything to be gained by going over the ground."

"No," said Perry Mason, almost dreamily, "I was just wondering how much time the two men had to quarrel."

"What do you mean?" asked Judge Purley with sudden interest.

"If," said Perry Mason, "the murder was committed by the time your car had arrived at the top of the hill, and if during that time Norton had summoned the chauffeur, and there had been a quarrel, the quarrel would, of necessity, have been of long standing."

"That doesn't follow at all," Judge Purley said. "The quarrel could have started right then. In fact, it isn't reasonable to suppose that Norton would have retained Devoe in his service if there had been a previous quarrel between them."

Perry Mason's eyes glinted.

"Then," he said, "you must agree that there wasn't opportunity for a great deal of premeditation."

Judge Purley regarded him quizzically.

"Just what are you leading up to?" he asked.

"Nothing," said Perry Mason noncommittally.

"In the eyes of the law," said Judge Purley, as though he were pronouncing some judgment, "there is no particular time required for premeditation. An instant's premeditation is all that is necessary to make a crime first degree murder."

"All right," said Perry Mason. "Now, let's look at the case from another angle. As I understand it, one of the windows had been jimmied open, and there were the marks of footprints under the window. These things tended to indicate that a burglar had entered the place."

"All a frame-up," said Judge Purley. "The police have demonstrated that."

"Precisely," said Perry Mason. "But it took some time to plant these clews. Now, the point I am getting at is that there is nothing in the evidence to show whether they were done before the murder, or afterwards. The police have been inclined to the theory that they were done afterwards. But it is barely possible they were done before."

Judge Purley looked at him through the blue haze of his cigar smoke, with a forehead that was washboarded in thought.

"In that case," he said, "the fact that Norton sent for the chauffeur would have had nothing to do with it. The chauffeur would have been waiting our departure, in order to enter Norton's study."

"Now," said Perry Mason, nodding his head, "you're commencing to get to the meat of the situation."

Judge Purley studied the tip of his cigar.

Perry Mason said, in a low tone of voice: "You were in the room where the crime was committed, Judge?"

"Yes. The police allowed me to look through the place. Because of my position, they gave me every liberty."

"Then," said Perry Mason, "if it's a fair question, did you notice anything unusual?"

Judge Purley acted as though the question had given him a great deal of satisfaction. He settled back in his chair, and spoke in slow, deliberate tones, gesturing once in a while with the tip of his cigar.

"The man had been struck from behind," he said, "apparently while he was seated at his desk. He had fallen forward across the desk, and had never moved after the blow crushed in his head. The telephone instrument was at his left hand. There were some papers on the desk, an envelope, I think, and a blank sheet of paper, and an insurance policy for the stolen automobile."

"Ah," said Perry Mason, in a voice that was purring. "The stolen car was insured then?"

"Of course it was insured," said Judge Purley. "Naturally, it would be."

"Are you certain the policy was for the stolen car?" asked Mason.

"Yes, said Judge Purley. "I checked it, and the police checked it. The policy covered a Buick sedan numbered 6754093. It was a policy of full coverage."

"Did you," asked Perry Mason, "know Edward Norton in his lifetime, Judge?"

"No, I had never met him. I am quite well acquainted

with Mr. Crinston, Mr. Norton's business partner, and Mr. Crinston has spoken to me so often about Mr. Norton and his peculiarities that I feel as though I had known him personally. But I had never met him. Mr. Norton was a bit difficult to approach, and I had never had any business dealings which would have caused me to make his acquaintance.''

Perry Mason suddenly turned to face Judge Purley.

''Judge Purley,'' he said, ''Edward Norton wasn't killed as the result of a quarrel.''

Judge Purley shifted his eyes.

''You're referring again to the time element?'' he said. ''The fact that there wasn't time for a quarrel?''

''Partially,'' said Perry Mason. ''Devoe wouldn't have had time to get to the room, have a quarrel with the man, and work himself up into the frenzy of rage necessary to result in murder. Furthermore, the clews which were planted, and were for the purpose of directing suspicion toward a couple of burglars, indicate the murderer knew the logical motive for the killing was that of robbery.''

Judge Purley fidgeted uncomfortably. He seemed struggling with the desire to make a statement, and a reluctance to do so. Perry Mason watched him as a sailing hawk might study a sloping hillside.

''Well,'' said Judge Purley, at length, ''I must say, counsellor, that you have done a very nice bit of reasoning. I wasn't supposed to mention it, but inasmuch as you seem to know, there can be no harm in my confirming your suspicions, or perhaps I should say, your deductions.''

''The motive, then,'' asked Perry Mason, ''was robbery?''

''The motive was robbery,'' said Judge Purley.

''Money?'' asked Mason.

''A very large some of money. Mr. Norton had on his person at the time of his death, something over forty thousand dollars in currency. That money was in a wallet in his inside pocket. When the body was found, the pockets had been rifled and the wallet was gone. That is, it had been lifted from the inside pocket and lay near the body, empty.''

"Were any of the other pockets disturbed?" asked Perry Mason.

"Yes. They had all been turned wrong side out," Judge Purley said.

"Have the police found any of the money?" asked the lawyer.

"That is something which probably won't come out until later, counsellor," said Judge Purley. "But I don't mind telling you in confidence that they have. They found two one thousand dollar bills in Devoe's trouser pocket. Those bills can be identified by their numbers as being part of the currency which Norton had in his possession, and Devoe has made the mistake of stating, in his maudlin way, that he doesn't have any idea how the bills got there."

"Has it been brought out why Norton had such a large sum of cash in his possession?" Mason wanted to know.

Judge Purley started to speak, then checked himself.

"I think, counsellor," he said, "that I have given you all of the information which I should give you. After all, your interest in this matter, while it is parallel with that of the police, is not, of course, identical. Much of the information which was given to me was given to me in confidence because of my judicial position, and I do not think that I should disseminate it carelessly."

There was a faint twinkle of amusement in the eyes of the attorney as he surveyed the ponderous form of the magistrate. Judge Purley radiated a sense of exaggerated self-importance.

"Of course, judge," said Perry Mason, "one must understand and respect your position. I didn't want you to think I was merely curious. I was trying to get a mental picture of what had happened. I am advised by the interested parties that I will be in charge of the estate, and, under those circumstances, I wanted to have complete information."

"That's true, of course," said Judge Purley, nodding his head, "and that's the reason that I gave you as much of the inside information as I did. You will, however, counselor, regard it as strictly confidential."

"Oh yes, of course," said Perry Mason, and there was

just a trace of mockery in his voice, which caused the judge to look up quickly. But the face of the lawyer was bland and innocent.

Chapter 9

Sun streamed in through the window of the room, and shone upon Edward Norton's massive desk.

A police representative sprawled in one of the chairs, a cigarette drooping from his lips, a pencil poised over a notebook. Don Graves, the efficient secretary of the dead man, checked off the documents.

The furniture in the room was in exactly the same position it had occupied the night of the murder. According to police orders, things were to be disturbed as little as possible.

Perry Mason, as the attorney representing the interested parties, was engaged in making a survey of the business affairs of the murdered man.

Don Graves, standing in front of the safe, turned to Perry Mason.

"This compartment of the safe, sir, contains all of the documents relating to the partnership business of Crinston & Norton."

"Very well," said Mason. "You're familiar with the details of those documents, I take it?"

"Oh, yes, sir."

"Generally, what is the financial state of the partnership?"

"The partnership had a few rather unfortunate investments, sir. There were some commitments which ran into rather a large deficit, amounting to something around a million dollars. But, aside from that, the affairs were in good shape. There was, I believe, something like eight hundred thousand dollars on deposit in various banks. Would you like the exact figures?"

"You might give them to me," said Mason. "I want to get just a general idea of the financial set-up."

Graves took a book from the safe, opened it, and read off a column of figures.

"The account was in a little better shape than I thought, sir. There's a balance of eight hundred and seventy-six thousand, five hundred and forty-two dollars and thirty cents at the Seaboard Second National Trust Company, and two hundred and ninety-three thousand, nine hundred and four dollars and fifty cents in the Farmers and Merchants National.

"There are notes, representing the partnership loss, which are held at the Wheeler's Trust and Savings Bank in an amount of nine hundred thousand dollars, with some interest due on them, I believe, and there's a deposit in that bank of seventy-five thousand dollars."

"How about the trust funds?" asked Mason. "The funds representing the trust in favor of Frances Celane?"

"Those are in excellent shape," said Graves. "There is over a million dollars in stocks, bonds, and securities. There's a list of them in this ledger. Mr. Norton was particularly careful about his trust obligations, and kept the account right up to date."

"Are there any liabilities in the trust account?" asked Mason.

"No, sir. There's not a dollar of indebtedness. The assets are all net."

"Then how about Mr. Norton's individual account; that is, outside the partnership of Crinston & Norton?"

"That's something that I can't tell you very much about," said the secretary. "Mr. Norton kept his private business in such shape that it required but little bookkeeping, and carried most of it in his head. Virtually all of the commercial transactions were in the partnership of Crinston & Norton. Mr. Norton's private affairs were confined to the purchase of gilt-edged stocks and bonds, which he kept in a safety deposit box."

"How about a will?" asked the lawyer.

"Yes, sir, there's a will. I don't know where it is. I think it's somewhere in the safe here. I understand generally it leaves everything to Miss Celane. Mr. Norton had no close relatives, you understand."

The police representative said casually, the words coming through an aura of cigarette smoke which seeped out from his mouth as he talked: "Pretty good thing for this Celane woman all around. She gets her trust account free and clear, and also gets a gob of money from the old man, himself."

Perry Mason made no reply to the comment, but continued to address Don Graves.

"Just where is the will?" he asked. "Can you find it?"

"Most of her personal papers were kept in this pigeon-hole in the safe," said Graves, indicating a pigeon-hole.

Perry Mason walked over to the safe, reached in the pigeon-hole, and pulled out a bundle of papers.

"Life insurance policy with the Prudential," he said. "Amount, five hundred thousand dollars. The beneficiary is the estate."

"Yes, sir," said the secretary. "You'll find several life insurance policies in cash to the estate. Those were taken out in order to have sufficient ready cash in the estate to pay inheritance taxes without necessitating a sale of securities at a loss."

"Good idea," said the lawyer. "Here are some more policies. You can list those."

He pulled out a small pasteboard-backed notebook from underneath the policies.

"What's that?" asked the police representative.

Perry Mason turned it over slowly.

"Looks like a car register," he said, "of mileage."

Don Graves laughed.

"Yes," he said, "that's one of the things about Mr. Norton. He always wanted appointments kept to the minute; always carried watches that were adjusted to the second; always kept an account of every mile that was traveled by one of his automobiles. He wanted to know exactly how much mileage he was getting to every gallon of gas and oil. I presume you can tell to within a fraction of a cent how much it cost him to operate every automobile."

"How many cars did we have?" asked Mason, fingering the notebook carelessly.

"He had three: The Buick sedan, a Ford coupe, and a Packard roadster."

"The Packard roadster was the one that Miss Celane usually drove?" asked the lawyer.

"It was," said Graves, "and you won't find any figures on that. That was the despair of his life. Miss Celane simply wouldn't turn in mileage figures."

"I see," said Mason. "But the others are accurately accounted for?"

"Yes."

"Miss Celane wasn't in the habit of operating the others?"

Don Graves flashed the lawyer a meaning glance.

"No," he said, shortly.

Perry Mason carelessly opened the notebook to the division which had to do with the Buick sedan, and noticed the different mileage reports which were in there. Apparently for every mile the Buick had traveled, there was a note as to the kind of road it had gone over, the place to which it had been driven, the general average speed, and much other data which represented a mass of detail that would have been considered useless to any save a mind that gloried in figuring costs to a fraction of a cent.

Perry Mason maintained a pose of casual interest as he fingered the pages until he came to the last entry covering the Buick sedan, which was as follows: "15,294.3 miles. Left house and drove to bank. Arrived bank at 15,299.5 miles. Left bank and returned to house at 15,304.7 miles. Instructed Devoe to fill tank."

Perry Mason glanced at the date, and saw that it was the date on which Norton had met his death.

"I see," he remarked casually, "that he went to the bank the day of his death."

"Did he?" said Don Graves.

"I wonder," said Perry Mason, "if that was when he got his money . . . that is, the cash that he carried."

"I'm sure I couldn't tell you, sir."

"Does anyone know why he had such a large sum of cash in his possession?" asked the lawyer.

"No," said Graves, emphatically.

"Almost looks as though he might have been blackmailed or something," said Mason, his patient eyes peering out from under his level brows at the face of the secretary.

Don Graves met his glance without changing expression by so much as the flicker of an eyelash.

"I hardly think so, sir," he said.

Mason nodded and slipped the book into his pocket. "Just a minute," said the police officer. "Shouldn't that book be kept here with the rest of the papers?"

Mason smiled.

"That's right," he said. "It looks so much like a notebook that I sometimes carry, I mechanically dropped it into my pocket."

He handed the book to the secretary, got up, and yawned.

"Well," he said, "I guess I've covered about everything I need to, as a first preliminary survey. Of course, we'll have to take a detailed inventory later on."

"We can take the detailed inventory now if you want," said Graves.

"Oh, I don't think so," said Mason, yawning again. "There's going to be a lot of detailed stuff to check over here, and I'll probably want my own stenographer here to take notes when I go into it in detail. I hate detail work."

"How about the will? Should we make any further search for the will?" asked Graves.

"Oh, let's close things up now, and I'll have my secretary come out and we'll tackle it to-morrow," said the attorney.

"Very well, sir, just as you say," said Don Graves.

The police representative flipped away his cigarette and remarked, "Any time suits me. I'll be around here all the time."

"Fine," said Mason, without enthusiasm. He lit a cigarette, and walked casually from the office.

He went down the broad flight of stairs, opened the front door, and stood in the sunshine, inhaling the fresh morning air. When he was certain he was not observed, he stepped off the porch, walked to the driveway, and went up the driveway to the garage. He slid back the door of the garage, slipped inside, and walked over to the Buick sedan which stood,

69

obviously well cared for and polished by the chauffeur who was now in jail, charged with murder.

Perry Mason opened the door of the sedan, slid in behind the steering wheel, switched on the dashlight and looked at the speedometer. The figures showed 15,304.7 miles.

The lawyer stared at them for a moment, then switched off the dashlight, slid out from behind the wheel, and carefully closed the door. He walked out of the garage, looked to see if anyone had been observing him, then retraced his steps to the front door.

As he stepped inside, he encountered the form of the housekeeper.

Her glittering black eyes surveyed him uncompromisingly.

"Good morning," she said.

"Good morning," said Perry Mason.

She lowered her voice slightly.

"I'm going to be wanting an answer, sir," she said, "very soon."

"You shall have it," said the attorney, "and, by the way, where is Miss Celane? Is she up yet?"

"Yes, sir, she's up. She's having breakfast in her room."

"Give her my compliments," said the lawyer, "and ask her if I can see her at once."

The glittering black eyes of the housekeeper surveyed his face searchingly, and Perry Mason met her stare with a look of weary patience.

"I'll see," said the housekeeper. She turned and walked with swift, aggressive steps toward the girl's bedroom.

Perry Mason lit a cigarette with a steady hand, took only a single appreciative inhalation, then stood studying the smoke as it eddied from the tip of the cigarette.

He heard the steps of the housekeeper as she pounded toward him.

"Miss Celane says you can talk to her while she's eating breakfast," said the housekeeper. "Right this way, please."

The lawyer followed the housekeeper down the corridor and to the door of the girl's room.

The housekeeper held it open.

"There you are, sir," she said. "Step right in," and added in a lower tone, "and remember, I want an answer."

Perry Mason walked in and heard the door slam viciously behind him.

Frances Celane, in a silken negligee, sat curled in an overstuffed chair. A small stand at the side of the chair held a tray containing empty dishes. A huge coffee pot had been pushed to the side of the tray, and a steaming cup of coffee was at the fingertips of her right hand. Her left held a cigarette.

Her dark eyes, seeming purposely expressionless, surveyed the attorney. Her face showed a hint of rouge, but there was no lipstick on her mouth. The negligee seemed to have been chosen for appearance rather than warmth.

"Good morning," he said, barely sweeping his eyes over the negligee. "Did you sleep any?"

"After I finally got to bed, I did," she said, staring at him steadily. She took the cigarette from her mouth and tapped the ashes into the edge of the saucer under the coffee cup.

Perry Mason moved over and dropped ashes from his own cigarette into the saucer.

"I presume," she said, "that you want money."

"What makes you ask that?" he inquired.

"I understand attorneys always want money."

He made a gesture of impatience with his hand, and said: "That isn't what I meant. Why did you choose this particular time for bringing up the subject?"

"Because," she said, "I have some money for you."

His eyes were coldly cautious. "A check?" he asked.

"No," she said, "cash. Would you mind handing me my purse? It's over there on the dresser."

Mason reached for the purse and handed it to her. She held it at such an angle that he could not see the contents. She opened it and fumbled with her fingers for a few moments, then produced a sheaf of currency.

"Here," she said, "is something by way of retainer."

He took the money, crisp new one-thousand dollar bills. There were ten of them. He looked at her for a few moments, then folded and pocketed the money.

"All right," he said, "where did you get it?"

Her eyes suddenly contained expression. "That's none of your business," she snapped. "You're an attorney paid to represent me; not to inquire into my personal affairs."

He stood with his feet apart, smiling down at her rage.

"Your temper," he told her, "is going to get you into trouble some day."

"Oh, you think so, do you?" she flared.

"I know it," he said. "You're getting on thin ice. You've got to learn to keep your temper and use your head."

"Just what do you mean by that crack about thin ice?"

"I was referring," he said, in cold tones, "to the reason that you were spared more detailed questioning last night, or, rather, early this morning."

"What was that?"

"The fact that you had taken your uncle's Buick sedan without his permission, and were, as I remember your story, speeding around the country trying to settle your nerves."

"I always do that," she said, her voice suddenly cautious, "after I've been in a rage. It calms me down."

He continued to smile frostily at her.

"Do you know how far you drove the automobile?"

"No. I drove it an hour or so. I had my foot pretty well down on the throttle. I drive like that most of the time."

"How unfortunate," he said, "that the speedometer was disconnected."

She stared at him, with her eyes suddenly wide and very dark.

"What are you talking about?" she asked, slowly.

"About the fact that your uncle's notebook shows every mile that the Buick was driven."

"Does it?" she asked, warily.

"Yes," said Mason dryly. "He made a note of driving the car from the bank to the house, showing that he started with the speedometer registering 15,299.5 miles, and arrived at the house registering 15,304.7 miles."

"Well," she asked, "what if he did?"

"When I inspected the speedometer on the Buick sedan this morning," he said slowly, "it showed 15,304.7 miles."

She stared at him with her eyes dark with panic. Her face had suddenly gone white. She tried to set down the coffee cup, but missed the saucer. The cup balanced for a moment on the edge of the tray, then crashed to the floor, spilling its contents over the rug.

"You hadn't thought of that, had you?" asked Perry Mason.

She continued to stare at him mutely, her face white to the lips.

"Now," said Perry Mason suavely, "you will perhaps pardon a repetition of my question. Where did you get this money that you gave to me just now?"

"I got it," she said slowly, "from my uncle."

"Just before his death?" asked Mason.

"Just before his death," she said.

"Oh," said the lawyer meaningly, "*before* his death."

The significance of the accented word suddenly dawned upon her.

"You don't think," she began. . . .

There was a knock at the door of the room, and the housekeeper walked in. She stared at them.

"Did I hear you drop something?" she asked.

The girl indicated the coffee cup on the floor.

"You have," said Perry Mason meaningly, "rather remarkable ears."

She met his stare with her eyes snapping and defiant.

"I was given a good pair of ears," she said, "and I *use them*."

"Even to the extent of listening at doors?" said the lawyer.

Frances Celane spoke steadily.

"That will do, Mr. Mason," she said. "I think that I am perfectly capable of disciplining the servants when they need it."

The housekeeper stooped, picked up the coffee cup, set it back on the tray, turned her back to the attorney, and said to Frances Celane: "Shall I bring you another cup and saucer?"

"Yes," she said, "and a hot pot of coffee."

The housekeeper picked up the tray, and swept from the room.

Perry Mason's tone was rasping. "If I'm going to handle this case," he said, "I don't want you interfering. That woman was spying on us. She tried to blackmail me early this morning."

Frances Celane seemed hardly interested.

"Indeed?" she said, absently.

Perry Mason stood, staring down at her.

"Yes, indeed," he said, "and I'm still waiting for an explanation of why your trip made in the Buick sedan at such a high speed, didn't show on the speedometer."

Frances Celane jumped from the chair, and, totally ignoring the presence of the lawyer, started pulling garments from her slender body.

"What are you doing?" he asked.

"Going to get dressed and put some mileage on that Buick, you fool!" she blazed at him.

"And are you going to tell me anything about where you were last night at the time of the murder?"

She whipped off the last of her lounging garments and started dressing.

"Don't be a fool," she said.

"I can help you a lot more," said Mason, "if you let me know the facts."

She shook her head. "Get out," she said.

Perry Mason turned to the door with dignity.

"Very well," he said, and jerked the door open.

The housekeeper was on the other side of the door, regarding him with malevolent, glittering eyes, and a smile which held a trace of sardonic triumph. In one hand she held a coffee cup and saucer, and in the other hand a pot of coffee.

"Thank you, sir," she said, "for opening the door," and slipped into the room.

Chapter 10

George Blackman tried to present an impressive appearance. He combed his hair well back from his high forehead, cultivated a deep, booming voice, and wore nose glasses from which dangled a wide, black ribbon. He might have been a congressman or a banker, but was, in fact, a criminal lawyer.

Only a slight uneasiness of the eyes belied the picture of stolid, intellectual respectability which he tried to present to the public.

He stared across the desk at Perry Mason. "I understand that you're the attorney for the family," he said.

Perry Mason's eyes were hard, and patient.

"I'm representing Miss Celane in the termination of her trust matter," he said, "and I'm representing Arthur Crinston, who is the surviving partner of the partnership. There's some talk about having me represent the executor under the will, but I can't very well represent both the surviving partner and the executor."

Blackman grinned, and there was a trace of envy in his grin.

"Pretty soft for you," he said, "with all of those fees coming in."

"Was that what you came to talk about?" asked Mason, coldly.

Blackman's expression changed.

"I came to tell you," he said, "that I'm representing Peter Devoe, the chauffeur, who is charged with the murder."

"Got a good case?" asked Mason casually.

The other man winced.

"*You* know all about the case," he said.

"To tell you the truth," said Mason, speaking with elaborate carelessness, "I don't. I've been so busy with other angles of the matter that I haven't had time to look into the murder case at all.''

Blackman said, "Baloney!" explosively.

Mason looked dignified and resentful.

Blackman leaned forward and tapped the desk impressively.

"Look here, Mason," he said. "You're playing things pretty foxy. But I just want you to know that you're up against somebody who's going to play just as foxy."

"Meaning?" asked Perry Mason.

"I mean that you can't sit back and rake in all the money, and keep all *your* people out of it, while you railroad Devoe to the gallows."

"I'm not railroading anybody to the gallows."

Blackman squirmed under the cold glare of the man across the desk.

"Look here," he said, "I'm talking facts now. There's nobody here to hear us. It's just a conference between us two. You know the game as well as I do. You defend persons accused of crime whenever there's a good fee in it, and so do I. When you defend a person, you're representing him and nobody else on earth. You'd fight the whole world to protect the rights of your clients."

"Sure," said Mason, patiently, tonelessly, "that's the duty of an attorney."

"All right," Blackman said. "I just want you to know that *I'm* going to be faithful to *my* duties."

"Go on," said Mason. "You've said too much or not enough. I can't tell which yet."

"All right," Blackman told him. "I mean just this. You're keeping this Celane woman pretty much in the background. You've managed to do it rather adroitly. After all, the only case against Pete Devoe is one of circumstantial evidence, and it's pretty weak circumstantial evidence, at that. He was lying there in bed, drunk, and *anybody* could have planted that club in his room and the two thousand dollars in his clothes."

"You overlook," said Mason, "the testimony of Don Graves, who actually saw the murder being committed. You overlook the fact that, according to Crinston's testimony, Edward Norton was sending for his chauffeur as Crinston left the place."

"I overlook nothing," said Blackman impressively, his eyes boring belligerently into Mason's face. "And I don't overlook the fact that there was a woman mixed up in the thing somewhere."

"Yes?" asked Mason in a tone of polite but surprised interest.

"Yes," said Blackman, "and don't be so damned surprised at it. You know it, as well as I do."

"Know what?" asked Mason.

"Know that Don Graves saw a woman in that room at the time the murder was being committed."

"Don Graves doesn't say so in the statement that he made to the police, as I understand it," Mason remarked.

"The statement he made to the police hasn't got anything to do with it," said Blackman. "It's the statement he is going to make on the witness stand that counts."

Mason looked at the ceiling and said, impersonally: "In the event, however, that the statement he makes on the witness stand doesn't coincide with the first statement he made to the police, it might have a tendency to weaken his testimony, particularly as far as the woman was concerned."

"Yes, it *might*," said Blackman.

There was silence for a moment, then Blackman lowered his voice and said emphatically, "All right. You know where I stand now. You're controlling all the money in this case, and I'm representing the man who has been picked for the fall guy. I want the family to coöperate in this thing, and I want some money. Otherwise, I'm going to tear the lid off."

"What do you mean by coöperation?" asked Mason.

"I mean that I want the family to convey the impression to the police that they're not at all vindictive; that if Devoe did anything, he was drunk when he did it, and that if the District Attorney will take a plea of manslaughter they'll be just as well satisfied. And then I'm going to want some of the gravy."

"You mean," said Mason, "that you want Frances Celane

77

to see that you get paid to plead Pete Devoe guilty of manslaughter so as to hush up any scandal? Is that what you're trying to convey to me?''

Blackman got to his feet with ponderous dignity.

''I think, counselor,'' he said, ''that you understand my errand perfectly. I think that I have stated my position fairly and frankly, and I do not care to commit myself by replying to the rather crude summary which you have attempted to make.''

Perry Mason pushed back the chair from his desk, stood with his feet planted well apart, his eyes staring at Blackman.

''Don't think you can pull anything like that, Blackman,'' he said. ''We're here alone. You're going to tell me what you want, and tell it in so many words.''

''Don't be silly,'' Blackman told him. ''You know what I want.''

''What do you want?''

''I want money.''

''What are you going to give in return for it?''

''I'll coöperate with you in keeping Miss Celane in the background.''

''To the extent that you'll have Pete Devoe plead guilty to manslaughter?''

''Yes. If I can get a plea.''

''Is he guilty of manslaughter?'' asked Perry Mason.

''Why the hell bother about that?'' said Blackman irritably. ''I told you that he'd plead guilty to manslaughter.''

''How much money do you want?''

''I want fifty thousand dollars.''

''That's too much money for a fee,'' Mason remarked, in a voice that was almost casual.

''Not for the work I'm going to do it isn't.''

''The work for Devoe?'' asked Mason.

''The work for Frances Celane, if you want to put it that way,'' Blackman told him.

''All right,'' Mason went on, ''as you, yourself, expressed it, we're here alone. There's no reason why we can't talk frankly. Did Pete Devoe kill Edward Norton?''

''You ought to know,'' said Blackman.

"Why should I know?"

"Because you should."

"I don't know. I'm asking you if he did."

"Why worry about that? I'll get him to plead guilty to manslaughter."

"For fifty thousand dollars?"

"For fifty thousand dollars."

"You're crazy. The District Attorney wouldn't accept any such plea. This is a murder case. Second degree murder would be the best you could get."

"I could get manslaughter," Blackman said, "if the family would coöperate, and if Graves would change his story a little bit."

"Why should Graves change his story?" Mason inquired.

"Why should anybody do anything?" Blackman asked in a sarcastic tone of voice. "Why should I do anything? Why should you do anything? We're not mixed in it. We're doing things for money. Don Graves would do things for money too."

Slowly, almost ponderously, Perry Mason walked around the big desk toward Blackman. Blackman watched him with greedy eyes.

"Just say it's all right," said Blackman, "and you won't hear anything more about it."

Perry Mason came to a stop in front of Blackman. He looked at him with eyes that were cold and sneering.

"You dirty scum," he said, his voice vibrant with feeling.

Blackman recoiled slightly. "What the hell are you talking about?"

"You," said Mason.

"You've got no right to talk to me like that."

Perry Mason took a swift step forward.

"A dirty shyster," he said, "who would sell out his client for a fifty thousand dollar fee. Get out of this office, and do it right now!"

Blackman's face twisted in surprise.

"Why," he said, "I thought you were going to listen to my proposition."

"I listened to it," Mason told him, "and heard all I wanted to."

Blackman suddenly bolstered up his courage, and brandished a rigid forefinger in front of Mason's face.

"You're mixed in this thing pretty deep yourself," he said. "You're either going to accept this proposition, or you're going to hear a lot more about it."

Perry Mason reached up and grasped the extended forefinger in his left hand. He twisted the other's hand down and around, until the lawyer exclaimed with pain. Mason abruptly released the forefinger, spun the other lawyer halfway around, grasped the back of the lawyer's coat with his big, capable hand, and propelled the lawyer to the door. He jerked open the door of the private office, gave Blackman a shove that sent him sprawling off balance, into the outer office.

"Get out, and stay out!" he said.

Blackman almost ran for half the distance across the outer office, then turned, with his face livid with rage, his glasses dangling at the end of the black ribbon.

"You're going to regret that," he said, "more than anything you ever did in your life!"

"Get out!" said Perry Mason, in a slow, even tone of voice, "or I'm going to do some more."

Blackman groped for the knob of the outer door, pulled it open, and stepped into the corridor.

Perry Mason stood in the doorway of his private office, shoulders squared, feet planted widely apart, staring belligerently at the slowly closing door.

"What happened?" asked Della Street, in sudden concern.

"I told the cheap heel where to get off," Mason remarked, without looking at her, his cold eyes still fastened on the door from the outer office.

He turned and walked back to his private office, leaving Della Street staring at him with wide, apprehensive eyes.

The telephone was ringing as he reached his desk. He scooped the receiver to his ear, and heard the voice of Frances Celane.

"I've got to see you at once," she said.

80

"All right," he told her, "I'm in my office. Can you come in?"

"Yes, unless you can come out here."

"Where are you?"

"Out at the house."

"All right," he told her, "you'd better get in that Buick and come in here."

"I can't come in the Buick," she said.

"Why not?" he asked.

"The police have sealed it up. They've locked the transmission and padlocked the wheels."

Perry Mason gave a low whistle over the telephone.

"In that event," he said, "you'd better get in the Packard and come here just as fast as you can. You'd better grab a suitcase and put some clothes in it, but do it without attracting too much attention."

"I'll be in in twenty minutes," she said, and hung up.

Perry Mason put on his hat, and paused for a moment to talk with Della Street as he went out.

"I'm expecting Miss Celane in here," he said, "in about twenty or twenty-five minutes, and I think I'll be back by the time she arrives. But if I'm not, I want you to put her in my private office and lock the door. Don't let anyone in. Do you understand?"

She looked up at him, swiftly apprehensive, and nodded her head in a gesture of affirmation. "Has anything gone wrong?" she asked.

He nodded curtly, then smiled and patted her shoulder.

He walked out of the door, took the elevator down, and walked a block and a half to the Seaboard Second National Trust Company.

B. W. Rayburn, vice president of the bank, regarded Perry Mason with hard, watchful eyes, and said: "Yes, Mr. Mason?"

"I'm representing Miss Frances Celane, the beneficiary under a trust fund which was administered by Edward Norton," said Mason. "Also, I'm representing Mr. Arthur Crinston, who is the surviving partner of Crinston & Norton."

"Yes," said Mr. Rayburn. "So I understand from a conversation I had this morning with Mr. Crinston."

"On the day of his death," said Mason, "Mr. Norton made a trip from his home to a bank and back again. I am wondering if the trip was to this bank, or to the Farmers and Merchants National, where I understand he also had an account."

"No," said Rayburn slowly, "he came here. Why do you ask?"

"I understand," said Mason, "he came here to secure a large sum of money in one thousand dollar bills. I am anxious to know if there was anything peculiar about his request for that money, or anything peculiar about the bills."

"Perhaps," said Rayburn significantly, "if you could be a little more explicit, I could give you the information you wanted."

"Did Mr. Norton," asked the lawyer, "say specifically for what purpose he wanted those bills?"

"Not specifically," said Rayburn, with the secretive manner of one who is determined only to answer direct questions.

Mason took a deep breath.

"Did he ask you in advance," he said, "to get for him a certain number of thousand dollar bills bearing consecutive serial numbers?"

"He did," said the vice president of the bank.

"And did he further state to you that, through your banking affiliations, he would like very much to have you make note of the numbers of those bills and ascertain when the bills were presented for deposit at any bank in the city?"

"Not exactly in those words," said Rayburn cautiously.

"Did he state that he intended to use that money to make a payment to a blackmailer, and would like to find out the identity of the person who deposited the currency?"

"Not in exactly *those* words," said the banker again.

"I think," said Perry Mason, smiling, "that I have all of the information I can ask you to give me, and sufficient for my purpose. Thank you, Mr. Rayburn."

He turned and walked from the bank, leaving behind him

a cold-eyed individual who surveyed his back in a gaze of shrewd speculation.

Mason returned to his office and beckoned Della Street to his inner office.

"Get Drake's Detective Bureau for me," he said, "and say that I want Paul Drake, himself, to handle a matter of the utmost importance. Say that I want Drake to come to my office posing as a client, and that I want him to wait in the reception room until I give him a line on what he's to do. During the time he's waiting, he is to appear merely as a client."

She looked at him with eyes that showed grave apprehension.

"Is that all?" she asked.

"That's all," he told her.

"And you don't want that Celane woman to know anything about who Paul Drake is?"

"Get this straight," Perry Mason told her. "I don't want *anyone* to know who Drake is. As far as anyone who comes into the office is concerned, Drake is a client who is waiting to see me."

"Okay," she said.

She paused for a few moments, watching him with eyes that made no effort to conceal their concern.

He grinned reassuringly.

"Don't worry," he said, "it's okay."

"You're not getting in trouble?" she asked.

"I don't think so."

"Is Miss Celane?"

"She's in already—up to her neck."

"Does she know it?"

"I think so."

"You won't let her drag you into it?"

He shook his head slowly.

"No," he said. "I don't think so. I can't tell just yet."

"When can you tell?" she asked.

"Not until Miss Celane tells me the truth."

"When will that be?"

"Not until she gets worse frightened than she is now."

Della Street frowned, then said, quickly: "Suppose we frighten her?"

Perry Mason shook his head and smiled.

"No," he said, slowly, "I don't think we'll have to."

Chapter 11

Perry Mason, thumbs hooked in the armholes of his vest, paced back and forth across the floor of his private office.

Frances Celane, perched in the big black leather chair which she had occupied on her first visit to the office, regarded him with eyes that moved steadily back and forth, following the pacing of the lawyer.

"Well," she said at length, "you haven't asked me anything about why I wanted to see you."

"I don't have to," he said, "I know what's happening better than you do. What I'm trying to do is to think far enough ahead so I can find the proper place to head them off."

"I'm in an awful mess," she said.

"Of course you are," he snapped, and resumed his steady pacing of the floor.

There was a period of silence, then he paused in his walk to plant his feet far apart and stare down at her.

"Where did you get that money you gave me?" he asked.

"Just as I told you before, I got the money from my uncle," she said, in a thin, weak voice.

"Before he was murdered or afterwards?" pressed Perry Mason.

"Before."

"How much before?"

"Not very much before. That is, just before Mr. Crinston came to the house."

"What happened?"

"There was forty-eight thousand dollars," she said. "He gave it to me, and told me he was sorry he'd been holding out my regular allowance. He said he'd decided to change his mind."

"Had he accused you of being blackmailed before that?"

"No."

"And he gave you this money in cash?"

"Yes."

"You came to him and told him that you needed cash?"

"I told him that I simply had to have some money and have it right away."

"And he didn't say anything about you being blackmailed?"

"No."

"*Were* you being blackmailed?"

She bit her lip and looked down at the floor.

"Is that any of your business?" she asked.

"Yes," he said.

"Yes," she said, "I was being blackmailed."

"All right," he said. "Was it by the housekeeper?"

She started, and raised her eyes to his with a look of alarm.

"How did you know?"

"I suspected," he said. "How much did you give her?"

"I gave her all of it," she said. "All except the ten thousand dollars that I gave you."

"Does that mean," he said, "that *you* haven't any of those thousand dollar bills in your possession?"

"That's right."

"Now listen. Let's not have any misunderstanding about this, and let's get it straight. You're in a jam, and I'm going to get you out, but it's important I know *exactly* what happened with that money. You haven't *any* of it in your possession?"

"Not a bit," she said.

Perry Mason took the ten thousand dollars which she had given him from his wallet and fingered the bills.

"You knew," he asked, "that all of these bills were numbered consecutively, and that various banking institutions in this city had been given a list of those numbers?"

"No," she said in a wan, frightened voice.

"Well," he told her, "that's a fact. Thousand dollar bills aren't so numerous but what they attract attention when they're deposited, and it's almost necessary to take them to

86

a bank to change them. Merchants don't ordinarily carry change for a thousand dollars in their tills.''

Perry Mason went to the desk, picked up a long envelope of heavy manila paper, sealed the ten thousand dollars in currency in the envelope, unscrewed the cap from a fountain pen, and addressed the envelope to Carl S. Belknap, 3298 15th Street, Denver, Colorado, and jabbed his forefinger on the button on the side of his desk, which summoned his secretary.

When Della Street opened the door, Perry Mason tossed her the envelope with a careless gesture.

''Stamp and mail this,'' he said. ''First Class.''

She looked at the address.

''I didn't know we had any correspondence with a Mr. Belknap,'' she said.

''We have now,'' he told her. ''Send it registered mail.''

She nodded, flashed one swiftly appraising glance at Frances Celane, then slipped back through the door to the outer office.

Perry Mason turned to Frances Celane.

''All right,'' he said. ''That envelope will be in the mail for the next few days. Eventually it will come back to me. In the meantime, nobody is going to find that money on me. Now why didn't you tell the police about that in the first place?''

Her eyes suddenly snapped black fire.

''That's my business!'' she said. ''I hired you as an attorney to represent my interests. Don't think that you can stand here and tell me what I'm going to do, and what I'm not going to do. . . . ''

He took a stride toward her and said: ''You're either going to control that temper, or you're going to march up the gallows and have a black bag put around your neck. Did you ever think of how you would like to be hung?''

She got to her feet and drew back her hand as though she intended to slap him.

''You've been a spoiled spitfire all your life,'' Perry Mason told her. ''Now you're facing a situation you can't handle by yourself. Just as sure as you're standing there, you're going to be arrested within the next forty-eight hours, and the case that's going to be built up against you is going to be so black that I don't know whether I can get you out of it or not."

Sheer surprise pushed her rage to one side, and showed in her dark eyes.

"Arrested? Me, arrested?"

"Arrested," he told her, "for murder."

"Devoe was arrested for murder," she said. "He's the one that did it."

"Devoe didn't do it," said Perry Mason, "any more than I did. That is, if he did do it, no one is ever going to prove it. He's got an attorney that knows the ropes, and he's going to drag you into this."

"How do you know?" she asked.

"Because he was here in this office less than an hour ago and told me so."

She sank back in the chair and stared at him, all of the temper gone from her eyes, which were now dark and pathetic.

"What did he want?" she asked.

"Money," he said.

Her face showed a trace of relief.

"All right," she said. "We'll give it to him."

"We will *not*," he said.

"Why?"

"Because," he said, "he'd blackmail you to death. He doesn't know for sure that you are in a bad jam, but he suspects it. He wanted to make sure. If I'd talked terms with him, he'd have been sure. He's heard whispers somewhere. He wanted to verify them. If I'd given in to him on the money end of it, he'd have been sure."

"But," she asked, "what did you do?"

His voice was grim.

"I threw him out of the office," he said.

"How much does he know?" she asked.

"Not much, but he suspects a lot."

"I'm afraid of him," she said, in a voice that was almost a wail.

"You've got a right to be," he said. "Now I want to get at the bottom of this thing. Tell me *exactly* what happened when your uncle was murdered."

She took a deep breath and said in a low monotone, "I was in the house. I had had a quarrel with him. He had been very bitter, and I lost my temper and said things that hurt."

"You would," said the lawyer drily.

"I did," she said, without expression.

There was a moment of silence.

"Go on," said the lawyer.

"He took some money from his wallet," she said. "It wasn't all of the money that was in there. There were some bills left. I don't know exactly how many, but he pushed the currency toward me and told me to take it. He said that he had intended to cut down on my allowance to bring me to my senses, but that he'd come to the conclusion I would never come to my senses. He said it was really my money and if I wanted to throw it away, that was my business."

"So you took the money," he told her.

"Yes, of course."

"Then what?"

"Then," she said, "I gave all of it except ten thousand dollars to Mrs. Mayfield."

"Why did you do that?" he asked.

"Because she knew I had been married, and was threatening to tell my uncle about it."

"Was that before Crinston came to the house, or afterwards?"

"You mean when I gave her the money?"

"Yes."

"Afterwards."

"Who saw you give the money to her . . . anyone?"

"Rob Gleason."

Perry Mason whistled.

"So Gleason was there, eh?" he asked.

"Yes," she said slowly, "Gleason was there. That's why I said I wasn't there."

"All right," he said grimly, "tell me about *that*."

"You know that we are married," she said. "Rob drove

89

up in his car, a Chevrolet. There's a porch which opens out from my room, and he came to that porch and I let him in. He was worried about Mrs. Mayfield and about what my uncle was going to do. I told him that I'd seen my uncle and I thought things were all right.

"While we were talking, Mrs. Mayfield came in and demanded money. She had been listening, and knew that my uncle had given me some money. She didn't know how much.

"I told her I'd give her all I had. I opened my purse and let her take it out. But, before I did that, I had ditched ten of the one thousand dollar bills, because I knew you were going to need some money, and I was saving it for you. That was all I needed money for—just you and her. I thought then that things would be all right, with you representing me, and Mrs. Mayfield keeping quiet. I thought we could work the thing out some way."

"And Crinston had arrived by that time?" asked Mason.

"Yes," she said, "he had come before that. I heard him drive up. In fact, I was leaving my uncle's office when Crinston came up."

"And Graves, the secretary, was in the outer office all the time?" asked the lawyer.

"Yes, he was there all the time, and knows pretty much what happened. He knows a lot more than he lets on. He knows a lot about my uncle's affairs, and I have an idea he knows something about what Mrs. Mayfield is doing."

"All right," said Mason, "then what happened?"

"Well," she said, "Mrs. Mayfield went out, and I went out and sat on the porch with Rob. Then there was a commotion, and I heard running steps from the front of the house, and shouts, and heard something about my uncle having been murdered. I knew that it would never do for Rob to be there, so I told Rob to get in his car and drive away."

"And you went with him?"

"Yes, I went with him."

"Why did you do that?"

"Because I didn't want to be there."

"Why?"

"I thought that I could fix up an alibi for Rob."

"How did you get out of the grounds?"

"There's a way out through an alley in the back, to the driveway. We went out there, and nobody heard us, I guess."

"All right, then what happened?"

"Then I came back home; that is, I had Rob drive me to a place about two blocks from the house, and got out there. I sneaked into my bedroom and talked with Don Graves. I found out from him that my uncle had reported the Buick as having been stolen, and they thought that I was driving it. I figured that was a good alibi for me, and would let Rob out of it, so I said that I had been driving that Buick, and nobody questioned my word."

"All right. Then what happened?"

"You know the rest. Everybody took it for granted that I had been driving the Buick, and I thought everything was all right until you came and told me about the speedometer records not checking up. I went out to put some mileage on the Buick, and found an officer there, who grinned at me and told me that the Buick was going to be held for evidence."

"They'd sealed it up?" asked Perry Mason.

"Yes. They put a padlocked chain around the front axle and through the spokes of the wheel, and they'd also locked up the transmission."

"That," said Mason drily, "makes it nice."

She said nothing.

After a moment Mason resumed his regular pacing of the floor, and the girl watched him with dark, anxious eyes, her head never moving, but the eyes following him back and forth as he paced rhythmically.

"You," he said, at length, "are going to have a nervous breakdown. I know a doctor I can count on. He's going to examine you and order you to a sanitarium."

"What good will that do?" she asked.

"It's going to give me a little time," he said.

"But won't that make them more suspicious when I run away?"

"They can't get any more suspicious," he told her. "The minute they sealed up that Buick, it showed they were working on this other angle of the case. I tried to slip that notebook

91

containing the mileages into my pocket, and make it appear I was doing it casually; but the officer wasn't so dumb. He called me on it, and I had to put the notebook back.''

"Did you know about the mileage then?" she asked.

"I suspected it.''

"How did it happen you suspected it?"

"Because I knew you'd been lying to me.''

Her eyes blazed.

"Don't talk to me like that!" she said.

He simply grinned at her. After a moment the angry light left her eyes.

"You've got to figure you're trapped on that car business,'' he told her. "You've got to switch around on that.''

"But," she said, "that's going to bring Rob into it. If they know Rob was there, that's going to make an awful mess, because there was bad blood between Rob and my uncle.''

"Did Rob see your uncle the night he was murdered?'' asked Mason.

She shook her head, hesitated a moment, then nodded it.

"Yes," she said, "he did.''

"And the reason you changed your story just now and admitted it,'' he said, "is that you suddenly remembered there is someone who knows Rob saw your uncle. Who is that someone—Don Graves?''

She nodded her head again.

Perry Mason stepped to the door of the outer office.

"Dell,'' he said, "get me Doctor Prayton on the telephone right away. Tell his nurse that it's vitally important—a matter of life and death. Get him on the telephone personally, and do it now.''

"Yes," she said. "There's a Mr. Paul Drake in the office who wants to see you about a personal matter. He won't tell me what it is.''

"All right," snapped Perry Mason. "Tell him to wait," and he stepped back into the office, slamming the door.

"Now," he told the girl, "you're going to have a nervous breakdown. You'll be sent to a sanitarium under another name. The police will find you sooner or later. But I want it to be later. Don't let anyone know who you are, don't show any undue interest in the newspaper reports of the case, and, no matter what happens, don't get stampeded.''

She stared at him searchingly.

"How do I know I can trust you?" she asked.

He met her gaze with a steady stare.

"That's one of the things you can use your own judgment about," he said, "and it's going to make a hell of a lot of difference what you do."

"All right," she told him, "I'm going to trust you."

He nodded.

"Under those circumstances," he said, "I'll order the ambulance right now before Doc Prayton gets here."

Chapter 12

Paul Drake, the detective, bore no resemblance whatever to the popular conception of a private detective, which was, perhaps, why he was so successful.

He was a tall man, with a long neck that was thrust forward inquiringly. His eyes were protruding, and glassy, and held a perpetual expression of droll humor. Nothing ever fazed him. In his life, murders were everyday occurrences; love nests as common as automobiles, and hysterical clients merely part of an everyday routine.

He sat in the big high-backed leather chair in Perry Mason's office, and turned sideways, so that his long legs were crossed over the right hand arm of the chair. A cigarette was in his mouth, hanging pendulously at an angle from his lower lip.

Perry Mason, seated back of the big desk, stared at the detective with patient eyes that were calmly watchful. His manner was that of a veteran fighter relaxed in his corner, waiting for the sounding of the gong. He looked like a man who would presently lose his relaxed watchfulness, spring from the chair, and engage in swift conflict, with the ferocity of a tiger.

"Well," said Drake, "what's eating you?"

"Awhile back," said Perry Mason, "you were telling me something about a rough shadow."

Paul Drake inhaled placidly on his cigarette. His glassy, protruding eyes watched Perry Mason with an expression of quizzical humor.

"You must have a good memory," he said. "That was a long time ago."

"Never mind when it was," Mason told him. "I want to get the lowdown on it."

"Somebody trying it on you?" asked the detective.

"No," said Mason. "But I have an idea I can use it. Give me the sketch."

Paul Drake removed the cigarette from his mouth, pinched it out, and dropped it into an ashtray.

"It's a stunt in detective work," he said. "We don't ordinarily talk about it—not to outsiders, anyway. It's a psychological third degree. It's predicated on the idea that a man who has something on his mind that he's trying to conceal, is likely to be nervous."

"How does it work?" Mason asked tonelessly.

"Well, let's figure that you're working on a case, and you figure somebody has got some knowledge—not just ordinary knowledge, but a sort of guilty knowledge that he's trying to conceal. You've got two or three ways of approaching him in order to get him to spill the beans. One of them is to use the routine stunt of getting an attractive woman to get acquainted with him, and start him boasting. Another one is to plant some man who becomes friendly with him, and gets his confidence.

"Usually one of those ways works out. But sometimes they don't work. Sometimes a man won't fall for a woman, or, if he does, won't start boasting, and he'll get suspicious if one of your operatives starts getting friendly with him. That's when we use the rough shadow. It takes two men to work a rough shadow job. First, you have your contact man who makes a contact with the suspect, but can't seem to get under his hide, can't get him to talk.

"Well, you pick the time and a suitable place, and have your rough shadow trailing along behind. The contact man starts the fireworks by giving a signal.

"Of course, you understand, shadowing is a job in itself. The public gets goofy ideas about the work of a shadow, and how he operates. The public gets the idea that a shadow puts on disguises and ducks into doorways or hides behind telephone poles, and all that sort of stuff. They get that way from looking at the movies and reading a lot of detective stories written by guys that don't know anything about the detective business.

"As a matter of fact, your real shadow is a smooth guy who almost never uses a disguise. He's just a casual, innocent-looking bystander. No matter what happens, he never gets rattled and never does any of this business of ducking in a doorway. He looks so matter-of-fact that the suspect always takes him as part of the general scenery, and never thinks of him as an individual."

"I know all that, in a general way," Perry Mason told him. "What I want to get straight is just how this rough shadow game is worked."

"Well, that's simple," said the detective. "It's like all of the good things—they're simple when you come right down to analyze them. The rough shadow simply acts the way the suspect figures a shadow should act. In other words, he quits being a regular shadow, and becomes crude. He does all the things that the suspect naturally expects a detective would do. He hides behind telephone poles and ducks in doorways, and all of that stuff."

"So that the suspect knows he's being shadowed?" asked Perry Mason.

"That's the idea," said Drake, taking another cigarette from a case in his pocket, and tapping it gently on his thumb nail.

"You see, the contact man has established a certain amount of friendly relations with the suspect. The suspect, however, is a guy who won't talk about the thing that the contact man wants him to talk about, so the contact man gets a shadow to tail along behind. The suspect never knows that he's being tailed, because the shadow is a smooth worker. But, when the circumstances are right, the contact man gives a signal, and then the shadow gets crude about his methods. He starts ducking around behind telephone poles, putting on disguises, and doing the hundred and one amateurish things which defeat the very purpose of a skilled shadow. Naturally, the suspect takes a tumble that he's being tailed.

"Now, it's a funny thing about a man finding out that he's being shadowed, particularly a man who ain't used to it. As soon as he finds that somebody's tailing him around, he starts getting nervous. Usually the first thing he does is to start

96

walking faster, and looking back over his shoulder. Naturally, the contact man has the rough shadow game sprung when he's walking with the suspect, and the contact man always slows down and saunters along.

"So the suspect wants to hurry things up a little bit, and he's nervous and jumpy all over. After a while, ninety-nine chances out of a hundred, he'll turn to the contact man and say that there's a detective following him and he wants to ditch the shadow. The contact man helps him to do it, and that makes the suspect loosen up and take the contact man into his confidence."

"Suppose the suspect doesn't say anything to the contact man?" asked the lawyer.

"Then," said Drake, "the contact man says something to the suspect. He taps him on the shoulder, and says: 'Listen, old man, I don't want to get personal, but do you know there's somebody shadowing you?' Or else, he may say: 'Say, look at that fellow behind us. I believe he's shadowing me.' If it's a crime he's working on, the contact man usually pretends that the rough shadow is tailing him, and opens up and confesses to the suspect that he's been guilty of a crime somewhere, and that he's afraid the dicks are on his trail. He asks the suspect to help him ditch the rough shadow. They rush into buildings, go up and down elevators, mingle with crowds, and all that sort of stuff, and when the contact man gives a signal, the rough shadow steps out of the picture, and the suspect thinks he's been ditched.

"It's just an angle of the game that sometimes brings results. You can nearly always get a man talking when you pull a rough shadow on him."

"All right," said Perry Mason, "I want to work a rough shadow game."

"Maybe you won't need a rough shadow," Drake pointed out. "It's something we use only as a last resort. Usually we can build up a friendship and get people to talk. A slick operative has a knack of making people spill facts."

"No," said Mason, "this is an unusual case, and I want a contact operative who is of a certain type."

"What's the type?" asked the detective.

"A middle-aged woman who can pretend she has had to work hard all her life. Get somebody who hasn't any particular beauty or figure; who has wrinkled hands and a heavy figure."

"Okay," said Drake. "I've got just the woman. She's clever, and she's hard-boiled. Who do you want to have her contact?"

"Mrs. Edna Mayfield, the housekeeper for Edward Norton."

"The man who was murdered?"

"The man who was murdered."

Drake whistled.

"Think she's mixed up in the murder?" he asked.

"I don't know just what she's mixed up in," Perry Mason said slowly, "but she's got information. I want that information."

"They've got the fellow that did the murder, haven't they?" asked the detective, his glassy eyes suddenly losing their expression of droll humor, and containing a glint of quick appraisal. "Wasn't it the chauffeur or somebody that pulled the job?"

"So I understand," said Mason noncommittally.

"You're representing Frances Celane, the young woman who's the beneficiary under the trust fund and the will?"

"Yes."

"Okay, now just what do you want me to get out of her?"

"Anything that she knows," said Perry Mason slowly.

"You mean about the murder?"

"About anything."

Paul Drake let his glassy eyes study the tip of the cigarette and the smoke which eddied upward from it.

"Look here," he said, "let's be frank with each other. I know you well enough to know that if you're getting me to start work on this murder case, that there's an angle to it that the police haven't got."

"I didn't say I wanted you to work on the murder case," Perry Mason said slowly.

"No," said Drake significantly, "you didn't *say* that."

There was a moment or two of silence, then Perry Mason

said, slowly and impressively: "I want you to find out every-thing that that housekeeper knows. I don't care what it's about."

Paul Drake made a gesture with his shoulders.

"Don't get me wrong," he said. "I'm not curious, and I don't want you to misunderstand me. But just suppose that some of the information this woman spills wouldn't look so well for your client?"

"I want to get the information," said Perry Mason.

"Sure, I know," said Drake. "But suppose that we get it through a couple of operatives that I'll put on the case. And suppose the information should be something you would want to keep under cover? I try to get dependable people to work for me, but things have a habit of leaking out in time."

"Yes," said Perry Mason slowly, "in time."

Once more there was an interval of silence.

"Well?" asked the detective.

"I think," said Mason, "that this is another case where I'm going to be working against time. I don't think there's any information that your operatives will get that the police won't get sooner or later. I want to have it sooner, and want the police to get it later."

Drake nodded.

"All right," he said. "I get the sketch. I just wanted to be certain there wasn't any misunderstanding between us. Misunderstandings in my business make for dissatisfied clients, and I want to keep my clients satisfied."

"All right," Mason told him. "We understand each other on that.

"Now, there's one other thing. A fellow by the name of Don Graves, secretary to Edward Norton, was a witness to the murder itself. He's told the police one story, and me another. He may be dangerous. I want to find out confidentially whether he really did see a woman in the room at the time the murder blow was struck, or whether he's going to say he did, which amounts to the same thing.

"Now, do you suppose that you could get someone to contact him without creating too much suspicion, and find out just what he's really going to testify to? If there's any way of doing it, I'd like to get a written statement out of him.''

"Any money for expenses?" asked the detective.

"Plenty of it," said the lawyer.

"Well, suppose I get somebody to go to him and tell him he's representing a tabloid newspaper, or a true detective story magazine, and wants the account of an eye-witness, get him to submit the manuscript signed and sworn to, and offer to pay him by the word?"

"Okay," said Mason, "provided there aren't too many words."

The detective grinned.

"You mean, provided the words are of the right kind."

"Well," said the lawyer, "I guess that amounts to about the same thing."

Drake got up and flipped his cigarette into a brass cuspidor.

"Okay," he said, "I'll get started."

"You'll let me know progress?"

"I'll let you know progress."

"Concentrate heavy on that housekeeper. She's a tartar and you'll have to watch her."

"Mail reports?" asked the detective.

"No. Make them orally or not at all."

There was a knock at the door, and Della Street glanced significantly at Perry Mason.

"That's okay," he said, "tell me what it is, Della."

"Mr. Crinston is out here. He says his business is important and he can't wait."

"Very well," said Mason, "I'll see him."

He flashed a meaning glance to Drake and said to the detective in a tone of voice sufficiently loud to carry into the outer office, "That's quite all right, Mr. Drake. I'm busy on an important matter right now, and I can't give it my immediate attention, but you've got ten days within which to make an appearance, and I'll draw up a demurrer and file it in court. That'll carry the thing along and keep you from being in default until we can go into greater details."

He shook hands with Drake in the doorway, and beckoned to Mr. Crinston.

"Come in," he said.

Crinston pushed his way into the inner office with that aggressive suggestion of booming authority which characterized him. He gave the impression of sweeping away all obstacles from his path by the very blast of his forceful personality.

"Hello, Mason," he said, shaking hands. "Glad to see you. Guess you've been pretty busy, haven't you?"

Mason watched him with speculative eyes.

"Yes," he said. "I've been busy."

Crinston sat down in the big chair, and filled it completely. He took a cigar from his pocket, clipped off the end, scraped a match on the sole of his shoe.

"Well," he said, "it's been a mess all around."

"Yes," the lawyer told him, "it's still a mess."

"Oh, I think it's going to come out all right," said Crinston, "but why didn't you follow my instructions?"

"What instructions?"

"About keeping Frances out of it."

"I have kept her out of it the best I could. The poor girl is hysterical. She came to the office and had a complete breakdown. I called a physician, and he prescribed complete rest. He's taken her to a sanitarium somewhere, and won't tell even me where it is, for fear that I might call her."

Crinston puffed out the first whiffs of blue smoke from the cigar, and stared at the lawyer thoughtfully.

"Not bad, that," he said.

"Her nerves were really on the ragged edge," said Mason with dignity.

"Yes, yes, I know," Crinston said impatiently. "No need to waste your time and my time with that stuff. I understand. What I dropped in to find out was whether you know a man by the name of George Blackman, an attorney here?"

"Yes, I know him," said Mason.

"He got in touch with me on the telephone and told me I should see you right away on a matter of great importance."

101

Mason kept his voice flat and expressionless in an even monotone.

"Blackman came to see me earlier in the day," he said, "and suggested that it might make matters better for the family all around if Devoe should plead guilty to manslaughter."

"Why, damn it!" stormed Crinston. "He's a murderer! That was a dastardly cold-blooded murder!"

"That attitude on the part of the family was the thing that Blackman wanted to speak to me about," said Mason, still speaking in the same even cautious monotone. "He said that if the family were going to adopt a vindictive attitude toward his client, it would be necessary for him to adopt a vindictive attitude toward the family and try to show that the case was a frame-up against his client."

"How could he do that?" asked Crinston.

"Oh, there are various ways," said Mason, in his steady monotone. "It's an axiom of criminal law that a man should try everyone except the defendant. You know, sometimes you can try the prosecuting attorney. Very frequently you can try the prosecuting witness. You can start digging around, cross-examining on extraneous matters, trying to show some sort of a motive for murder. Then, if you can get a motive before the jury, you start showing opportunity, and if you can get motive and opportunity, you suddenly switch the accusation and claim there's just as much ground to suspect the prosecuting witness as there is the defendant."

"You mean to switch the guilt to Fran Celane?" asked Crinston.

"I didn't mention any names," said Mason. "I simply told you how criminal lawyers play the game."

"Look here," said Crinston. "Did you find out *exactly* what he wanted?"

"He *said* that he wanted a fee," said Mason, "and the assurance that a request would go to the District Attorney to look at the matter as leniently as possible and accept a plea of manslaughter."

Crinston studied the lawyer thoughtfully.

"You say that's what he *said* he wanted?" he commented.

"Yes."

"You act as though you didn't think it was what he really wanted."

"I don't."

"Why?"

"Because I don't think the district attorney would consider a plea of manslaughter. I think he'd prosecute either for first degree murder, or not at all."

"Then what *did* Blackman want?" Crinston demanded.

"I think he wanted to find out what our reactions would be to a proposition of that kind. If we'd been willing to go ahead, he'd have taken as much money as he could get, and then blackmailed us for as much more as possible, and then double-crossed us at the time of trial."

Crinston studied his cigar thoughtfully.

"He didn't impress me as being that kind of a man," he said slowly. "Not from the impression he made over the telephone, anyway."

"If you'd seen him, he'd have made a better impression," Mason told him.

Crinston put the cigar back in his mouth and chewed on it thoughtfully.

"Look here," he said suddenly, placing his parted fingers to his mouth, and jerking out the chewed cigar, "I don't like the way you're handling this case."

"No?" asked Perry Mason coldly.

"No!" said Crinston explosively.

"And what don't you like about it?" asked the lawyer.

"I think you're letting a golden opportunity slip through your fingers. I think there's a good chance to get this thing all cleaned up by playing ball with Blackman."

Mason's answer was curt and without explanation.

"I don't," he said.

"Well I do, and I'm giving you orders right now to get in touch with Blackman and give him what he wants. Anything within reason."

"He doesn't want things within reason," Mason said. "His type never does. He'd find out what we consider reasonable, and then raise his sights."

103

"All right. Let him raise them. There's a hell of a lot of money involved in this thing, and we can't afford to bungle it."

"Are you afraid," asked Perry Mason, "that Frances Celane can't stand too much pressure?"

"That's a great question to ask me!" Crinston almost shouted. "When you've had to let her have a nervous breakdown in order to keep her out of the hands of the police."

"I didn't say that I did it to keep her from the police," Mason reminded him.

"Well, I said it," said Crinston.

"Yes," Mason told him, "I heard you, and furthermore, you don't need to shout."

Crinston got to his feet, flung the half smoked cigar into the cuspidor, and glowered at Mason.

"All right," he said, "you're finished."

"What do you mean I'm finished?"

"Just what I say. You're not representing me anymore, and you're not going to represent Frances Celane anymore."

"I think," Mason told him slowly, "that Miss Celane will be the best judge of that. I'll wait until she tells me that I'm not to represent her anymore."

"She'll tell you fast enough, as soon as I get in touch with her."

"Where," asked Mason, smiling thoughtfully, "are you going to get in touch with her?"

"Don't worry," Crinston told him, "I'll get in touch with her all right, and then you're going to be finished. You're a bungler. You've been smart enough on some things, but you've let the case get into a hell of a mess. I'm going to get some attorney, and . . ."

Abruptly, Perry Mason got to his feet. He strode purposefully around the desk. Crinston watched him come with eyes that remained steady, but seemed to hold just a trace of panic. Mason planted himself firmly in front of the other man, his eyes cold, hard, and ominous.

"All right," he said, "let's not have any misunderstanding about this. From now on I'm not representing you, is that right?"

104

"You bet that's right!"

"And don't think," said Mason, "that your business is so damned important. Miss Celane would have let me handle the estate if it hadn't been for the fact that I couldn't place myself in the position of acting as attorney both for the estate, and for the surviving partner."

"Well," Crinston told him, "you don't need to worry about that anymore. On the other hand, don't think you're going to represent the estate. You aren't going to represent anything or anybody. I'm going to get another attorney to represent me, and he's going to represent Frances Celane, as well."

Perry Mason said, slowly, ominously: "Just to show you what a fool you are, and how you've walked into a trap, the man that you're going to get to represent you is one that was suggested to you by Blackman."

"What if he is?" Crinston demanded.

Mason's smile was frosty.

"Nothing," he said. "Go right ahead. Walk into the trap just as deeply as you want to."

Crinston's eyes softened somewhat.

"Look here, Mason," he said, "I've got nothing against you personally, but this is a business matter. I think you're bungling things, and I think you're too damned ethical. I don't want you to misunderstand me. Frances Celane means a lot to me. I'm just like an uncle to her. She's a kid that I've taken a lot of interest in, and I'm going to see that she gets a square deal. I think that this case requires someone who can deal with Blackman. He says he wouldn't deal with you anymore if you were the last man left on earth."

Perry Mason laughed a bitter, mirthless laugh.

Crinston went on doggedly. "No matter what happens, I'm for Frances Celane. I don't know what the evidence may disclose before it gets done, but I'm going to stick by the kid no matter what happens. Get that, and get it straight. I'm a business man, and she doesn't know a thing about business. I'm going to see that she gets a square deal, beginning immediately."

He turned and walked with ponderous dignity toward the door.

Perry Mason watched him with thoughtful concentration.

"What a sucker you are," as Crinston jerked the door open.

Crinston whirled on him. "I hate that word!" he said. "I don't let anybody call me a sucker."

"You'll hate it a lot worse before you're done," said Mason, and, turning on his heel, walked back to his desk.

Crinston hesitated a moment, then turned and walked back into the room.

"All right, wise guy," he said, "now I'm going to tell you something.

"You've bungled this case from the time you started in on it. I know that *I* can't fire you as Miss Celane's lawyer. That's something that's entirely up to her. *I'm* going to advise her to let you go. In the event she doesn't, however, I'm going to give you one tip, and that's watch Purkett, the butler."

"Now," said Perry Mason, "you interest me. Go ahead and tell me what you're driving at."

"Oh," said Crinston sarcastically, "you *do* want to take a little advice, eh?"

"I want you to tell me why you made that remark about Purkett," said Perry Mason, his eyes cold.

Crinston's eyes surveyed the lawyer in thoughtful appraisal.

"If I told you," he asked, "would you have sense enough to use the information?"

Perry Mason said nothing, but held his head slightly on one side, after the manner of a person anxious to hear that which is about to be said.

"The evidence in this case," said Crinston, "pointed unmistakably to Devoe. A *good* lawyer would have seen that the police never had a chance to consider the possibility that such evidence wasn't conclusive. However, you sat back and did nothing while the police began to doubt that evidence and make other investigations.

"Then, when that investigation was under way, you did nothing to keep them from involving your client. Now, if

106

Devoe is guilty, that's the end of it. If he isn't guilty, someone else is. There's a stronger probability that that someone else is Purkett than anyone else. Yet you're letting him keep entirely in the background.''

Crinston stopped speaking and stood in an attitude of glowering belligerency.

''Is that all you have to say?'' asked Perry Mason.

''That's all.''

Perry Mason smiled.

''Blackman's address,'' he said, ''is in the Mutual Building. I thought I would save you looking it up in the telephone book.''

Crinston's face showed a slight flicker of surprise, then set in grim lines.

''Very well,'' he said, jerked the office door open, and slammed it behind him.

Perry Mason sat for a few minutes, then clamped his hat down firmly on his head. He walked through the outer office, saying to his secretary as he went past, ''I don't know just when I'll be back, Della. Close up the office at five o'clock.''

Chapter 13

Perry Mason walked into the garage where he stored his automobile and asked for the mechanic.

"How much of a job would it be," he said, "to turn a speedometer back a few miles? That is, suppose you had a speedometer that registered around 15,350 miles, and you wanted to turn it back to 15,304.7 miles. How much of a job would it be?"

"Not much of a job," said the mechanic grinning, "only, if you were going to turn it back that far, you should make a good job of it and turn it back to 3000 miles and sell the car as a demonstrator."

"No," said the lawyer, "I didn't mean to slip one over on the car dealer or on a customer. I was trying to find out about evidence. How long would it take to set the speedometer back?"

"Not so very long," said the mechanic. "It's a simple job."

Perry Mason gave him half a dollar and walked from the garage, his head bowed in thought.

He stepped into a drug store and telephoned the number of Edward Norton's residence.

The voice that answered the telephone, apparently that of the butler, was filled with that type of formality which comes when one has answered a telephone innumerable times in connection with some tragedy which has attracted much public interest.

"I want to talk with Mr. John Mayfield, the gardener," said Mason.

"I beg your pardon, sir," said the voice, "but it's rather unusual for calls to come through for Mr. Mayfield. I don't know whether he's supposed to take calls on this telephone or not, sir."

"That's all right," said Mason, without disclosing his identity. "This is in connection with some police business. Get him on the phone, and don't waste time."

There was a moment of hesitant silence at the other end of the line, and then the butler's voice said: "Very good, sir. Just a moment, sir."

After a delay of several minutes a heavy, stolid voice said: "Hello," and Perry Mason spoke rapidly.

"Don't tell anybody who this is," he said, "but this is Mason, the lawyer, who represents Frances Celane. Your wife spoke to me about getting some money for her, and I can't locate her. Do you know where she is?"

"I think," said the man, "she went to the District Attorney's office. They called for her in a car and took her there."

"All right," said Mason. "It's important that I get in touch with you and talk with you about this business matter which your wife took up with me. Now, the question is, can you take one of the cars and come in to meet me?"

"Maybe I could, sir, but I'm not certain. I'd much rather walk up and meet you at the corner of the boulevard if you could drive out here, sir."

"All right," said Mason, "I'll do that. You meet me at the boulevard, and don't tell anybody that you're meeting me there."

Mason returned to the garage, got his car, and made time out to the place where the curving roadway which led to the Norton residence intersected the boulevard.

A man who was stooped of shoulder, heavily framed and big-boned, stepped out from the gathering dusk as Mason parked the car.

"You're Mr. Mason?" he asked.

"Yes," said the lawyer.

"I'm John Mayfield. What was it you wanted?"

Mason got partially out of the car and stood with one foot on the running board, and surveyed the man with keen scrutiny.

He saw a stolid, unemotional face, with sullen eyes and heavy, unsmiling lips.

"Did you know what your wife spoke to me about?" he asked.

"My wife told me she had had a talk with you," said the man, cautiously.

"Did she tell you what she talked about?"

"She told me that maybe we were going to get some money."

"All right," said Mason. "Now, in order to know where I stand on this thing, you've got to tell me about that speedometer."

"About what speedometer?" said the man.

"About the speedometer on that Buick car. You set it back, didn't you?"

"No, sir," said the gardener.

"Would you say that you set it back if I completed the business arrangements with your wife?" asked Mason.

"What do you mean?"

"Never mind what I mean," said the lawyer. "You simply tell your wife that if business arrangements are going to be completed between us, I would want to know first whether there would be testimony that the speedometer of that Buick automobile had been set back."

"What's that got to do with it?" asked the gardener.

"Just this," said Mason, making little jabbing motions with his forefinger to emphasize his statements. "We know that Edward Norton telephoned in to the police that his Buick had been stolen.

"Now that means that the Buick most certainly wasn't in his garage at the time he telephoned. *Somebody* had that Buick out. It doesn't make any difference whether Miss Celane was home or not. Somebody had the Buick out. That Buick was missing at the time Norton telephoned. Now, when the police got there, the Buick was in the garage, and the speedometer on the Buick was set back to the same mileage that it showed when it was taken out. So somebody set that speedometer back. Now, the question is, *who did it*?"

"I didn't, sir," said the gardener.

110

"How about Devoe, the chauffeur?"

"I don't know about him, sir."

"How about the butler?"

"I don't know about him."

"All right," said Mason. "You don't know very much about anything, but your wife has a pretty good idea about what's going on. I want you to tell her that *if* we are going to do business *she has got to find out who set the speedometer back* on that car."

"You mean the person that had it out, sir?"

"No," said Mason, "I don't care a damn about the person who had it out. I'd just as soon the police figured it was Miss Celane who had the car out. What I want to do is to prove that the speedometer was set back, and I want to find out who set it back. Do you understand?"

"Yes, I think I do now. Yes, sir."

"When is your wife coming back?"

"I don't know. Some men from the District Attorney's office came and talked with her. Then they told her they wanted her to go to the office and make a statement."

"All right," said Mason. "Do you think you can give her my message?"

"Yes, sir, I know I can."

"All right. See that you do," Mason told him. "Now there's one other thing that I want to find out about, and that's where you were at the time the murder was committed."

"Me?" said the man. "I was asleep."

"You're certain about that?"

"Of course I'm certain. I woke up with all of the commotion going on."

"Your wife wasn't asleep," said Mason.

"Who says she wasn't?" demanded Mayfield, his sullen eyes showing some trace of emotion.

"I do," said Mason. "Your wife was around the house. She hadn't gone to bed when the murder was committed. You know that."

"Well, what of it?' said Mayfield.

"Just this," Mason remarked, lowering his voice impressively, "there was a woman in the room with the man who

111

struck that blow. Now your wife had intimated that woman was Miss Celane, or may have been Miss Celane. I want you to tell your wife that I now have evidence which leads me to believe that *she* was the woman who was in the room at the time.''

''You mean,'' said the man, bristling, ''that you're accusing my wife of murder?''

''I mean,'' said Mason, standing his ground and staring at the belligerent gardener, ''that I'm telling you I have evidence that indicates your wife was the woman who was in the room at the time the blow was struck. That doesn't mean that she struck the blow. It doesn't mean she knows anything at all about the fact that a blow was going to be struck. But it does mean that she was in the room at the time.''

''You want me to tell her that?'' asked Mayfield.

''I want you to tell her that,'' said Mason.

''All right,'' said Mayfield, ''I'll tell her that, but she won't like it.''

''I don't care whether she likes it or not,'' said Mason. ''I told you to tell her that.''

''All right,'' said Mayfield. ''Is there anything else?''

''No,'' Mason told him, ''except that you want to be sure and tell her about this interview when no one is listening. In other words, I don't want the representatives of the District Attorney's office to know about it.''

''Oh, sure,'' said Mayfield, ''I know enough for that.''

''All right,'' said Mason, and got in his car and drove down the boulevard.

He drove in to a cafe, where he dined leisurely and thoughtfully.

By the time he had finished dinner, the newsboys were crying papers on the street, and Perry Mason bought one, took it to his automobile, lounged back against the cushions, turned on the domelight and read the headlines which spread across the top of the page.

''NEW MYSTERY IN MILLIONAIRE MURDER. . . . WOMAN IN ROOM AT TIME OF CRIME IS CLAIMED. . . . POLICE TRACING MARKED

MONEY TAKEN FROM BODY OF MILLION-
AIRE. . . . HEIRESS SECRETLY MARRIED AND
HUSBAND SOUGHT AS MATERIAL WITNESS. . . .
BEAUTIFUL NIECE MYSTERIOUSLY DISAPPEARS
FOLLOWING VISIT TO PROMINENT LAWYER.''

Perry Mason read through each word of the sensational
story which followed; a story in which the reporters told as
much as they dared in between the lines; a story which
stopped short of actual accusation, yet which left the public
to infer that the police were far from satisfied with the case
against Pete Devoe, the chauffeur, and were considering a
sudden change of front which would involve persons of wealth
and prominence.

Perry Mason carefully folded the paper, thrust it into the
door pocket of the car, and drove, not to his bachelor apart-
ment, but to a downtown hotel where he registered under an
assumed name and spent the night.

Chapter 14

Perry Mason walked into his office, said good morning to Della Street, then went into his private office where the morning newspapers were spread on his desk.

Della Street opened the door and followed him into the private office.

"Somebody broke in and searched . . ."

He whirled on her, placing his finger to his lips. Then, while she ceased talking, started making a round of the office. He moved pictures, peering behind them, swung out the revolving bookcase and inspected the wall space, then crawled under the desk. He straightened, smiled, and said: "Looking for a dictograph. There's just a chance that they'd have one planted."

She nodded.

"Somebody broke into the office last night," she said, "and went through everything. The safe was opened."

"Did they smash it?"

"No, he must have been some clever crook who knew how to work the combination. The safe was opened, all right. I could tell, because the papers were disturbed."

"That's all right," he told her. "What else is new?"

"Nothing," she said, "except three police detectives watching the office, and I have an idea they're waiting for someone to come in."

He smiled wisely and said: "Let them wait. It will teach them patience."

"Did you read the papers?" she asked.

"Not the morning papers," he told her.

"The late editions say that they've identified the club that killed Norton," she told him.

"Yes?"

"Yes. It was a heavy walking stick, and they've found out that it belonged to Rob Gleason, the husband of our client."

"That'll mean," said Perry Mason, "that they'll charge him with first degree murder, and let the charge against Devoe go."

"They're also going to charge the woman," she said, "unless they have already."

"So?" he asked.

"Yes. This secretary, Don Graves, has given some additional information which has changed the entire complexion of the case, according to the *STAR*. Graves was shielding some one. The police broke him down and he gave additional evidence."

"Well," he said, "that makes it interesting. If anybody comes in, give them a stall."

She nodded her head, staring at him apprehensively.

"You're not going to get mixed into this thing, are you?" she asked.

"Why should I get mixed into it?" he inquired.

"You know what I mean," she said. "You do too much for your clients."

"What do you mean by that?"

"You know what I mean. You had Miss Celane have a nervous breakdown, and leave here in an ambulance."

He smiled at her. "Well?" he asked.

"Isn't it a crime," she said, "to conceal someone who is wanted by the police?"

"Was she wanted by the police then?" he inquired.

"No," she said, dubiously, "not then, I guess."

"Furthermore," said Mason, "I am not a physician. I might make an incorrect diagnosis. I thought she was having a nervous breakdown, but I called a physician to verify my impression."

She frowned at him and shook her head.

"I don't like it," she said.

"Don't like what?"

"Don't like the way you mix into these cases. Why can't you sit back and just do your stuff in a court room?"

"I don't know, I'm sure," he told her, smiling. "Maybe it's a disease."

"Don't be silly," she told him. "Other lawyers walk into court and examine the witnesses and then put the case up before a jury. You go out and mix yourself into the cases."

"Other lawyers," he told her, "have clients who get hung."

"Sometimes they deserve it," she pointed out.

"Perhaps. I haven't had one hung so far, and I haven't had one who deserved it."

She stood staring at him for a moment, then smiled, and there was something almost maternal in her smile.

"Are *all* your clients innocent?" she asked.

"That's what the juries say," he told her. "And after all, they're the ones to judge."

She sighed and shrugged her shoulders.

"You win," she said, and went back into the outer office.

As the catch clicked, Perry Mason sat down at his desk and spread out the newspapers. He read for fifteen minutes without interruption, and then the door opened.

"There's a Mrs. Mayfield out here," Della Street told him, "and I have an idea you'd better see her while the seeing is good."

Perry Mason nodded.

"Send her in," he said, "and make it snappy. There'll probably be a police detective following on her trail. Stall him off just as long as you can."

The girl nodded, opened the door, and beckoned to the woman who sat in the outer office.

As the broad form of Mrs. Mayfield hulked in the doorway, Perry Mason saw his secretary blocking as much of the passage as possible. Then, as the door was closing behind the housekeeper, he heard Della Street's voice saying: "I'm very sorry, but Mr. Mason is in an important conference right now and can't be disturbed."

Perry Mason nodded to Mrs. Mayfield, got up, crossed the office and turned the lock on the door.

"Good morning, Mrs. Mayfield," he said.

She stared at him in black-eyed belligerency.

"Good morning!" she snapped.

Perry Mason indicated the black leather chair, and Mrs. Mayfield sat down in it, her back very stiff and her chin thrust forward.

"What's this about the speedometer being set back on the Buick automobile?" she asked.

There was the sound of scuffling motion from the outer office, then the noise of bodies pushing against the door, and the knob of the door twisted. The lock held it shut, and Perry Mason kept his eyes fastened on Mrs. Mayfield, holding her attention away from the noise at the door.

"Mr. Norton," said the lawyer, "reported the Buick automobile as having been stolen. At the time, we thought that Miss Celane was driving it. Now it appears that she was not. Therefore, the Buick must have been gone at the time Norton reported its theft to the police. However, we have the mileage record of the car, and it shows that he returned it to his house at 15,304.7 miles.

"That means the person who was using it the night of the murder must have either set the speedometer back or disconnected the speedometer when he took it out."

Mrs. Mayfield shook her head.

"The car wasn't out," she said.

"Are you certain?" he asked.

"Purkett, the butler," she said, "sleeps right over the garage. He was lying awake in bed, reading, and he'd have heard anyone take a car out. He says that the garage doors were closed, and that no car went out."

"Could he have been mistaken?" pressed Mason.

"No," she snapped. "The doors make a noise when they're opened. It sounds very loud up in the room over the garage. Purkett would have heard it, and I want an explanation of this crack that you made to my husband about me being in the room when the murder . . ."

"Forget that for a minute," Mason interrupted. "We're talking about the car, and our time's short. I can't do any business with you unless I can prove that speedometer was set back."

She shook her head emphatically.

"You can't do any business with me anyway," she said. "You've got things in a fine mess."

"How do you mean?"

"You've handled things in such a way that the police have dragged Frances Celane into it."

The black eyes snapped at him in beady indignation, and then suddenly filmed with moisture.

"You mean *you're* the one that got Frances Celane into it," said Mason, getting to his feet and facing her accusingly. "You started it by blackmailing her about her marriage, and then you wanted more blackmail to keep her out of this murder business."

The glittering black eyes now showed globules of moisture.

"I wanted money," said Mrs. Mayfield, losing her air of belligerency. "I knew it was an easy way to get it. I knew that Frances Celane was going to have plenty. I didn't see any reason why I shouldn't have some of it. When she hired you, I knew you were going to get plenty of money, and I didn't see any reason why I shouldn't have some.

"All my life I've been a working woman. I've married a husband who is a clod, and hasn't ambition or sense enough to come in out of the rain. All my life I've had to take responsibilities. When I was a girl I had to support my family. After I was married, I had to furnish all the ambition to keep the family going. For years I've waited on Frances Celane. I've seen her live the life of a spoiled lady of leisure. I've had to slave my fingers to the bone doing housework and seeing that she had her breakfast in bed, and I'm tired of it. I didn't see any reason why I shouldn't have some money too. I wanted lots of money. I wanted people to wait on me. I was willing to do anything to get the money, except to get Frances into real trouble.

"Now I can't do anything about it. The police cornered me and made me talk, and they're going to arrest Frances Celane for murder. For murder! Do you understand?"

Her voice rose almost to a shriek.

There was an imperative pounding on the door of the office.

"Open up in there!" gruffed a voice from the outside.

Perry Mason paid no attention to the commotion at the door, but kept his eyes fixed upon Mrs. Mayfield.

"If it would help clear up this mystery," he said, "do you think you could find someone who would testify that the car was taken out and that the speedometer was either disconnected or set back?"

"No," she said, "that car didn't go out."

Mason started pacing the floor.

The knocking at the outer door was redoubled in intensity. Someone shouted: "This is a police detective. Open up that door!"

Suddenly Mason laughed aloud.

"What a fool I've been!" he said.

The housekeeper blinked back the tears and stared at him with wide eyes.

"Of course," said Mason, "that car didn't leave the garage. No car left the garage." And he smacked his fist down upon his palm.

He whirled to the housekeeper.

"If you want to do something for Frances Celane," he said, "talk with Purkett again, and in detail. Go over the case with him and strengthen his recollection so that, no matter what happens, he can't be shaken in his testimony."

"You want him to say that the car didn't leave the garage?" asked the housekeeper.

"I want him to tell the truth," said Perry Mason. "But I want him to tell it with sufficient firmness so that he won't be rattled on the witness stand by a lot of lawyers. That's all I want him to testify to—just the fact that the car did *not* leave the garage at any time on that night; that the garage doors were closed, and that they remained closed, and that no person could have taken a car from the garage without his hearing it."

"Well," she said, "that's the truth. That's what he says."

"All right," he told her, "if you want to do Frances Celane a favor, you get to him and see that no pressure on earth can change that testimony of his."

"I'll do it," she said.

He asked hastily: "What did you tell the police about getting money from Frances Celane?"

"Nothing," she said. "I told them that she gave you money but I didn't know how much, or whether it was in large bills or small bills."

The door creaked under the weight of a body which had been thrown against it.

Perry Mason walked to it, snapped back the lock, and opened the door.

"What the hell do you mean," he demanded, "by trying to bust into my private office?"

A burly man with square shoulders, thick neck and scowling forehead, pushed his way into the room.

"I told you who I was," he said. "I'm a police detective."

"I don't care if you're Mussolini," said Perry Mason. "You can't break into my office."

"The hell I can't," said the detective. "I'm taking this woman into custody."

Mrs. Mayfield gave a little scream.

"On what charge?" asked Perry Mason.

"As a material witness in a murder case," said the detective.

Mason remarked: "Well, you didn't get the urge to take her into custody as a material witness until after she came to this office."

"What do you mean?" asked the detective.

"Exactly what I say," said Mason. "You sat outside and watched this office until you saw Mrs. Mayfield come in. Then you telephoned your superior for instructions, and he told you to pick her up as a material witness before she had a chance to talk with me."

"Pretty smooth, ain't you?" sneered the detective.

Mrs. Mayfield stared from one to the other and said: "But I haven't done anything."

"That ain't the question, ma'am," said the detective. "It's a question of keeping you as a material witness where you won't be annoyed or inconvenienced."

"And," sneered Perry Mason, "where you won't have a

chance to talk with anybody except representatives of the District Attorney's office.''

The detective glowered at Perry Mason.

"And we understand,'' he said, "that you received ten one thousand dollar bills that were stolen from the body of Edward Norton.''

"Is that so?'' said Mason.

"That's so,'' snapped the detective.

"Just where do you think those bills are?'' asked the lawyer.

"We don't know, but we intend to find out,'' the detective told him.

"Well,'' said Mason, "it is a free country, or it used to be once. Go ahead and find out.''

"When we do,'' said the detective, "you're likely to find yourself facing a charge of receiving stolen property.''

"Well, you've only got three things to do,'' said Mason.

"What three things?'' asked the detective.

"Prove that the money was stolen, prove that I received it, and prove that I knew it was stolen when I received it.''

"You know it's stolen now.''

"How do I know it's stolen?''

"Because I've told you it was. You're on notice.''

"In the first place,'' said Mason, "I'm not admitting that I have any ten thousand dollars. In the second place, I wouldn't take your word for anything.''

The detective turned to Mrs. Mayfield.

"Come along, ma'am,'' he said, "we'll handle this lawyer later.''

"But I don't want to go,'' she said.

"It's orders, ma'am,'' he told her. "You won't be annoyed. We're simply going to keep you where you'll be safe until after we can get your testimony.''

Perry Mason watched the pair depart from his private office. His rugged face was expressionless, but there was a glint of smouldering hostility in his patient eyes.

When the door of the outer office had closed, Perry Mason walked to his secretary's desk and said: "Della, I want you to ring up the *STAR*. Tell them who you are. They've got a reporter there named Harry Nevers. He knows who I am. Tell the city editor to have Nevers come and see me. I'll see that he gets some sensational news.''

She reached for the telephone.

"You want me to tell that to the city editor?" she asked.

"Yes," he told her. "I want Nevers sent here right away."

"You don't want to talk with the editor?"

"No, he'd plug a rewrite man in on the line, listen to what I had to say, call it an interview, and let it go at that. I want you to tell them who you are, tell them to send Nevers over here for a hot yarn. They'll try to pump you about what it is. Tell them you don't know, and that I'm not available."

She nodded and lifted the receiver from the hook. Perry Mason walked back to his private office and closed the door.

Chapter 15

Harry Nevers was tall and thin, with eyes that looked at the world with a bored expression. His hair was in need of trimming, and his face had that oily appearance which comes to one who has gone long without sleep. He looked as though he had been up all night, and had, as a matter of fact, been up for two.

He walked into Perry Mason's office and perched himself on the arm of the big black leather chair.

"I'm going to give you a break," said Perry Mason, "and I want a favor."

Nevers spoke in a dull monotone of low-voiced comment.

"Sure," he said. "I had that all figured out a long time ago. Where is she?"

"Where's who?" asked Mason.

"Frances Celane."

"Who wants to know?"

"I do."

"What's the big idea?"

Nevers yawned and slid back over the arm of the chair, so that he was seated cross-wise in the chair.

"Hell," he said, "don't try to surprise me. That's been tried by experts. I doped out the play as soon as I got the call. There was nothing to it. Frances Celane had a nervous breakdown and was rushed to a sanitarium. Last night the District Attorney uncovered evidence which made him decide to put a first degree murder rap on her. She was secretly married to a chap named Gleason. They've picked up Gleason, and they're ready to go after Frances Celane.

"You're Frances Celane's attorney. You've got her under cover somewhere. It's a cover that's deep enough to keep her

123

from walking into a trap until you're ready to have her surrender. But you can't keep her under cover when the newspapers broadcast that she's wanted for murder. You've got a doctor mixed up in it, and a hospital. They wouldn't stand for it, even if you wanted them to. So it's a cinch you've got to turn her up, and you just picked on me to get the news, because you wanted something. Now tell me what you want, and I'll tell you whether we'll make a trade."

Perry Mason frowned thoughtfully, and made little drumming noises with his fingertips on the edge of the desk.

"I don't know what I want, Harry," he said.

Harry Nevers shook his head lugubriously.

"With the hardboiled bunch I'm working for, brother, if you don't know what you want, you're never going to get it. If you're going to make a trade you've got to make a trade right now."

"Well," said Perry Mason slowly, "I can tell you generally what I want. Somewhere along the line I'm going to try to get two or three people back at the Norton residence, under conditions that were similar to those which existed at the time of the murder. I don't know just how I'm going to do it. Somewhere along the line I'm going to make a point about the fact that the Buick automobile, which was reported stolen, wasn't taken out of the garage. All I want you to do is to see that I get a reasonable amount of publicity on those two points."

"Wait a minute," said Nevers, speaking in that same dull monotone, "you said you were going to make a point that the Buick car hadn't been taken out of the garage. You mean that you're going to claim that it was taken out, but the speedometer was either disconnected or set back, ain't that right?"

"No," Mason told him. "I'm going to make a point that it wasn't taken out of the garage."

For the first time since he had entered the office, the voice of Harry Nevers showed a trace of interest; a touch of tone.

"That's going to be a funny angle for *you* to play," he said.

"All right," said Mason, "we'll talk about that when the

124

time comes. I'm just telling you now what I want. The question is, do we make a trade?''

"I think so," said Nevers.

"Have you got a photographer lined up?"

"Sure. He's down in the car waiting, and I've got a space held on the front page for a picture."

Perry Mason reached for the telephone on his desk, took down the receiver, and said to Della Street, in a low voice:

"Get Doctor Prayton on the line. Find out what sanitarium he put Frances Celane in. Get him to make out a discharge from the sanitarium, and telephone it over. Tell him that Frances Celane is going to be charged with murder, and I don't want him to get mixed up in it. Get the telephone number of the sanitarium, and after he's telephoned in the discharge, get Frances Celane on the line for me."

He hung up the telephone.

"Now listen," said Nevers earnestly, "would you do me a favor?"

"What is it?" asked Mason cautiously. "I thought I was doing you one. You're getting exclusive photographs and all that."

"Don't be so cagy," Nevers told him. "I was just asking an ordinary favor."

"What is it?"

Nevers straightened up slightly in the chair, and said in his low monotone: "Get that jane to show a little leg. This is a picture that's going to make the front page, and I want to have a lot of snap about it. Maybe we'll take a close-up of her face for the front page, with a leg picture on the inside page. But I want to take back some photographs that have got a little leg in them."

"Well," said Perry Mason, "why not tell her so? You can be frank with her."

"I'm going to be frank with her all right," said Nevers, "but you're her lawyer, and she'll have confidence in you. Sometimes we have a little trouble getting these janes to pose right when they're excited. I want you to see that I get a break."

"Okay," Mason told him, "I'll do the best I can."

Harry Nevers took a cigarette from his pocket, lit it, and looked appraisingly at the attorney.

"If we could get her to come down to the *STAR* office and surrender herself to our custody," he said, "we'd see that she got a better break."

Mason's tone was firm.

"No," he said, "you're going to get the exclusive story and photographs. That's the best I can give you. She's going to surrender to the District Attorney, and I want to be sure there isn't any misunderstanding about that. In other words, I want the newspaper account to tell the public the truth."

Nevers yawned and looked at the telephone.

"Okay," he said. "I wonder if your secretary's got the calls through yet. . . ."

The telephone rang, and Mason took down the receiver. He heard Frances Celane's voice, eager and excited, at the other end of the line.

"What is it?" she asked. "They won't let me have newspapers here."

"All right," said Mason. "The show's starting."

"What do you mean?" she asked.

"They've arrested Rob Gleason for murder." He heard her gasp, and went on, "They've identified the club that killed Edward Norton. It was a walking stick that belonged to Rob Gleason."

"Rob Gleason never did it," she replied swiftly. "He called on my uncle, and they had quite an argument. He left that walking stick in Uncle's study, and . . ."

"Never mind that,' interrupted Perry Mason. "There's a chance this line is tapped. They may have detectives listening in on us. You can tell me when you get here. I want you to get in a taxicab and come to the office right away, prepared to surrender yourself for murder."

"You mean they're going to arrest me too?"

"Yes," he said. "I'm going to surrender you into custody."

"But they haven't charged me with murder yet, have they?"

"They're going to," he said. "I'm going to force their hand."

"*Must* I do it?" she asked.

"You said you were going to have confidence in me," he told her. "I say you must do it."

"I'll be in there," she said, "in just about half an hour."

"Okay," said Mason, and hung up the telephone.

After a moment he jiggled the receiver and said to his secretary: "Get me the office of the District Attorney. I want to talk with Claude Drumm if he's in."

He hung up the telephone and faced the reporter.

"Listen," Nevers told him, "you're going to step on your tonsil there. If you tell the D.A. you're going to surrender the broad, they'll cover your office and pick her up when she comes in. They'd rather have her picked up than have her surrender."

Mason nodded.

"That's why you're going to listen to my talk with the D.A.'s office," he said. "It'll avoid misunderstandings."

The telephone rang, and he picked up the receiver.

"Hello," he said. "Hello, Drumm? This is Mason talking. Yes, Perry Mason. I understand that Rob Gleason has been charged with the murder of Edward Norton."

Drumm's voice came cold and cautious over the telephone.

"He is charged as *one* of the principals."

"There's another one then?" asked Mason.

"Yes, probably."

"Have charges been filed?"

"Not yet."

"A little birdie," said Mason, "tells me that you want to charge Frances Celane as being the other principal."

"Well?" asked Drumm, his voice still cold and cautious. "What did you call me up for?"

"I called you up to tell you that Frances Celane is on her way to surrender herself into custody at your office."

There was a moment of silence, then Drumm said: "Where is she now?"

"Somewhere between where she is and your office. That is, she's on the road."

Drumm asked cautiously: "Is she going to make any stops in between times?"

"I'm sure I couldn't tell you," said Mason.

"All right," said Drumm. "When she comes in, we'll be glad to see her."

"Will there be bail?" asked Mason.

"We'll have to talk that matter over after she makes a statement to us."

Mason smiled into the telephone.

"Don't misunderstand me, Drumm," he said. "I told you that she was going to surrender into custody. There won't be any statement."

"We want to ask her some questions," said Drumm.

"That's fine," said Mason. "You can ask her all the questions you want. She'll be only too glad to have you do so."

"Will she answer them?" asked Drumm.

"She will *not*," said Mason. "If there's any talking to be done, I'll do it."

He heard Drumm's exclamation of exasperation, and hung up the receiver.

Nevers looked over at him with bored eyes.

"They'll double-cross you," he said. "They'll figure that she's going to come to the office, and they'll send men to arrest her here. They'll make it appear she was arrested, rather than giving herself up."

"No," Mason said, "they think she's going directly from the sanitarium to the D.A.'s office. And, anyway, you've heard the conversation. That'll eliminate misunderstandings."

Mason opened a desk drawer, took out a flask of rye, and set out a glass. The reporter slid the glass back to him along the desk and tilted the bottle to his lips.

When he lowered the bottle, he grinned at the lawyer. "My first wife hated to wash dishes," he said, "so I got out of the habit of dirtying them. You know, Mason, this may be a hard morning, and I haven't had any sleep for a couple of nights. If I put this bottle in my pocket, it might keep me awake."

Mason reached out and took the bottle.

"If I keep it in the desk," he said, "I'll know that you don't get an over-dose."

"Well," Nevers told him, "under those circumstances, there's nothing to keep me from going down and getting the photographer," and he slid down from the arm of the chair and walked through the door which led to the outer office.

He was back in five minutes with a photographer who carried a camera in a canvas case in one hand, and tripod in the other.

The photographer wasted no time in greetings, but scrutinized the office with an eye that soaked in the lighting arrangements.

"What sort of complexion has she got?" he asked.

"Spun silk hair," said Mason. "Dark eyes, high cheeks, and a good figure. You won't have any trouble with her when it comes to posing. She's expert at placing herself where she looks well."

"I want her in that leather chair," said the photographer.

"That's where she'll go," Mason told him.

The photographer raised the shades on the windows, set up the tripod, adjusted and focused the big camera, poured some flashlight powder into a flashgun.

"Why don't you use electric bulbs?" asked Perry Mason, eyeing the photographer with interest. "I understand they do better work, and they don't get a room all filled with smoke."

"Try telling that to the eagle-eyed bird that audits the expense account," said the photographer, "and it's *your* office. *I* don't care about the smoke."

Nevers grinned at Mason.

"That's the sweet spirit of coöperation that we have over at the *STAR*," he said.

Mason looked at the ceiling of the room and muttered: "I presume I can move out of here for a half an hour just because you fellows want to save the cost of a flashlight globe."

"Give him a shot out of that bottle," said Nevers, "and maybe he won't load the flash quite so heavy."

Mason slid the bottle over to the photographer.

"Listen," Nevers said, almost moodily, "something seems to tell me you've got a trick up your sleeve, Mason."

"I have," Mason told him.

Nevers nodded to the photographer.

"All right, Bill," he said, "better get a photograph of the lawyer at his desk. Drag out some law books. Get that bottle out of the way, and get a couple of shots."

"Don't waste your film," Mason told him. "They won't publish my picture unless it's in connection with a courtroom scene, or walking down the street with Frances Celane, or something like that."

Harry Nevers looked at him moodily, and said, in that bored monotone: "I'm not so certain. It depends on what you've got up your sleeve. You've pulled a couple of fast ones lately, and I'll have these pictures for the morgue in case we need 'em. You can't ever tell what's going to happen."

Perry Mason looked at him shrewdly.

"In other words," he said, "you've heard that there's some talk of arresting me as an accessory after the fact."

Nevers chuckled, a dry, rasping chuckle.

"You've got a good mind, Mason," he said. "But you've got funny ways of trying lawsuits and representing clients. Now that you mention it, it seems to me I *did* hear something about some stolen money that you'd received on a fee and hadn't surrendered."

Mason's laugh was scornful.

"If I *had* received any money, what a sweet spot it would put my client in if I walked into the D.A.'s office, and laid the money down on the table and said, virtuously: 'Here it is.' "

"Did you receive any one thousand dollar bills from your client?" asked Harry Nevers, in the tone of one who asks a question without expecting an answer.

Perry Mason made a gesture with his hand.

"If I did," he said, "I'd either have the bills on me, or some place in the office. The office has been searched from top to bottom."

"This morning?" asked Nevers.

"Some time last night," Mason told him.

Nevers jerked his head toward the photograph.

"Better take three pictures, Bill," he said. "Get him at the desk, get him standing up, and get a close-up."

Chapter 16

Fran Celane sat in the big, black leather chair, stared at the camera on the tripod, looked at the face of Perry Mason, and smiled, a wan, pathetic smile.

"Hold that smile," said the photographer.

"Wait a minute," said Nevers, "there's going to be a sex angle to this, and I want a little more leg."

Fran Celane continued to smile wanly. She reached down with her left hand and moved her skirt up an inch or two.

"Face the camera," said the photographer.

Harry Nevers said: "Wait a minute. It still ain't right. I want a little more leg."

The smile left her face, her black eyes blazed furiously. She reached down and pulled the skirt far up over the knee with an angry gesture.

"That's too much, Miss Celane," the photographer said.

"All right," she blazed at Nevers, "damn you, you wanted leg! There it is!"

Mason explained patiently.

"You understand, Miss Celane, that these men are friendly to our side of the case. They're going to see that you get some favorable publicity, but, in order to do that, they've got to have a picture that will attract the interest of the public. Now, it's going to help your case a lot if you can get just the right kind of a smile on your face, and at the same time, show just enough of a sex angle to appeal to the masculine eye."

Slowly the glitter faded from her eyes. She adjusted her skirt down over her knee, and once more the wan, pathetic smile came on her face.

"That's oke," said Nevers.

"Hold it," said the photographer, and, "don't blink your eyes."

A puff of white light mushroomed up from the flashgun and a little cloud of smoke twisted and turned as it writhed toward the ceiling.

"All right," said the photographer, "let's try one with a slightly different pose. Handkerchief in the left hand as though you'd been weeping, face mournful. Let the mouth droop a little bit. Not quite so much leg."

Frances Celane flared: "What do you think I am, an actress or a mannequin?"

"That's all right," soothed Perry Mason. "You'll have a lot of this to go through with, Miss Celane. And I want to caution you to keep your temper. If you flare up and show temper, and the newspaper reporters start playing you up as a tiger-woman, it's going to be a bad thing for your case. What I'm trying to do is to get the case brought on for trial, and get a quick acquittal. You've got to cooperate or you may have some unpleasant surprises."

She stared at Perry Mason, sighed, and took the pose they had suggested.

"Chin a little lower and to the left," said the photographer. "Eyes downcast, but not so far that they give the impression of being closed. Get the point of that shoulder a little bit away from the camera, so I can get the sweep of your throat. All right, that's fine. Hold it!"

Once more the shutter clicked, and once more the flashlight gave forth a puff of white smoke.

"Okay," said the photographer. "That's fine for those two."

Perry Mason crossed to the telephone.

"Get me Claude Drumm at the District Attorney's office," he said.

When he had Drumm on the line, he said: "I'm awfully sorry, Drumm, but Miss Celane is very much indisposed. She's had a nervous breakdown and was ordered to a sanitarium by her physician. She left the sanitarium to come in and surrender herself into custody when she knew that the police were looking for her. She's at my office now, and she's suffering from nervousness. I think you'd better arrange to pick her up here."

"I thought you said she had left your office when you telephoned before," said Drumm, with a trace of annoyance in his voice.

"No," said Mason, "you misunderstood me. I said that she had started for your office. I told you I didn't know what stops she intended to make on the way. She was nervous, and stopped in here because she wanted me to go with her."

Drumm said: "All right, the police will be there," and slammed down the telephone.

Mason turned and grinned at Nevers.

"If I'd let them know she was coming here to surrender herself, they'd have had men parked around to grab her before she got here," he said.

"Oh, well," said Nevers. "It's all in the game. I could stand another drink of that whisky if you've got it handy."

"I could stand a drink myself," said Fran Celane.

Mason shook his head at her.

"No, we're going to be in the middle of action pretty quick, and I don't want you to have liquor on your breath, Miss Celane. You've got to remember that every little thing you do, and everything you say, will be snapped up and dished out to the public.

"Now remember that under no circumstances are you to talk about the case or to lose your temper. Those are two things *you've got* to remember. Talk about anything else, give the reporters plenty of material. Tell them about the romance of your secret marriage with Rob Gleason. Tell them how you admire him and what a wonderful man he is. Tell them all about the childhood you had, the fact that your parents died and that your uncle was the same as a father and a mother to you. Try to get the note of the poor little rich girl who has neither father nor mother, but is rolling in coin.

"Give them all the material that they want to write sob sister articles and character sketches, and that stuff. But the minute they start talking about the case, or what happened on that night, simply dry up like a clam. Tell them that you're awfully sorry, that *you'd* like to talk about it, and you don't see any reason why you couldn't, but that your lawyer has given you specific instructions that he's to do all the talking.

134

Tell them you think it's silly, and that you can't understand why your lawyer feels that way, because you've got nothing to conceal, and you'd like to come right out and tell the whole circumstances as you remember them, but you've promised your lawyer, and you're not going to break your promise to anybody.

"They'll try all sorts of tricks on you, and probably tell you Rob Gleason has made a full confession, or that he has told the officers he has reason to believe that you committed the murder, or that you made certain incriminating statements to him, or they'll tell you that he has come to the conclusion that you are guilty and has made a confession in order to take the jolt so that you'll be spared. They'll try all sorts of stuff. Simply look at them with a dumb expression on your face, and say nothing. And for God's sake, don't lose your temper. They'll probably do things that will make you want to kill them, but if you lose your temper and fly into one of your rages, they'll spread it all over the front pages of the newspaper, that you've got an ungovernable temper, and are one of these tiger women."

"I understand," she said.

There was the sound of a siren drifting up through the windows of the office.

Frances Celane shuddered.

"Well," said Nevers to the photographer, "get your camera all loaded up, boy, because some of these cops will want to get their picture in the paper, taking the suspect into custody. Probably Carl Seaward will show up from the Homicide Squad. He's one of those birds that likes to stick his stomach in front of a camera and put his hand on the shoulder of the prisoner, with a photograph for the front page labeled: *'Carl Seaward, intrepid investigator of the Homicide Squad, taking the suspect into custody, marking the termination of a case which has baffled the entire police force for the past forty-eight hours.'*

"Maybe I'd better get in this picture too. I wonder if my hair is on straight. I can pose as the *STAR* reporter who assisted the police in locating the suspect."

135

And Nevers struck a pose in front of the camera, grinning.
Frances Celane surveyed him in scornful appraisal.
"Show a little leg," she said.

Chapter 17

Paul Drake perched on the edge of Perry Mason's desk and shook tobacco from a cloth sack into a brown paper which he held expertly between cigarette-stained fingers.

"Well," he said, "we've got our contact with Mrs. Mayfield. But it isn't getting us anything. We had one devil of a time. The police had her in custody as a material witness for a while."

"Have you worked the rough shadow business on her yet?" inquired Mason.

"Not yet. We're building up to it. We've got a woman operative who's posing as a woman who's been abroad as a governess, and is now out of work. We've checked back on Mrs. Mayfield and found all about her early associates. We managed to run one of them down and got all the dope from her about the names of the people she knew, and all that sort of stuff."

"This woman is getting across all right?" asked Mason.

"I'll say she's getting across. She's got Mrs. Mayfield confiding in her, all of her troubles with her husband, and all that sort of stuff."

"But she hasn't said anything about the murder?" asked Mason.

"Not a peep so far. That is, of course, she mentions that she was taken to the District Attorney's office and held for awhile as a material witness until they got a signed statement out of her, and a lot of that stuff. But she isn't going into details. All that she's telling is simply a rehash of what she's told the newspapers."

"How about Don Graves?" inquired the attorney. "How are you getting along with him?"

Paul Drake put the finishing touches on the cigarette.

"We're making some *real* progress there," he said, "We've got a young lady operative who has contacted him, and Graves is falling for her like a ton of brick. He's telling her everything he knows."

"About the case?" asked Mason.

"About the case, about everything. He's turning himself inside out."

"This woman must be good," said Mason.

"I'll say she's good," explained Drake enthusiastically. "She'd knock your eye out. She's got one of those confiding techniques that snuggles up and looks at you with big eyes, and seems to listen all over. You just naturally ache to tell her things. My God, every time I go out with that broad, I sit down and start telling her all of *my* troubles; about the girl that jilted me in my childhood, so that I never got married, and all that stuff.

"You've seen a guy when he's about nine-tenths drunk, going around and weeping on the necks of total strangers and telling all of his private affairs? Well, that's just the way this jane works. She affects the fellows just about like nine-tenths of a drunk. They fall all over her and spill everything."

"That's fine," said Mason. "What have you found out?"

"So far, just stuff you don't want to hear," said the detective. "It don't help your client a damn bit."

"All right," said Mason, "give me the lowdown, and don't try to put a sugar coating on it. Give me the facts."

"The facts are," said Drake, "that this Celane girl had on a pink negligee the night the murder was committed. Graves was sent by Edward Norton to ride up with Judge Purley and Arthur Crinston to get some documents. He kept looking back toward the house as they went around the curves in the road and when they got to the point in the road where he could look up at the window in Edward Norton's study, he saw somebody standing back of Norton, who was seated at his desk.

"More than that, he says that he saw the man swing a club down on Edward Norton's head, and Norton collapsed across the desk. He says that he saw the arm, shoulder and head of a woman, and that he thinks he is positive of the identity of

138

both the man and the woman. The woman had on a pink negligee."

"He made that statement to the District Attorney's office?" asked Mason.

"Yes, he's made it, and subscribed and sworn to it."

"That isn't the statement he made the first time," Mason pointed out. "When they were making their first investigation, Graves said that he saw the man in the room, who struck the blow, and didn't see anyone else except Norton."

"That won't help you any," said Drake casually. "You can't prove that."

"They took the statement down in shorthand," said Mason.

Drake laughed.

"Those notes have been lost. I'm just telling you in the event you don't know it," he said. "I made it a point to ask one of the newspaper reporters to inquire of the shorthand stenographer who took down the statements there that night. Strange as it may seem, something happened, and the notebook had been misplaced. It's disappeared."

He grinned at the lawyer.

Perry Mason stared down at the surface of his desk, his brows in straight lines of frowning concentration.

"The dirty crooks," he said. "The D.A. always howls to high heaven about the crooked criminal lawyers who manipulate the facts. But whenever the D.A. uncovers any evidence that gives the defendant a break, you can bet something happens to it."

The detective shrugged his shoulders.

"The D.A.'s want convictions," he said.

"Can your operative get into Mrs. Mayfield's room in Norton's residence, Paul?" Mason asked.

"Sure. That's a cinch."

"All right, I want her to make a report on every dress that's in there. In other words, I want to see if there's a pink dress or a pink negligee in there."

Paul Drake squinted at the lawyer significantly.

"It wouldn't be such a hard job to *put* one in there," he said.

"No," said Mason, "I'm going to play fair."

"What's the use of playing fair?" asked Drake. "They didn't play fair with you."

"I can't help that," said Mason. "I think I've got an out in this case, and I'm going to play it fair and square. I think I can beat the rap if I can get a decent break."

"Listen," said Paul Drake, drawing his feet up to the desk, and sitting cross-legged on the corner of it, "you haven't got an out in this case. They've got your client as good as convicted right now. Look what they've got on her. She's the one that would have benefited by the old man's death. In fact, with that marriage hanging over her head, she either had to kill him, or lose an estate that's worth a big bunch of money.

"This fellow, Gleason, may have married the woman because he loved her, or he may have married her because he wanted her money. Nobody knows which, but he gets all the credit for marrying her for money. The theory of the prosecution is that when he found out about the trust provision, he and the girl tried to reason with Norton. When Norton wouldn't listen to reason, Gleason made up his mind he'd bump him off. They had a big squabble. He'd have killed Norton right then if it hadn't been for Crinston coming to keep an appointment. So Gleason waited around until Crinston left, then jimmied a window to make it look as though burglars had broken in from the outside. Then he cracked down on Norton's head.

"He probably hadn't figured on any robbery at the time. He just wanted to make it look like robbery, so he turned the pockets inside-out. He found so much money in the wallet, he decided to keep it. Then he heard Crinston coming back, and had to do something quick. He knew the chauffeur was drunk, so he dashed down and planted as much of the evidence on him as he could, and then beat it.

"Frances Celane was with Gleason when the murder was committed. She's got the devil of a temper when she gets aroused. Probably she was in a rage, but Gleason married her for her dough. It was a deliberate crime on his part. He'd probably worked out the burglar plant while Crinston was talking with Norton. When he heard the car coming back, he realized he must have been seen, or that something had gone wrong, so then he framed the chauffeur, just as a second string to his bow.''

Perry Mason stared at the detective with his eyes cold and hard.

''Paul,'' he said, ''if they go into court on that theory, I'm going to bust it wide open.''

''You're not going to bust anything wide open,'' Drake told him. ''They've got all kinds of circumstantial evidence. They've caught the girl in half a dozen lies. Why did she say that she was out in the Buick sedan when she wasn't? They can prove that the car never left the garage. Mrs. Mayfield has worked up that end of the case for them, and the butler will swear positively that the car was there all the time. They can prove the ownership of the club that killed Norton, and they can prove that the girl had some of the money that came from Norton. . . .''

Perry Mason jerked to rigid attention.

''They can prove the girl had the money?'' he asked.

''Yes,'' said Drake.

''How?'' asked the lawyer.

''I don't know exactly how, but I do know that it's part of their case. They've got it all worked up. I think it's through the Mayfield woman.''

''Well,'' said Mason wearily, ''we're going to have a chance to find out. I'm going to force them to bring that case to an immediate trial.''

''Force them to an immediate trial?'' exclaimed Drake. ''Why I thought you were stalling for delay. The newspapers say that you are.''

Perry Mason grinned at him.

''That,'' he said, ''is the way I'm forcing them to a trial. I'm yelling for continuances, and asking for additional time, as though my clients would be stuck if I didn't get them. Naturally, they're opposing my continuances. After I've got the D.A.'s office to make that opposition sufficiently vigorous, I'm going to admit that I'm licked, and let them bring the case on for trial.''

Drake shook his head.

"They won't fall for that one," he said, "it's too old."

"It won't be old the way I dress it up," said Mason. "What I want you to do is to play this rough shadow business on Mrs. Mayfield, and also on Don Graves. I want to see if we can't frighten some facts out of them. Neither one of them is telling the truth—not yet. And I want to find out more about that money, whether the District Attorney had proof or just suspicions."

"You going to try and saddle the murder off on Mrs. Mayfield and her husband?" asked Drake.

"I'm going to represent my client to the best of my ability," Mason insisted.

"Yeah, I know that line," the detective told him, "but what does it mean?"

Mason tapped a cigarette end on the polished surface of the desk.

"The way to get to the bottom of a murder," he said, "is to pick out any pertinent fact which hasn't been explained, and find the real explanation of that fact."

"Sure," said Drake, "that's another generality. Get down to earth. What are you talking about?"

"I'm talking about the reason Norton had for claiming the Buick sedan was stolen," said the lawyer.

"What's that got to do with it?" Drake wanted to know.

"Everything," insisted Perry Mason. "That's an unexplained fact in that case, and until we get the explanation of that fact, we haven't got a solution of the murder."

"That's a good line of hooey for the jury," commented the detective, "but it doesn't really mean anything. You can't explain everything in any case. You know that."

"Until you can explain it," doggedly insisted Mason, "you haven't got a complete case. Now remember that the prosecution is going to rest its case on circumstantial evidence. In order to get a conviction on circumstantial evidence, you've got to exclude every reasonable hypothesis other than that of guilt."

The detective snapped his fingers.

"A lot of lawyer talk," he said. "That doesn't mean

anything to the newspapers, and the newspapers are going to be the ones who will determine whether or not your client gets convicted.''

"Well, before I get done with this case," Mason remarked, "the newspapers are going to figure that Buick car is the most important fact in the entire case.''

"But the automobile wasn't stolen. It didn't leave the garage.''

"That's what the butler says.''

Drake's face suddenly became hard with concentrated attention.

"You mean that the butler is lying?" he asked.

"I'm not making any statements right now," said Mason.

Drake spoke in a monotone, as though thinking out loud.

"Of course if the butler had taken the car and disconnected the speedometer, and maybe gone for a little drive, and Norton had telephoned the police that the car was stolen, and he wanted the driver picked up, no matter who it might be, and then the butler had come back and found out about that telephone call . . ."

His voice trailed off into silence. He sat motionless for a few minutes, then shook his head sadly.

"No, Perry," he said, "that won't work.''

"All right," said Mason, smiling, "I'm not asking you what'll work and what won't work. I want facts out of you. Get the hell off of my desk, and let me go to work. Put your rough shadows to work just as soon as you can. I'm anxious to find out what they uncover.''

"You're representing both Gleason and the woman, eh?" asked Drake.

"Yes, I am now. Frances Celane is going to stand by her husband. She's told me to represent him.''

"All right, I'm going to ask you something that's been asked me by a dozen different people, I hope you won't take any offense, but it's for your own good, because everybody in town is talking about it. They're saying that if the lawyer for the defense has any sense why doesn't he try to get separate trials and try the man and the woman separately? In that way they'd have to try the man first, and you'd have a chance to find out all their evidence and cross-examine all their witnesses before they got down to a trial of the woman.''

''I couldn't get separate trials for them,'' said Mason. ''The court wouldn't allow it.''

''Well, you could at least make the attempt,'' said the detective.

''No,'' said Mason with a smile, ''I rather think I'm satisfied the way things are now. I think we'll try them together.''

''Okay,'' said Drake, ''you're the doctor. I'll get the rough shadows at work just as soon as I can.''

Chapter 18

Perry Mason appeared at the entrance to the visitors' room in the huge jail building.

"Robert Gleason," he told the officer in charge.

"You're Gleason's attorney?" asked the officer.

"Yes."

"You didn't appear for him as his attorney when he first came in."

Perry Mason frowned. "I'm his attorney now," he said. "Do you want to bring him out, or do you want me to go into court and show that the officers have refused to permit me to talk with my client?"

The officer stared at Mason, shrugged his shoulders, turned on his heel without a word, and vanished. Five minutes later he opened a door and escorted Mason into the long room.

A table ran the length of this room. Along the middle of the table, stretching to a height of some five feet above it, was a long screen of heavy iron mesh. The prisoners sat on one side of this screen. The attorneys sat on the other. Robert Gleason was seated about half way down the table. He got to his feet, and smiled eagerly as he saw Perry Mason approaching. Perry Mason waited until the officer had moved out of earshot, then dropped into the chair, and looked searchingly across at the man accused of murder.

"Keep your voice low when you answer questions, Gleason," said Mason, "and tell me the truth. No matter what it is, don't be afraid to tell me the exact truth."

"Yes sir," said Gleason.

Mason frowned at him.

"Did you make a statement to the District Attorney?" he asked.

Gleason nodded his head.

145

"A written statement?"

"It was taken down in shorthand by a court reporter, and then written up and given to me to sign."

"Did you sign it?"

"I haven't yet."

"Where is it?"

"It's in my cell. They gave it to me to read. That is, they gave me a copy."

"That's funny," said Mason. "Usually they try to rush you into signing it. They don't let you have a copy."

"I know," said Gleason, "but I didn't fall for that. They tried to rush me into signing it, and I told them I was going to think it over."

"It won't do you much good," the lawyer told him, wearily, "if you talked in front of a court reporter, he took down everything you said, and he can testify to the conversation from his notes."

"That's what the District Attorney's office told me," said Gleason. "But I'm not signing, just the same."

"Why not?"

"Because," said Gleason, in a low voice, "I think that I'll repudiate what I said."

"You can't do it," the lawyer told him. "Why the devil did you have to shoot off your mouth?"

"I can do it the way I intend to," Gleason told him.

"Can do what?"

"Repudiate the confession."

"All right, show me," said the lawyer.

"I intend to take the entire responsibility for the murder," Gleason told him.

Perry Mason stared at the man through the coarse screen of the partition.

"Did you commit the murder?" he asked.

Gleason bit his lips, turned his head so that his eyes were averted from those of the attorney.

"Come on," said Perry Mason. "Come through, and come clean. Look up at me and answer that question. Did you commit the murder?"

Rob Gleason shifted uncomfortably in the chair.

146

"I'd rather not answer that question just yet," he said.

"You've got to answer it," Perry Mason told him.

Gleason wet his lips with the tip of a nervous tongue, then leaned forward so that his face was almost against the coarse iron screen.

"Can I ask you some questions before I answer that?" he inquired.

"Yes," Mason said, "you can ask me all the questions you want, but you've got to come clean on that before I leave here. If I'm going to act as your attorney, I've got to know what happened."

"The District Attorney's office told me that Frances had been caught with some of the money that Mr. Norton had in his possession when he was killed."

"Don't believe everything the District Attorney's office tells you," Mason answered.

"Yes I know. But the point is, *did* she have that money?"

"I'll answer that question by asking you another," said Perry Mason. "Did Mrs. Mayfield make any statement to the District Attorney about having money in her possession, that she had received from Frances Celane?"

"I don't know," said Gleason.

Perry Mason chose his words carefully, *"If,"* he said, "the District Attorney's office has any *proof* of Frances Celane having any of that money, it came through Mrs. Mayfield. In other words, they found Mrs. Mayfield with the money, and she passed the buck to Frances Celane. Now, if that happened, there's just as much reason to believe that Mrs. Mayfield was in the room at the time of the murder, and took the money from the body of the dead man, as to believe that Frances Celane gave it to her."

"Are they *sure* that there was a woman in the room at the time of the murder?" Gleason inquired.

"Don Graves says there was."

"He didn't say that the first night."

"We can't prove what he said the first night because the police have torn up the notes of the statement he made."

"He says now that there was a woman there?"

"Yes, he says there was a woman. I think he's going to say it was a woman who wore a pink negligee."

"Did he see her plainly enough to identify her?"

"He saw her shoulder and arm, and part of her head—probably the back of her head."

"Then Mrs. Mayfield is trying to pin this crime on Fran?" asked Rob Gleason.

"I'm not saying that," said Mason. "I'm simply giving you the facts as I know them. If the District Attorney's office has proof of any money, that's where they got it."

"How much chance do you stand of getting Fran off?" asked Gleason.

"One never knows what a jury is going to do. She's young and attractive. If she keeps her temper and doesn't make any damaging admissions, I stand a pretty good chance."

Gleason stared through the screen at the lawyer for a few moments, and then said: "All right, I'm not attractive. I haven't got any of the things in my favor that Frances has. How much chance do you stand of getting me off?"

"It depends on the kind of a break I can get, and on what you've told the District Attorney," said Mason. "Now, I'm going to tell you what I want you to do. You go back to your cell and get some paper. Say that you want to write out what happened, in your own handwriting. Take that paper and scribble a lot of meaningless stuff on a few pages of it, and then tear it up. Let them believe that you used up all the paper, but take the rest of the paper and write out a copy of the statement that the District Attorney has given you to sign. In that way, I'll know exactly what you said, and what you didn't say."

Rob Gleason swallowed twice painfully.

"If," he said, "you don't get the breaks, they may convict Fran?"

"Of course, she's charged with first degree murder, and there's some circumstances in the case that don't look so good."

"Would they hang her?"

"Probably not. She'd probably get life. They don't hang women, as a rule."

"Do you know what it would mean to a girl of her fire and temperament to be shut up in a penitentiary for the rest of her life?" asked Gleason.

Perry Mason shook his head impatiently.

"Of course I know," he said. "Let's not start worrying about that now. Let's get down to facts. Tell me, did you, or did you not, murder Edward Norton?"

Gleason took a deep breath.

"If," he said, "the case commences to look hopeless for Fran, I'm going to confess."

"Confess to what?" asked Mason.

"Confess to the murder of Edward Norton; confess that I married Frances Celane for her money; that I didn't care very much about her. I liked her well enough, but I wasn't crazy about her. She had a great big bunch of money, and was a good catch. I wanted the money bad enough to marry her, and I married her. Then I found out that because she had married, her uncle had the right to cut her off with almost nothing. Her uncle didn't know about the marriage until the night he was killed. He found it out then. He was going to exercise the discretion given to him under the trust, and turn everything over to the charitable institutions, leaving Fran with just a lousy thousand or two. I went in and argued with him. He wouldn't listen to reason. Fran went in and argued with him, and that didn't do any good. Then Crinston came, and he had an appointment with Crinston, so we had to let our matter go. Fran and I went back down to her room. We sat and talked things over. Mrs. Mayfield came in, and was furious. She'd been blackmailing Fran, threatening to tell Mr. Norton about the marriage, unless she got a bunch of jack. Edward Norton had found out about the marriage, and that had killed the goose that laid Mrs. Mayfield's golden eggs.

"I heard Crinston drive away. He took Don Graves with him. I went out to have a last word with Mr. Norton. I went up to his study, and on the stairs I ran into Mrs. Mayfield. She wore a pink negligee, and she was still weeping about the money that she'd lost. I told her if she'd keep her head, we could have lots of money. She wanted to know what I meant, and I told her I was going to give Norton one more chance to come through. If he didn't take it, I was going to smash his head for him before he had a chance to give Frances Celane's money to charity. She went with me up the stairs and into his study. I gave Edward Norton his ultimatum. I told him that if he didn't give Frances her money, he was going to be sorry. He told me that he was not going to give her a cent; that he was going to turn it all over to charity, and then I cracked him on the head. I went through his pockets, and he had a big bunch of dough in his pockets. I took some, and Mrs. Mayfield took some. We were talking about how we were going to make the murder look as though burglars had done it. Mrs. Mayfield said we could pry up a window and leave some footprints outside in the soft loam. I wanted to plant it on the chauffeur because I knew he was drunk. While we were talking it over, we saw the lights of an automobile coming down the hill, and I figured it must be Crinston coming back. Mrs. Mayfield ran down and fixed the window so it looked as though burglars had come in, and I ran down and planted a stick and a couple of the thousand dollar bills in Devoe's room. Then I jumped in my car and beat it.''

Perry Mason looked at the young man thoughtfully. ''What did you do with the money that you had?'' he asked.

''I buried it,'' said Rob Gleason, ''where it will never be found.''

Perry Mason drummed with the tips of his fingers on the table. ''So help you God,'' he asked, ''is that what happened?''

Gleason nodded his head.

''That's in confidence,'' he said. ''I'm going to beat the rap if I can. If I can't, I'm going to come clean so that Frances Celane won't have to take the jolt.''

''Did you,'' asked Perry Mason, ''take out the Buick automobile on the night of the murder? Did you use it at all?''

''No.''

Perry Mason pushed back the chair.

''All right,'' he said. ''Now I'm going to tell you something. If you ever spill that story, you're going to get Frances

Celane sent up for life, if you don't get her hung. Probably you'll get her hung."

Rob Gleason's eyes grew wide.

"What ever in the world do you mean?" he asked.

"Simply," said Perry Mason, "that nobody will believe the story the way you tell it. They'll believe just half of it. They'll believe that you committed the murder all right, but they'll figure that it wasn't Mrs. Mayfield that was with you. They'll figure that it was Fran Celane, and that you're trying to protect her by dragging Mrs. Mayfield into it."

Gleason was on his feet, his face white, his eyes wide.

"Good God!" he said. "Can't I save Frances by telling the truth?"

"Not that kind of truth," said Perry Mason. "Now go back to your cell and get me a copy of that statement the District Attorney wants you to sign. In the meantime, keep your head and don't tell anybody anything."

"Not even the truth, the way I told it to you?" asked Gleason.

"The truth is the last thing in the world you want to tell," said Perry Mason, "the way you're situated. Because nobody's going to believe you if you do tell the truth, and you're a rotten liar."

He turned on his heel and walked away from the screen meshed table, without a single backward glance. The officer opened the locked door, and let him out of the visiting room.

Chapter 19

It was the first time Frank Everly had ever been in court with Perry Mason; the first time he had ever been behind the scenes in a big murder case.

He sat at the side of Perry Mason and stared surreptitiously at the crowded courtroom, at the nine men and three women who were in the jury box, being examined as to their qualifications as jurors. He strove to give the impression of being thoroughly at home, but his manner betrayed his nervousness.

Perry Mason sat at the counsel table, leaning back in the swivel chair, his left thumb hooked in the armhole of his vest, his right hand toying with a watch chain. His face was a cold mask of rugged patience. Nothing about the man gave any indication of the terrific strain under which he labored.

Behind him sat the two defendants: Frances Celane in a close fitting costume of black, with a dash of white and a touch of red, her head held very erect, her eyes calm and a trifle defiant.

Robert Gleason was nervous, with the nervousness of an athletic man who finds himself fighting for his life under circumstances that necessitate physical passivity. His eyes smouldered with the sullen fires of suppressed emotions. His head jerked from time to time as he turned to face the various speakers in the drama which so intimately concerned him.

The courtroom was filled with that peculiar atmosphere which permeates a crowded room where spectators are in a state of emotional unrest.

Claude Drumm was acting as the trial deputy for the state, but there was a rumor that the District Attorney himself would come into the case as soon as the jury had been selected, and the routine evidence disposed of.

Drumm had been on his feet much of the time in his examination of the jurors. He was tall, well-tailored and self-contained, yet forcefully aggressive, without displaying too much force. His manner held the easy assurance of a professional who is fully at home and who is driving steadily toward a predetermined goal which he is assured of reaching.

Judge Markham, beneath the cloak of his austere judicial dignity, held himself with wary watchfulness. Perry Mason had the reputation of being able to "stampede," every case he tried, and Judge Markham was determined, that while the trial would be conducted with impartiality, it would be conducted with a proper regard for the dignity of law and order; that there would be no errors in the record, no opportunities for the dramatic manipulation of emotions which so frequently turned trials in which Perry Mason participated into spectacular debacles for the prosecution, crashing across the front pages of newspapers in glaring headlines.

"The peremptory," said Judge Markham sternly, "is with the people."

Claude Drumm dropped back to his chair and engaged in a whispered consultation with his assistant. He interrupted, to glance up at the court.

"If I may have a moment's indulgence, Your Honor."

"Very well," said the judge.

Everly looked at Perry Mason inquiringly, and caught a glint in the lawyer's eyes.

Mason leaned forward and whispered:

"Drumm wants to get number three off of the jury, but he thinks we have got to get off jurors nine and eleven. We've got twice as many peremptory challenges as he has, so he's wondering if he dares to pass his peremptory and hold it in reserve until he sees what the jury looks like later on."

"Does he dare to do it?" asked Everly.

"That," said Perry Mason, "remains to be seen."

There was a moment of tense silence, then Drumm got to his feet and bowed to the court.

"The people," he said, "pass their peremptory."

Judge Markham looked down at Perry Mason, and his lips moved to form the words: "The peremptory is with the defendants."

But the words were never uttered, for Perry Mason, turning toward the jury with a casual glance of appraisal, as though the entire matter had just claimed his attention, said, in a clear voice: "Your Honor, this jury seems *entirely* satisfactory to the defendants. We waive our peremptory challenge."

Claude Drumm was caught by surprise. Eyes of those who were wise in courtroom technique, saw the quick intake of his breath as he started unconsciously to register a protest which his consciousness knew would be futile.

Judge Markham's voice rang out through the crowded courtroom:

"Let the jurors stand and be sworn to try the case."

Claude Drumm made an opening statement to the jury which was remarkable for its brevity.

"Gentlemen," he said, "we expect to show that, at the exact minute of eleven thirty-two on the twenty-third day of October of this year, Edward Norton met his death; that he was murdered by a blow on the head, struck with a club held in the hand of the defendant, Robert Gleason; that at the time of the murder, there was present as an active accomplice, the defendant, Frances Celane; that at the time of the murder, Edward Norton had a large sum of money on his person in the form of one thousand dollar bills.

"We expect to show that at the hour of eleven fourteen on that date, Edward Norton telephoned to the police station, reporting the theft of one of his automobiles, a Buick sedan; that Frances Celane was, in fact, presently in the study of Edward Norton at the hour of eleven thirty-two P.M., on the date of the murder, but that, for the purpose of trying to establish an alibi, and knowing that Edward Norton had reported this Buick sedan as having been stolen at the hour of eleven fourteen, the said defendant, Frances Celane, then and there stated falsely and wilfully that she had been distant from the scene of the crime, in the said Buick automobile, from the hour of approximately ten forty-five until approximately twelve fifteen.

"We expect to show that immediately following the commission of the crime, the defendants left the bloody club with which the crime had been committed, and two of the one thousand dollar bills which had been stolen from the body of the deceased, in the bedroom of one Pete Devoe, who was then and there asleep and in an intoxicated condition; that this was done for the purpose of directing suspicion to the said Pete Devoe.

"We will also show that the defendants forced open a window and made footprints in the soil beneath the window, in an attempt to lead the police to believe burglars had entered the house.

"We also expect to show that immediately thereafter the defendant Robert Gleason fled from the scene of the crime; that both defendants gave false and contradictory accounts as to their whereabouts; that the club with which Edward Norton was struck down was a walking stick belonging to the defendant, Robert Gleason.

"We expect to show that an eye-witness actually saw the murder committed, and will identify Robert Gleason as the man who struck the blow, and will identify Frances Celane as the young woman who, attired in a pink dress or negligee, aided and abetted the commission of the crime."

Claude Drumm stood staring at the jurors for a moment, then sat down. Judge Markham looked inquiringly at Perry Mason.

"If the court please," said Perry Mason, "we will withold our opening statement until the time we start to present our case."

"Very well," said Judge Markham. "You may proceed, Mr. Drumm."

Claude Drumm started building up the case with that calm, deadly efficiency for which he was noted. No detail was too small to claim his attention; no link in the chain of evidence was to be overlooked.

The first witness was a surveyor who had mapped and

155

photographed the premises. He introduced diagrams drawn to scale, showing the room in which the body had been found, the furniture in the room, the location of the windows. Then he produced a photograph of the room, other photographs of various corners of the room. Each of these photographs was identified by locating it on the diagram of the room. Then followed photographs of the house, and finally, a map showing the house with reference to the winding road which climbed up to the boulevard. Following that came a contour map showing the various elevations of the windows in the house, with reference to the road along which the automobile had traveled.

"So that," said Drumm, suavely, indicating a place on the diagram where a curve in the road was shown, "it would be perfectly possible for a person traveling along this section of the road which I am indicating, in an automobile, to glance back and see into the room marked number one on the map, People's Exhibit A?"

Before the surveyor could answer the question, Perry Mason got to his feet and raised his voice in protest:

"Just a moment, Your Honor," he said. "That question is leading. It also calls for a conclusion of the witness. It calls for a conclusion which the jury is to draw in this case. It is one of the points upon which we intend to convince this jury of the improbability of the People's case. Whether or not . . ."

The gavel of the judge banged down upon his desk.

"The objection," he said, "is sustained. The argument, Mr. Mason, is unnecessary."

Mason dropped back to his chair.

With the manner of one who has scored a victory even in defeat, Drumm bowed smilingly to Mason.

"Counsellor," he said, "you may inquire on cross-examination."

With the eyes of everyone in the courtroom riveted upon him, Perry Mason, fully aware of the dramatic advantage of the moment, and the interest which would attend upon his first question, strode to the map which had been fastened to the blackboard with thumb tacks, placed the index finger of his right hand upon the curve in the line which indicated the roadway from the house to the boulevard, placed the index finger of his left hand upon the location of the study in the house, and said, in a voice which rang with challenge: "Exactly how far is it from the point which I am indicating with my right forefinger, and which is the curve in this roadway, to the point which I am indicating with my left finger, and which is the point where the body was found?"

"If," said the witness in level tones, "your right forefinger is exactly at the point where the curve swings farthest south, and your left forefinger is at a point representing the exact point where the body was found, the distance is exactly two hundred and seventy-two feet, three and one-half inches."

Perry Mason turned, his face showing surprise.

"Two hundred and seventy-two feet, three and one-half inches?" he exclaimed incredulously.

"Yes," said the witness.

Mason dropped his hands to his sides with a gesture of finality.

"That," he said, "is all. I have no further questions to ask of this witness."

Judge Markham looked at the clock, and an anticipatory rustle of motion stirred the courtroom, as dead leaves on a tree are stirred by the first current of an advancing breeze.

"It has," said the judge, "approached the hour of adjournment. The court will adjourn until ten o'clock tomorrow morning, and during that time, the jury will remember the admonition of the court not to converse amongst themselves about this case, nor permit others to converse with them or in their presence about it."

The gavel banged on the desk.

Perry Mason smiled craftily, and remarked to his assistant: "Drumm should have carried on the examination until the hour for adjournment. Giving me the opportunity to ask that one question, will make the newspapers feature it tomorrow morning."

Everly had his eyes puckered in concentration.

"Two hundred and seventy-two feet is a long distance," he said.

"It won't," Mason assured him grimly, "get any shorter as the case goes on."

Chapter 20

The newspapers predicted that the first major witness for the prosecution would be either Arthur Crinston, the business partner of the murdered man, or Don Graves, who had been the only eye-witness of the murder.

In this, the newspapers showed that they underestimated the dramatic trial tactics of the chief trial deputy. Drumm would no more have plunged into the drama of that murder without preparing the minds of the jurors for the gruesome tidbit, than would a playwright have opened his presentation with a crisis lifted from the third act.

He called to the stand, instead, Judge B. C. Purley.

Necks craned as the Municipal Judge, coming in from the back of the courtroom, strode down the aisle with the stately bearing of one who realizes to the full the dignity of his appearance, and the importance of his position.

White-haired, ponderous, deep-chested and heavy-waisted, he held up his right hand while the oath was administered to him, and then took the witness chair, his manner indicating a respect for the tribunal and what it stood for, a dignified tolerance of the attorneys and jurors, a calm disregard of the restless spectators.

"Your name is B. C. Purley?" asked Claude Drumm.

"Yes sir."

"You are now a duly elected, qualified and acting Judge of the Municipal Court of this city?"

"I am."

"And, on the night of October twenty-third of this year you had occasion to be in the vicinity of the residence of Edward Norton?"

"I did."

159

"At what time did you arrive at the residence of Edward Norton, Judge Purley?"

"At precisely six minutes after eleven."

"And what time did you leave that vicinity?"

"At precisely thirty minutes past eleven."

"Will you explain to the jury, Judge Purley, why it is that you are able to testify with such exactness as to the time of arrival and departure?"

Perry Mason recognized the trap, yet had no alternative but to walk into it.

"Objected to, Your Honor," he said. "The witness has given his testimony. The mental processes which led up to it are incompetent, irrelevant, immaterial, and, at best, matter only for cross-examination."

"Sustained," said Judge Markham.

Claude Drumm's smile was ironically sarcastic.

"I will withdraw the question, Your Honor," he said. "It was an error upon my part. After all, if Counsellor Mason desires to go into the matter, he is at liberty to do so upon cross-examination."

"Proceed," said Judge Markham, pounding his desk with the gavel.

"Who was with you on the occasion of your visit?" asked the deputy district attorney.

"Mr. Arthur Crinston was with me when I went to the vicinity of the house, and both Mr. Arthur Crinston, and Mr. Don Graves were with me at the time I departed."

"What happened while you were there, Judge Purley?"

"I arrived at the grounds in the vicinity of the house, stopped my car to allow Mr. Crinston to get out, turned my car, shut off the motor, and waited."

"During the time that you were waiting what did you do?"

"Sat and smoked for the first ten or fifteen minutes, and looked at my watch rather impatiently several times during the last part of the period I was waiting," said Judge Purley.

And he glanced, with just a trace of subdued triumph, at Perry Mason, his manner indicating that, being fully familiar with court procedure, he was going to get the damaging parts of his testimony in, whether the defense wanted them in or not. The inference to be drawn from the fact that he had glanced several times at his watch was that he was aware of the exact minute of his departure, and he was sufficiently adroit to get that inference across to the jury without violating the ruling of the court.

Perry Mason eyed the witness with placid indifference.

"Then what happened?" asked Claude Drumm.

"Then Mr. Crinston came out of the house to join me. I started the motor of my car, and at that moment the window of the house in the southeast corner of the building was opened, and Mr. Norton thrust his head out of the study window."

"Just a moment," said Claude Drumm. "Do you know of your own knowledge that that was Mr. Norton's study?"

"No sir," said Judge Purley. "I only know it from the fact that it was the room in the southeast corner on the second story of the house, and is the room marked on the map and diagram as room number one, Mr. Norton's study."

"Oh," said Drumm, "then the room is that which is indicated on Plaintiff's Exhibit A by the figure one marked in a circle?"

"Yes sir."

"Very well," said Drumm, "what did Mr. Norton say?"

"Mr. Norton called down to Mr. Crinston, and said, as nearly as I can remember: 'Arthur, would it be all right for you to take Don Graves in to your house in your car and let him get the documents? Then I will send the chauffeur to pick him up.' "

"And," said Drumm, "what happened next?"

"Mr. Crinston said, as nearly as I can remember: 'I am not in my own car, but with a friend. I will have to ask my friend if it will be all right.' "

"Then what happened?"

"Mr. Norton said: 'Very well, do so, and let me know,' and withdrew his head from the window."

"Then what happened?"

"Then Mr. Crinston came to me and said that Mr. Graves was to get some documents . . . ."

"Objected to," said Perry Mason in a casual tone of voice. "Anything which took place without the hearing of this defendant is admissible only as a part of the *res gestae*. By no stretch of the imagination can this be considered as a part of the *res gestae*."

"The objection is sustained," said Judge Markham.

"Very well. Then what happened?" asked Drumm suavely, smiling over at the jury as much to say: "You see how technical the defense is in this case, ladies and gentlemen?"

"Then," said Judge Purley, "Mr. Crinston went back to a position under the study window, and called up, as nearly as I can remember his words: 'It's all right, Edward. He can go with us.' And at about that moment, the front door opened and the figure of Mr. Graves ran down the steps, Mr. Graves saying 'I am ready,' or words to that effect."

"And then what happened?"

"Then the three of us got in my automobile, Mr. Crinston sitting in the front seat with me, Mr. Graves sitting in the rear seat. I started the machine and started to drive up along the road, lettered on the map 'People's Exhibit B' as '*Winding Roadway*.' We traveled up that road until we were in a position on the curve . . ."

"Just a moment," said Claude Drumm. "Can you take a pencil and indicate the exact point on the curve which you had approached when the event took place, concerning which you were about to testify?"

Judge Purley nodded, got to his feet, and walked with ponderous dignity to the blackboard, turned up the map and marked a small oblong on the curve in the roadway.

"This represents the approximate position of the car."

"And what happened when the car was in that position?" asked Claude Drumm.

"Mr. Graves looked back through the back window and exclaimed . . ."

"Objected to," snapped Perry Mason. "Hearsay, incompetent, irrelevant, and immaterial, not part of the *res gestae*, not binding upon the defendant."

"Sustained," said Judge Markham.

162

Claude Drumm made a helpless gesture.

"But surely, Your Honor, in view of what is to take place . . ."

"The objection," said Judge Markham coldly, "is sustained. You may call Mr. Don Graves at the proper moment, counsellor, and let him testify as to anything he saw. As to anything which was said or done outside of the presence of this defendant, and which is not a part of the *res gestae*, the objection is well taken."

"Very well," said Drumm, turning to the jury, and all but bowing, "at the proper time I will call Mr. Don Graves, and Mr, Don Graves will testify as to exactly what he saw at that place.

"Go on, Judge Purley, and tell the jury exactly what was done at that time and place, with reference to what you, yourself, did in relation to the operation of the automobile."

"I did nothing at exactly that place, but proceeded along the winding road, as indicated there on the map, for a distance of several rods, until I came to a place in the road which was wide enough to turn. There I turned the car by backing and twisting, and went back down the winding roadway, stopping once more in front of the house of Edward Norton."

"And then what did you do?"

"Then Mr. Graves and Mr. Crinston entered the house, and at their request I accompanied them. The three of us went up the stairs and into the room marked by the number 'one' in a circle on People's Exhibit A, and saw there a body, which was subsequently identified to me as that of Edward Norton, lying sprawled across the desk, with its head badly crushed. The body was lifeless at the time of my arrival. There was a telephone near one hand, and several papers, including a a policy of automobile insurance, on the desk."

"Did you notice, Judge Purley, what automobile was covered in that policy of insurance?"

"Objected to as incompetent, irrelevant and immaterial," said Perry Mason.

"Your Honor," said Drumm, "this is vital, and I pro-

163

pose to connect it up. It is a part of the theory of the prosecution that the defendant, Frances Celane, made a statement to the effect that she was out driving this Buick automobile; that these statements were made after she had been advised that police had been notified that the Buick automobile had been stolen. In other words, she knew that Edward Norton had telephoned that the Buick automobile had been stolen. Frances Celane, knowing that . . ."

"Very well," said Judge Markham, "there is no necessity for further argument, counsellor, as to the relevancy of the testimony. Upon the assurance of the prosecution that the matter will be connected, I will overrule the objections as to its relevancy, and permit the question to be answered, subject to a motion on the part of the defense to strike out if the evidence is not subsequently connected.

"This ruling, however, goes only to the relevancy of the testimony. It is, of course, apparent that the evidence called for by the question is not the best evidence. The automobile insurance policy, itself, is the best evidence of its contents, but there seems to be no objection made upon that ground."

Judge Markham looked down at Perry Mason with a puzzled expression on his face.

Perry Mason seemed to smile, the faintest trace of a quiver at the corners of his lips.

"No, Your Honor," he said, "there is no objection upon *that* ground."

"Very well," snapped Judge Markham, "the objection, as made, is overruled. Answer the question."

"The policy," said Judge Purley, "as I noticed at the time, or a few minutes later, covered a Buick sedan number 6754093, with a license number 12M1834."

Claude Drumm made a gesture with his hand.

"You may cross-examine the witness, Mr. Mason," he announced.

Perry Mason regarded Judge Purley with a placid smile.

"Judge Purley," he said, "did I understand you to say that when you went into the study you saw the body of Edward Norton lying across the desk?"

"You did *not*," snapped Judge Purley. "I stated that I saw the body of a man who was subsequently identified to me as being that of Edward Norton."

Perry Mason looked crestfallen.

"My mistake," he said.

There was a moment of silence, during which Judge Purley gazed at the courtroom with an air of complacent self-satisfaction, the air of one who has given testimony in a very credible manner, and the manner of one who has confidence in his ability to avoid any trap which can be set for him by cross-examining counsel.

"You see," explained Judge Purley, "I had never personally met Mr. Norton, despite the fact that I was quite friendly with Mr. Crinston and had, upon at least one prior occasion, driven Mr. Crinston to Mr. Norton's house."

Perry Mason seemed to be smiling.

"Oh how many occasions had you discussed any business matters with Mr. Norton on the telephone?" he asked.

Judge Purley showed his surprise.

"Why, I never talked with the man on the telephone in my life," he said.

"Then you'd never discussed the trust fund of his niece, Frances Celane, with him?"

Judge Purley's eyes bulged with surprise.

"Good heavens, no! Of course not!"

"Had you," asked Perry Mason, "ever discussed this trust fund with anyone else?"

Drumm was on his feet.

"Your Honor, that is objected to, not proper cross-examination, hearsay, incompetent, irrelevant, immaterial. Counsel has simply started upon a round-about way of calling for conversations which could not possibly . . ."

"Sustained!" snapped Judge Markham.

Drumm sat down.

There was silence in the courtroom. Perry Mason's face was expressionless.

"Any further questions?" asked Judge Markham.

"No, Your Honor," announced Perry Mason, to the surprise of the courtroom. "There is no further cross-examination."

Chapter 21

"Call Sergeant Mahoney," said Claude Drumm.

Sergeant Mahoney, attired in a uniform, stepped to the front of the clerk's desk, held up his right hand to be sworn, then took the witness stand.

"Your name is Sergeant E. L. Mahoney, and you were, on the evening of October twenty-third of the present year, acting as desk sergeant at the Central Police Station in this city?" asked Claude Drumm.

"Yes, sir."

"You received a telephone call at about the hour of 11:14?" asked Drumm.

"Yes, sir."

"Just describe that call, Sergeant."

"Mr. Edward Norton called, sir, and . . ."

Perry Mason started to his feet, but Claude Drumm was the one who interrupted the witness.

"Just a moment, Sergeant," he said. "Let me caution you that you are under oath, and are to testify only to the things which you know of your own knowledge. You didn't know that that call came from Edward Norton. You only know that someone called."

"He *said* he was Edward Norton," blurted the sergeant.

There was a ripple of laughter, which ran through the courtroom, and was promptly silenced by a banging of the judge's gavel.

"Just tell what was said to you over the telephone," said Drumm, and glanced sidelong at Perry Mason, waiting for the attorney to object.

But Perry Mason remained placidly indifferent.

Judge Markham said: "Is it claimed that this is part of the *res gestae*, counsellor?"

Drumm looked uncomfortable.

"There is no objection to it, in any event, Your Honor," said Perry Mason.

"Very well," said Judge Markham. "Proceed, Sergeant."

"This call came in, and I noticed the time of it," said Sergeant Mahoney. "It was fourteen minutes past eleven. The man said that he was Edward Norton, and that he wanted to report a stolen automobile, that a Buick sedan, belonging to him, No. 6754093, with a license number of 12M1834 had been stolen, and that he wanted the car picked up and the driver arrested, no matter who the driver might be. I believe that he stated that even if the driver should be related to him, he wanted him or her arrested."

"You may inquire, counsellor," said Claude Drumm, with the smiling gesture of one who had landed a telling blow.

"Did that call come in all at once?" asked Perry Mason, casually.

"How do you mean, sir?"

"I am just testing your recollection," said Perry Mason.

"Of course it came in all at once," said the sergeant.

Perry Mason reached in his brief case and took out a newspaper.

"You made a statement to the newspaper reporters when this matter was more fresh in your mind, Sergeant?"

"Well, I believe I said something to them the next morning, yes."

"And didn't you state at that time that the call was interrupted?"

"Just a moment," said the Deputy District Attorney. "That is not the proper way to lay a foundation for an impeaching question."

"I am just refreshing the recollection of the witness, if the Court please," said Perry Mason.

Sergeant Mahoney made frantic gestures.

Judge Markham smiled and said: "I think from the demeanor of the witness that his recollection has been refreshed. Proceed, Sergeant."

"That's right," said Sergeant Mahoney, "I remember now. The call came in, and he was cut off right in the middle of the conversation—right at the first part of it, I think it was. He gave his name and address and wanted to know if he was talking with the police department, and said he had a crime to report. Then the line went dead. I looked up his telephone number in the book, to call him back, when the call came in again, and he went right along talking. He said he'd been cut off."

"That," said Perry Mason, with emphasis, "is all."

Claude Drumm looked puzzled.

"What's that got to do with it?" he asked sharply.

Judge Markham banged his gavel on the desk.

"Order!" he snapped. "Is there any redirect examination, counsellor?"

"None," said Claude Drumm, but his eyes were thoughtful as he stared at Perry Mason.

"The next witness," said Judge Markham.

"Arthur Crinston," snapped Claude Drumm.

Arthur Crinston arose from a seat within the bar, walked to the clerk, was sworn, and took the witness stand.

"Your name is Arthur Crinston, and you are the surviving partner of the firm of Crinston & Norton, the said firm being composed of yourself and Edward Norton?"

"That is correct, sir."

"Edward Norton is dead?"

"He is, sir."

"Did you see the body of Edward Norton, Mr. Crinston?"

"Yes sir. On the twenty-third day of October of this year."

"At about what time?"

"I saw his body at approximately eleven thirty-five or eleven thirty-six."

"Where was his body?"

"Lying across his desk in the study, with the top of the head crushed in."

"What did you do then?"

"I notified the police."

"Did you see the defendant, Frances Celane, on that night?"

"I did."

"At about what time?"

"At approximately midnight or a little before."

"Did you tell her anything about the death of her uncle?"

"I did."

"Did you mention anything about the reported theft of a Buick automobile?"

"I did."

"Did she make any statement to you at that time as to the said Buick automobile?"

"That can be answered yes or no," said Judge Markham, in a cautioning tone of voice. "It is preliminary merely."

"Yes, she did," said Arthur Crinston.

"At what time was this?"

"At about midnight."

"Who was present?"

"Miss Celane, Mr. Don Graves, and myself."

"There was no one else present?"

"No sir."

"What did she say?"

"She said that she had taken the Buick automobile at about ten forty-five o'clock and gone for a ride, returning at approximately fifteen minutes past twelve, midnight."

"What was Mr. Norton doing the last time you saw him alive, Mr. Crinston?"

"Standing in the window of his study calling down to me."

"What did he say?"

"He asked me if Don Graves could accompany me to the city; that is, to my residence."

"And what did you tell him?"

"I told him that I would have to ask Judge Purley, in whose car I was riding."

"Then what happened?"

"I stepped across to ask Judge Purley, and received an affirmative answer from him to my request. Then I returned to notify Mr. Norton. He was standing in his study—a few feet back from the window at that time. I called up to him that it was all right, and Mr. Graves, who had anticipated Judge Purley's consent, was then coming down the steps from the front doorway to join me.''

''Then what happened?''

''Then I got in the front seat of the automobile with Judge Purley, Mr. Don Graves got in the rear seat, we started up the winding road shown on the map, until we came to a certain point, where we turned around and went back to the house. I take it that I cannot state any conversation that took place in the automobile?''

''That is the ruling of the court, Mr. Crinston.''

''Very well. I returned in the automobile, re-entered the house, and found Mr. Norton's body as described, whereupon I notified the police.''

''Cross-examine,'' snapped Claude Drumm unexpectedly, turning to Perry Mason.

Perry Mason surveyed Arthur Crinston with an expressionless face for a few seconds, then said abruptly: ''You had been in conversation with Mr. Norton during the evening?''

''Yes. I had an appointment and was a few minutes late for that appointment. I arrived there at six minutes past eleven, I think.''

''What,'' asked Perry Mason, ''did you talk with Mr. Norton about?''

Arthur Crinston made a swift grimace and shook his head at Perry Mason. The gesture seemed to be one of warning.

Claude Drumm, who had jumped to his feet to object, caught that gesture of warning, and suddenly smiled. He sat down.

Arthur Crinston looked at Judge Markham.

''Answer the question,'' said Perry Mason.

Arthur Crinston blurted: ''*You* don't want to have me answer that question.''

Judge Markham banged with his gavel on the desk.

''Is there any objection, Mr. Drumm?'' he asked.

The Deputy District Attorney shook his head smiling. ''None whatever,'' he said. ''Let the witness answer the question.''

"Answer the question," said Judge Markham.

Crinston fidgeted.

"Your Honor," he blurted, "it isn't to the advantage of the defendant, Frances Celane, that I should testify to what was said, and Perry Mason has reason to know that. I don't know what his idea is in asking any such question . . ."

The gavel of Judge Markham banged upon the desk.

"The witness," he said, in tones of icy frigidity, "will confine his comments to the answers of such questions as may be asked of him. The witness certainly should know that any such statement coming in court, particularly in a trial of this nature, is a contempt of court. The jury are admonished to disregard that statement, and are admonished to disregard any statements of the witnesses except those which are elicited as a part of the testimony. Mr. Crinston, you will answer that question or be held in contempt of court."

"We talked," said Crinston in a low voice, "about an attempt that had been made to blackmail Miss Celane."

A grin of triumph suffused Claude Drumm's face.

"An attempt at blackmail, made by the housekeeper, Mrs. Mayfield?" asked Perry Mason.

The grin faded from Claude Drumm's face. He jumped to his feet. "Your Honor," he said, "that is objected to as incompetent, irrelevant, and immaterial, leading and suggestive. Counsel well knows that Mrs. Mayfield is an important witness for the prosecution in this case, and this is an attempt to discredit her . . ."

"Leading questions are permitted upon cross-examination," said Judge Markham. "You did not object when Counsel asked the witness as to what the conversation consisted of, and since this is cross-examination, I am going to permit the question."

Claude Drumm slowly sat down.

Crinston squirmed uncomfortably in the chair.

"Mrs. Mayfield's name was not mentioned," he said at length, in a low voice.

"You're certain of that?" asked Perry Mason.

172

''Well,'' said Crinston, ''it *might* have been mentioned as a possibility.''

''Oh,'' said Perry Mason, ''so it was mentioned as a possibility? Is that right?''

''It might have been,'' said Crinston.

Perry Mason abruptly shifted his attack.

''Edward Norton had secured rather a large sum of money during the day of October twenty-third in one thousand dollar bills, had he not, Mr. Crinston?''

''So I understand,'' said Crinston, surlily.

''You didn't secure that money for him?''

''No, sir.''

''Did you go to any of the banks during that day in which the firm of Crinston & Norton had an account?''

Arthur Crinston scowled thoughtfully.

''Yes,'' he said, ''I did.''

''Which bank?''

''The Wheeler's Trust and Savings Bank.''

''Whom did you talk with there?''

Suddenly Crinston's face changed color.

''I would prefer,'' he said, ''not to answer that question.''

Claude Drumm jumped to his feet.

''The question is objected to,'' he said, ''as incompetent, irrelevant and immaterial, and not proper cross-examination.''

Perry Mason smiled, a slow, drawling smile.

''Your Honor,'' he drawled, ''if I may present a brief argument?''

''Very well,'' said Judge Markham.

''This witness has testified on direct examination that he was a surviving partner of Crinston & Norton. I let that question go in, although it probably calls for a conclusion of the witness. But I have the right to cross-examine him as to his activities as a co-partner, and the reasons upon which that conclusion was founded.''

''Not at a remote time,'' said Judge Markham.

''No, sir,'' said Perry Mason. ''That is why I am confining the question to the date of October twenty-third—the day of the death.''

Judge Markham stared at Perry Mason with eyes that were suddenly hard and wary.

Mason returned the gaze, his eyes wide with candor.

Claude Drumm was on his feet.

"The partnership affairs have nothing whatever to do with it," he said.

"But," said Judge Markham, "you, yourself, qualified him as a member of a partnership."

"But only for the purpose of showing the intimacy of his acquaintance, Your Honor."

Judge Markham shook his head.

"I am not convinced," he said, "that the question is proper cross-examination, but in a case of this nature I am going to err, if at all, on the side of the defendants. The witness will answer the question."

"Answer the question, Mr. Crinston," said Perry Mason. "Whom did you talk with?"

"With Mr. Sherman, the president."

"And what did you talk with him about?"

"About the partnership business."

"You talked with him about meeting the indebtedness of approximately nine hundred thousand dollars which the partnership had with that bank, did you not; an indebtedness which, as I understand the facts, was evidenced by notes which had been signed by you as an individual alone, isn't that right?"

"No sir, that is not right. Those notes were partnership notes, signed by Crinston & Norton."

"That is, signed by the partnership name of Crinston & Norton, per Arthur Crinston. Isn't that right?"

"I think that is right," said Arthur Crinston. "The main business of the partnership as far as banking activities were concerned, was transacted by me; that is, I signed the partnership name to notes, although in a majority of instances the checks were signed by both of us. No, I'll amend that statement. I guess that the Wheeler's Trust and Savings Bank notes were signed with the partnership name per myself, and that checks were drawn out in the same way."

"You went out to Mr. Norton's house to see him about the maturity of those notes, did you not?"

"That is correct."

"Then," said Perry Mason, "how did it happen that you talked about the blackmailing of Frances Celane by the housekeeper?"

"I didn't say it was by the housekeeper," snapped Arthur Crinston. "I said that her name was mentioned as a possibility."

"I see," said Perry Mason. "My mistake. Go ahead and answer the question."

"Because," said Crinston, "the business matter relating to those notes occupied but a few minutes of our discussion. The question of his niece's being blackmailed weighed very heavily on Mr. Norton's mind, and he insisted upon postponing all further business discussion in order to ask my advice about that."

"And why did he say she was being blackmailed?" asked Perry Mason.

"He thought that she was being blackmailed over something she had done."

"Naturally," said Perry Mason. "Did he mention *what* it was?"

"No, I don't think he did."

"Did he mention what it might have been?"

"He mentioned that she had an ungovernable temper," said Crinston suddenly, and then bit his lip and said: "Wait a minute, I'll withdraw that. I don't think he said that. That was my mistake."

"Your mistake," asked Mason, "or are you trying to protect the defendant, Frances Celane?"

Crinston's face purpled.

"I'm trying to protect her a lot better than you are!" he roared.

Judge Markham's gavel banged upon his desk.

"Mr. Crinston," he said, "the court cautioned you once before. The court now pronounces you in contempt of court, and assesses a fine of one hundred dollars for contempt of court."

Crinston, his face purple, bowed his head.

"Proceed with the case," said Judge Markham.

"Was anything else discussed by you and Mr. Norton, save the matter of indebtedness to the bank, the partnership affairs, and the possibility that his niece was being blackmailed?"

"No, sir," said Arthur Crinston, evidently with relief that the question was no more searching as to the possibilities of the blackmail.

Perry Mason smiled urbanely.

"I may desire to recall Mr. Crinston for further cross-examination later on, Your Honor," he said, "but I have no more questions at the present time."

Judge Markham nodded.

"Any redirect?" he asked.

"Not at this time," said Claude Drumm, "but if counsel reserves the right to recall the witness for further cross-examination, I would like to reserve the right to recall the witness for further redirect examination."

"Granted," snapped Judge Markham. "Proceed."

Claude Drumm raised his voice dramatically.

"Call Mr. Don Graves," he said.

Don Graves arose and pushed his way forward, while the spectators turned to exchange swiftly whispered comments. The murder trial was proceeding with a dispatch which was unusual, and the attorney for the defense seemed to be overlooking many opportunities in his cross-examination. Yet those who knew Perry Mason knew him as one whose trial technique was a by-word among attorneys.

And it was equally apparent that Judge Markham was mystified, as well as the spectators. From time to time, his eyes dwelt upon the placid face of Perry Mason with thoughtful speculation.

Don Graves cleared his throat and looked expectantly at Claude Drumm.

"Your name is Don Graves, and you were employed on the twenty-third of October of this year, and had been employed for some time prior thereto, as the confidential secretary of Mr. Edward Norton?"

176

"Yes, sir."

"You were with Mr. Norton on the evening of October twenty-third?"

"Yes, sir."

"When did you last see him on that evening?"

"At approximately eleven thirty in the evening."

"You had seen him before that?"

"Oh, yes. Mr. Crinston left about eleven twenty-seven or eleven twenty-eight, and Mr. Norton came out of his private office when Mr. Crinston left. They talked for a minute or two and Mr. Norton asked me to get some papers which Mr. Crinston had at his house."

"Then what happened?" asked Claude Drumm.

"Then Mr. Crinston went downstairs, and Mr. Norton told me to call Mr. Peter Devoe, the chauffeur, and get him to drive me to Crinston's residence. Then, just as I was starting for the stairs, he said: 'Wait a minute. I have another idea,' or words to that effect, and went to the window and called down to Mr. Crinston to ask if I could accompany him.

"Mr. Crinston said that he was with Judge Purley and would have to get Judge Purley's permission, and I, knowing that Judge Purley would give his permission and that time was valuable, ran down the stairs and was just coming out of the front door when Mr. Crinston called up that Judge Purley said he would be glad to accommodate me.

"I ran across and got in Judge Purley's automobile, getting in the rear seat, and then Judge Purley started the automobile and we drove up the winding road until we came to a spot, the approximate location of which Judge Purley has marked on the map."

"And then what happened?"

"At that point," said Don Graves dramatically, "I turned and looked back, and saw through the rear window of the automobile into the study window of Edward Norton."

"And what did you see?" purred Claude Drumm.

"I saw a figure raise a club and strike Mr. Norton on the head."

"Could you recognize who that person was?"

"I thought I could," he said.

"Who did you think it was?" asked Drumm.

"Just a minute," said Perry Mason, "that is objected to as calling for a conclusion of the witness, and as leading and suggestive. The witness has stated that he *thought* he could make the identification."

Judge Markham looked at Perry Mason as though expecting to hear an extended argument upon this crucial point. There was no argument.

He looked at Claude Drumm.

Claude Drumm shrugged his shoulders.

"He has stated that in his opinion he could make an identification," he said. "The word 'thought' is merely a colloquial expression."

"You'd better clear the matter up," said Judge Markham.

"Very well," said Claude Drumm.

"Mr. Graves," he said, "you say that you thought you could identify the witness. Just what do you mean by that?"

"I believe," said Don Graves, "that I know who that man was. I think that I recognized him. I did not see his face clearly, but I think that I could recognize him by the manner in which he held his head, from his shoulders and the general outline of his body."

"That is sufficient, if the court please," said Claude Drumm. "A man doesn't need to see the facial characteristics of another in order to make an identification. The objection goes to the weight, rather than the admissibility of the evidence."

Judge Markham looked expectantly at Perry Mason.

Perry Mason said nothing.

"I will overrule the objection," said Judge Markham. "Answer the question, young man."

"That man was Robert Gleason," said Don Graves in a low voice.

"Was there anyone else in the room?" asked Claude Drumm.

"Yes, sir."

"Who was that other person?"

"A woman, sir, who was attired in a pink garment of some sort."

"Could you see that woman?"

"I saw part of her shoulder, just a bit of her hair, and her arm."

"Could you recognize that woman from what you saw of her?"

Judge Markham interrupted.

"I think, counsellor," he said, "that while I permitted the first identification upon the ground that the objection went to the weight rather than the admissibility of the evidence, that where a witness can see only a relatively small portion of a woman's figure at the distance which was shown upon this map, the objection really should go to the weight as well as the admissibility of the evidence, and I will sustain the objection as to the identity of the woman."

"Your Honor," said Perry Mason softly, "there was no objection made as to the identity of the woman."

"No objection?" said Judge Markham.

"None, Your Honor," said Perry Mason.

"Very well," said Judge Markham, "I shall sustain an objection if one is made."

"There will be none made," said Perry Mason.

A rustle sounded throughout the courtroom.

"Very well," snapped Judge Markham, his face purpling, "answer the question."

"Yes, sir," said Don Graves. "I think that that woman was Frances Celane. I am not as certain in her case as I was in the case of the man, but I think it was Frances Celane. She was dressed like Frances Celane, and the color of her hair, and the contour of her shoulder made me think it was Frances Celane."

"How long have you known Frances Celane?" asked Claude Drumm.

"For more than three years."

"You have lived in the same house with her?"

"Yes, sir."

"Did she, at that time, to your knowledge, have a dress or some garment of the color which you saw upon the woman who was standing in that room?"

"Yes, sir."

"Very well," said Claude Drumm. "What did you do, if anything?"

"I told the other gentlemen what I had seen, and asked them to turn the car around."

"I will strike that out on my own motion," said Judge Markham. "It is incompetent, irrelevant, and immaterial. The question is what the witness did next, with reference to what had taken place in this room. Conversations between parties outside of the presence of the defendant which are not part of the *res gestae* will not be permitted."

"Very well," said Claude Drumm. "Then what happened? What did you do with reference to Mr. Edward Norton?"

"I returned to the house, climbed the stairs to his study, and found his body slumped across the desk, with the top of his head beaten in," said Don Graves.

"Cross-examine," snapped Claude Drumm.

Perry Mason got to his feet and stared slowly and fixedly at Don Graves. An electric tension ran around the courtroom. The spectators sensed that this was to be the crucial part of the trial.

"Your eyes are in good condition?" asked Perry Mason.

"Yes."

"You think that you were able to sit in a speeding automobile at this point on the road, and, in the momentary glance which you had through the rear of the automobile, recognize the occupants of the room in that study?"

"Yes, sir. I know I could."

"How do you know it?"

"Because I saw them at that time, and because in order to test my own ability, I have made subsequent tests."

"The last part of that answer may go out," snapped Judge Markham.

"There was no motion to strike it out," said Perry Mason. "If the court please, I would like to follow that point up."

"Very well," said Judge Markham.

"You say you have made subsequent tests?"

"Yes, sir."

"In an automobile?"

"Yes, sir."

"With occupants in the room?"

"Yes, sir."

"Who were the occupants in the room?"

"Mr. Drumm, the Deputy District Attorney, and two people from his office."

"You were able to recognize those people?"

"Yes, sir. You see, sir, the windows are very wide, and the lighting in that study or office is very good."

"The automobile in which those tests were made wasn't driven very rapidly, was it?" asked Perry Mason.

"Just about the same rate as the automobile in which I was riding on the night of the murder."

"That was Judge Purley's automobile?"

"Yes, sir."

"But you haven't made a test in Judge Purley's automobile, have you?"

"No, sir, in other automobiles."

"Then the tests weren't made under the same conditions; that is, the machine wasn't the same, the window in the rear wasn't the same."

"They were similar," said Don Graves.

Perry Mason stared accusingly at the witness.

"But the tests weren't made under *exactly* the same conditions."

"No, sir."

"Would you," thundered Perry Mason, "*dare* to make a test under the *same* conditions?"

"Objected to as argumentative," snapped Claude Drumm.

"I think," said Judge Markham, "that it may be argumentative, but it has a tendency to show the interest or bias of the witness. The question was, whether or not he would be *willing* to make a test under certain conditions."

"But such a test wouldn't prove anything more than has already been proven," said Drumm.

"The question," said Judge Markham, "is, whether or not he would be willing to make such a test. I think I will permit the witness to answer."

"Answer the question," said Perry Mason.

"Yes, I would be willing to make such a test."

"If Judge Purley will furnish his automobile, *will* you make a test while you are riding in such automobile?"

Claude Drumm was on his feet.

"The question is now different, Your Honor. It is not a question now of whether he is willing to make such a test, but if he *will* make such a test."

"Yes," said Judge Markham, "if you desire to object to that question, I think that I shall sustain an objection to it."

Perry Mason turned to face the jury.

"In that event," he said, "there is no further cross-examination."

"No further cross-examination?" asked Claude Drumm.

"No. The fact speaks for itself," snapped Perry Mason. "You are afraid to have a test made under identical conditions."

The gavel of Judge Markham banged sharply on the desk.

"Counsellor," he said, "you will please refrain from personalities and address your remarks to the court, rather than to opposing counsel."

"Your pardon, Your Honor," said Perry Mason, but his voice held no trace of humility, and his eyes twinkled with amusement.

Claude Drumm stared at Perry Mason, and his forehead creased in thought.

"Your Honor," he said, "might I ask at this time for an adjournment until to-morrow morning at ten o'clock? I have been rather surprised at the unexpected progress which this case has made."

"You are no more surprised than the court," said Judge Markham. "Agreeably surprised, I may say. It is customary for murder cases to be drawn out to such prolonged length that it comes as rather a startling innovation to have a case move with such rapidity as this. Your request is granted, Counsellor, and court will adjourn until ten o'clock to-morrow morning, during which time the jury will remember the usual admonition of the court against discussing the case or allowing it to be discussed in their presence."

The gavel banged.

Perry Mason swung about in his chair and turned to face the dark eyes of Frances Celane.

He smiled at her reassuringly.

Rob Gleason, sitting at her side, was haggard and drawn, showing the effects of the ordeal; his posture tense and strained, his eyes filled with a lurking fear.

The girl was calm and collected, her eyes gave no hint of her feelings. Her chin was up, and her head back.

Perry Mason leaned toward her.

"Have confidence in me, please," he said.

Only when she smiled at him was there evident the changes which had taken place in her during the ordeal preliminary to the trial. There was a touch of sadness in the smile; a hint of patience that had not been in her face before. She said nothing, but her smile spoke volumes.

Rob Gleason whispered: "A word with you, sir? And in private, please."

A deputy sheriff moved forward, touched Frances Celane on the shoulder. Perry Mason said to him: "Just a moment, please," and led Rob Gleason to one side.

Gleason spoke in hoarse whispers.

"Looks pretty black, doesn't it?"

Perry Mason shrugged his shoulders.

"If," whispered Gleason, "it's going against us, I want to take it all."

"Meaning?" asked the lawyer.

"Meaning," husked Gleason, "that I want to confess and take the sole blame. I want to free Fran of any responsibility."

Steadily, purposefully, remorselessly, Mason's eyes studied Gleason's features.

"It hasn't come to that yet, Gleason," he said. "And it won't. Keep your mouth shut."

He turned and signaled the waiting deputy that the conference was over.

Chapter 22

Perry Mason sat at his desk in the office, looking across at Harry Nevers.

Nevers, with his hair trimmed, his face clean-shaven, wearing a newly pressed suit, twisted his legs up over the arm of the leather chair, and let his eyes study Perry Mason in bored appraisal.

"Sure I'll do you a favor," he said, "if it's anything I can do. The office is friendly toward you. You gave us a nice break on Frances Celane's surrender."

"All right," said Perry Mason, his eyes hard and watchful. "I want you to bear down heavy on the fact that the District Attorney has conducted secret tests to determine whether Don Graves could be telling the truth."

Nevers nodded and yawned.

"I suppose you mean that you want to have an intimation between the lines, that the D.A. wouldn't have had those tests made unless he'd had a little doubt in his own mind about the testimony."

Perry Mason nodded.

"Well," said Harry Nevers, in that expressionless monotone which was so characteristic of him, "that's already been done. I gave you that much of a break in advance."

"All right," said Mason. "Now here's something else. I want you to emphasize the events that happened just before court adjourned; the fact that the District Attorney refused to make a test under identical circumstances."

Nevers inclined his head in a gesture of assent.

"All right," he said, "what's back of it?"

"Back of what?" asked the attorney.

"Back of this test business."

"You can see for yourself," said Mason. "The District

Attorney conducted tests. That shows he had some doubt of the ability of the witness to see the occupants of that room, as he claims he did. Furthermore, he has now refused to conduct a test, or permit a test to be conducted under exactly identical circumstances.''

"Baloney," said the reporter. "That's a good line to hand to the jury, but I'm asking you for the lowdown."

"There isn't any lowdown," Mason told him.

"The hell there ain't," said Nevers. "Don't think I'm going to pull chestnuts out of the fire for you. You've given me a break in this case, and I'm willing to give you a break. But don't think I'm going to run around playing cat's paw for you, and get my fingers burnt unless I know whether the chestnut is worthwhile reaching for."

Mason shook his head.

"You've got me wrong, Harry," he said. "I simply want to have a test arranged under exactly identical circumstances."

"Well," said Nevers, "we'll talk that over for a while. What do you mean by exactly identical circumstances?"

"Well," said Perry Mason, "here's the way I want the test arranged. I want it so that I'm riding in the front seat of the automobile with Judge Purley. I'll be in the position that Arthur Crinston occupied. I'm perfectly willing to allow Drumm, the Deputy District Attorney, to sit in the back seat with Don Graves."

Harry Nevers stared at him with eyes that showed a glint of surprise.

"Have you gone crazy?" he asked.

"No," said Perry Mason shortly.

"Why you poor damned innocent babe in the woods!" said Nevers. "Don't let Claude Drumm fool you with any of that bushwa about being fair. He's one of the crookedest campaigners in the game. He's the one that ditched the notes that contained the first statement Don Graves made to the police—the one in which he said he recognized Devoe as the murderer, and didn't say anything about there being some other person in the room."

186

"That's all right," said Mason. "What if he did?"

"Why, simply this: He'll have things arranged so that Don Graves could be blindfolded and still make a one hundred percent identification. If you let him sit within nudging distance of Don Graves or where he can whisper or signal to him, you're just a plain fool."

Perry Mason shook his head and smiled.

"All right, then," said Nevers, "tell me what's up or you don't get a bit of coöperation out of us."

"There are times," said Perry Mason, "when a person has to use a little strategy—for instance when one is stalking a flock of geese it's always advisable to get behind a horse to walk up on the geese."

"What does that mean?" Nevers inquired.

"It means that geese are wild things, and they take flight whenever they see something they can't understand, or something that looks like a hunter," said Perry Mason. "But they're accustomed to the sight of a horse and when they see a horse walking around them, they don't pay any attention to it."

"So you're walking behind a horse?" asked Harry Nevers.

Perry Mason nodded his head.

Nevers slid his feet off the arm of the chair, stood up, and looked steadily at Perry Mason.

"Look here," he said, "you've got a reputation among lawyers of being a fast worker, and a two-fisted campaigner. You've got the reputation of jockeying a case around so that you get in a position to give one knock-out punch and then concentrate on that one punch. You don't go around wasting your energy in a lot of little taps that don't mean anything. Now I want to know what the knock-out punch is in this case."

"I'm not certain yet," Perry Mason told him. "There may not be any."

"The hell there ain't," said Nevers. "Look at the way you've tried this case. You have sat back and let the prosecution put in every damned bit of evidence they wanted. You

187

haven't cross-examined the witnesses so as to bring out anything that's to the advantage of either of the defendants.''

"What do you mean by that?'' inquired Perry Mason in low, ominous tones.

"Keep your shirt on,'' Nevers drawled tonelessly. "You aren't fooling me any with that stuff. You know as well as I do that Don Graves made a statement to the police the night of the murder, in which he either said, or at least intimated, that the person who struck the blow was Devoe, the chauffeur. He said there wasn't a woman in the room at the time the blow was struck, or at least he failed to say he saw a woman in the room. You've gone ahead and let him testify in this case, and haven't brought that out, or even intimated that he ever made a contradictory statement.''

"It wouldn't do any good if I did,'' Perry Mason said. "The notes of that statement have been destroyed, and Graves would swear, either that he never made such a statement, or that Frances Celane asked him to give her a break, and he tried to leave her out of it.''

"Baloney,'' said Nevers.

Perry Mason slid open a drawer in his desk and took out a flask of whiskey.

"I'll tell you this much, Harry,'' he said. "If you'll play ball with me, you won't be sorry.''

"Meaning by that?'' asked Nevers.

"Meaning by that you can stick around on this test that's made and save a big slice of the front page for a blow-off.''

Harry Nevers pushed back the glass which Mason had handed him with the bottle, and tilted the bottle to his lips. He took half a dozen swallows, then handed the bottle back to the attorney.

"When's this blow-off going to come?'' he asked. "Right after the test?''

"I don't think so,'' said Perry Mason. "I think I'll have to do a little manipulation.''

The reporter spoke as though he might have been thinking out loud.

"We can force the D.A. into making that test,'' he said.

"It's a test that is bound to come out all right. But you've got something up your sleeve. You're trying this murder case with no more apparent fight about you than as though you were covering a coroner's inquest. You're going through it with a hop, skip and jump, and letting the prosecution get in all the damaging evidence they want. Everybody in town is talking about what a poor defense you're putting up."

"Yes?" asked Mason, raising his eyebrows.

"Oh forget it!" said Nevers, with a trace of feeling in his voice. "You know damned well they are. A kid out of law school would have tried this case better than you're trying it. Everybody is commenting on it. The town is divided into two camps—those that think you're shrewd as the devil, and have something up your sleeve, and those that think you've just been lucky on your other cases, and haven't got anything on the ball. Naturally, it's an important case. A woman who's got as many millions as Frances Celane at stake; a secret marriage; a sex angle, and all that sort of stuff makes front page news. It's the opportunity of your life to drag this case along, fighting every inch of the way, keeping your name on the front page of the newspaper for two or three weeks. In place of that you're acting like a dub. For a murder case, this thing is streaking through the court like a greased pig going between a farmer's legs."

Perry Mason corked the whiskey bottle, and slid it back in the drawer of his desk.

Nevers looked at him searchingly.

"Going to say anything?" he asked.

"No," said Perry Mason.

Nevers grinned and wiped the back of his hand across his lips.

"Okay," said Nevers. "I've done my duty. I'll tell the city editor I tried my damnedest to get something out of you. Maybe I'll fake some piece of inside information that the readers can pick out between the lines."

Perry Mason took the reporter's arm and escorted him to the door of the outer office.

"Listen, Harry," he said, "if you fake anything, be sure you fake it right."

Perry Mason paused in the doorway, suddenly turned and faced the reporter.

"All right," he said, "I'll give you a bit of inside information. Rob Gleason is intending to make a complete confession and take the blame for the crime, exonerating Frances Celane."

Nevers stared at him.

"You can't give me that for publication," he said.

"Why not?" asked Perry Mason.

"It would be violating every professional confidence."

"That's all right," said Mason easily, "you're not using my name, that's all. Simply put it down as coming from a source that is close to the inside."

"My God!" said Nevers. "That would be the worst kind of libel if we couldn't back it up!"

"You can back it up," said Mason. "If anybody calls you on it, you can disclose the source of your information."

"Meaning that it came from you?"

"Meaning that it came from me," Mason told him.

Nevers took a deep breath.

"Listen, Perry," he said, "I've seen 'em come, and I've seen 'em go. I've been in on all kinds of cases, interviewed all kinds of people. I've seen those that were foxy, and those that just thought they were foxy. I've seen those that were dumb, and didn't know it, and those that were dumb, and thought they were smart, but you've got the whole world cheated. This is the damnedest interview with a lawyer I ever had!"

Mason placed his right hand between the reporter's shoulder blades and gently pushed him into the outer office.

"All right," he said, "I've given you a break. Give me one."

Frank Everly was standing in the outer office, his manner filled with impatience.

"Did you want to see me?" asked Perry Mason.

Everly nodded.

"Come in," Mason told him.

Everly walked into the inner office. Perry Mason stood in

190

the door until Harry Nevers had gone out through the outer door, then Mason closed the door of the inner office, and turned to face Everly.

Everly coughed and averted his eyes.

"Didn't the case move rather expeditiously, Mr. Mason?" he asked.

Mason smiled at him with patient, tired eyes.

"In other words," he said, "you've been hearing some comments that I've stubbed my toe on the defense, and the prosecution is walking all over me, is that it?"

Everly turned red and said in a choked voice: "I didn't say anything like that, Mr. Mason."

"Did you ever hear the story," asked Perry Mason, in a kindly tone of voice, "of the man who brought suit against his neighbor, claiming to have been bitten by the neighbor's dog? The neighbor filed an answer in which he denied that his dog was vicious, denied that the dog had bitten the man, and denied that he ever had a dog."

"Yes," said Frank Everly, "I've heard that yarn. It's a classic around law school."

"All right," said Perry Mason. "The defense in that case became humorous because it took in too much territory. Now, when you've got a doubtful case, it's all right to try and have two strings to your bow. But remember that when you have two strings on a bow, while increasing the factor of safety, you lose the efficiency of the weapon. A bow that has two strings won't break a string, but it won't shoot an arrow one quarter of the distance that it would if it only had one string to it."

"You mean you're sacrificing everything in this case to concentrate on some one point?" asked the law clerk.

"Yes," said Perry Mason, "the innocence of Frances Celane and Rob Gleason is virtually shown by the evidence as it exists at the present time. The guilt of the defendants simply cannot be proved beyond a reasonable doubt. But I want to do more than raise a reasonable doubt in the minds of the jurors. I want to make a complete solution of the case."

Frank Everly stared at Perry Mason with wide, incredulous eyes.

"My heavens!" he said. "I thought that everything that went in to-day clinched the guilt of Frances Celane and Rob Gleason. I thought that unless we could break down the stories of some of those witnesses, we could just as well figure on a verdict of first degree murder."

Mason shook his head wearily.

"No," he said, "the big point I wanted in the case has already gone in. What I'm trying to do now is to crash that point home to the jury in such a dramatic manner they'll never forget it. And remember this—I've got Claude Drumm so badly rattled the way that case is going that he's on the verge of panic right now. He figures I must have an ace up my sleeve somewhere, or I wouldn't be giving him all the breaks."

"The jury," suggested Frank Everly, "looked rather unsympathetic."

"Of course they looked unsympathetic," said Perry Mason. "And they'll probably look more unsympathetic. You notice what Claude Drumm is doing. He's putting in the *corpus delicti* with just a smattering of testimony. Just before he gets ready to rest his case, he'll start introducing photographs of the dead body slumped over the desk, of the bloody blotter, of the insurance policy, spattered with the life blood of the dead man, and all of that stuff. Then, he'll throw the case into our laps, and leave us to face a jury that's hardened its heart to bring in a death penalty verdict."

"What I don't see," said Everly, "is how you're going to stop him."

"I'm not going to try to stop him," smiled Perry Mason, "I'm going to head him off."

Della Street walked into the room.

"Mr. Drake is out there," she said, "and says it's important."

Perry Mason smiled at her.

"He'll have to wait just a minute," he said, "I'm explaining something to Frank Everly."

Della Street looked at Perry Mason with eyes that were warm with tenderness.

"I can remember," she said softly, "when I made you explain something to me. After that, I've had enough faith in you so I don't need any explanations."

Perry Mason watched her with speculative eyes.

"You've read the papers?" he asked.

"The afternoon papers, yes."

"And you know how the trial is going?"

"Yes."

"You gathered that I was putting up a pretty weak defense?"

She stiffened slightly, and looked accusingly at Frank Everly.

"Who said that?" she asked.

"It's intimated in the newspapers," said Perry Mason.

"Well," said Della Street, "I just made a bet of half of my month's salary, with Paul Drake, that you were going to get both defendants acquitted. That shows how much faith I've got in you."

"Then," said Perry Mason, "Drake must have some bad news. You two get out of here and let me talk with him. You know he's doing some work for me on this case. He's probably got some inside information. It wasn't very sporting of him to bet on his inside information."

"That's all right," Della Street said. "He was square about it. He told me he had some inside information."

"Did he tell you what it was?"

"No, he just said he had it, and I told him I had some too."

"What did you have?" asked Perry Mason, staring speculatively at her.

"Faith in you," she said.

Mason waved his hand.

"All right," he said, "you folks get out and let me talk with Drake. We'll see what he's got to say."

Drake came into the inner office, sat down, grinned, and rolled a cigarette.

"Well," he said, "I've got the lowdown for you."

"All right," Perry Mason said, "what is it?"

"The rough shadow did it," said Drake.

"Never mind the methods," said Mason. "I want the facts."

"Well," said Drake, "the story goes like this. This Mrs. Mayfield is a hard-boiled baby."

"I knew she was," said Mason. "She tried to hold me up a couple of times."

"Yes, I got all the lowdown on that, too," said Drake. "The only trouble is, Perry, that it looks like hell for your clients."

"How do you mean?"

"Well, in the first place, Mrs. Mayfield doesn't know quite as much as she tried to pretend she did. She made the mistake of going to bed at the wrong time. She went to bed just about fifteen or twenty minutes before the murder was committed. But she'd spent the evening snooping around.

"It all starts in with the fact that she found out Gleason and Frances Celane were married. She started in trying to capitalize on that knowledge. She took quite a bit of money from Frances Celane; I don't know how much, around ten thousand dollars, I think. And then, in some way, Edward Norton got wise that Frances Celane was paying blackmail. He got her in and tried to make her tell him whom she was paying money to and why. Naturally, she didn't dare to let him know. But Norton was a pretty obstinate individual, and, in order to find out, he shut off the girl's allowance. That put her in the position of having no money with which to pay any blackmail.

"On the other hand, Mrs. Mayfield said that she could capitalize on the information elsewhere, and if Frances Celane wouldn't give her money, she was going to sell the information to some of the charitable institutions who would benefit by the knowledge.

"Of course, this was all bluff, but Frances Celane didn't know it. The whole situation came to a head on the night of the murder. Frances Celane had a stormy interview with Norton, and they quarreled bitterly. Norton said that before he went to bed that night he was going to execute a written

194

document terminating the trust and giving to Frances Celane the annuity provided by the terms of the trust, and letting the balance go to charity.

"Whether that was a bluff on his part or not I don't know. Anyhow, that's what he said. Then Mrs. Mayfield went to bed. Next morning Frances Celane had money, lots of it. She gave Mrs. Mayfield twenty-eight thousand dollars to keep quiet. Mrs. Mayfield promised she would.

"Rob Gleason was there in the house that night, and participated in at least a part of the interview with Norton. Norton was furious, and accused the girl of all sorts of things. She got mad and used language that must have raised a blister on his ears.

"Afterwards, Gleason went down to the girl's room. That was after Crinston came, and before the murder. Along about that time Mrs. Mayfield went to bed. She doesn't know exactly what happened, except that she's certain Frances Celane didn't go out in the Buick automobile. Therefore, she knows that the alibi Frances Celane was trying to make was false.

"She went to you and tried to shake you down for money to keep Frances Celane out of it. You turned her down hard, so she started concentrating on the girl, and actually collected from her. Then she found out that the money she'd taken from Frances Celane was in thousand dollar bills that were numbered consecutively, and knew that these bills would be traced in the event that she tried to change them for smaller bills. So she has these bills hidden, and has tried to create the impression that Frances Celane gave you twenty-eight thousand dollars to apply on a fee. She has told the District Attorney's office that that is what happened, and the District Attorney's office has been trying to locate the twenty-eight thousand dollars. They've made examinations at your banks, and have even gone so far as to search the office. They have now come to the conclusion that you must be carrying the twenty-eight thousand dollars on your person.

"The District Attorney is intending to use her as a surprise witness. She's going to testify as to the falsity of the girl's claim that she was out in the Buick automobile, and also to the quarrel that took place.

"It's the theory of the prosecution that a bitter quarrel was interrupted by Arthur Crinston; that the two people hatched out this murder plot and waited until Crinston had left to carry it into execution; that, as soon as Crinston drove away, they dashed up to the office and killed Mr. Norton, then planted the evidence in Pete Devoe's room in order to make it appear Devoe was the guilty party, in the event the officers didn't fall for the jimmied window and the footprints in the soft soil."

"How about Graves?" asked Perry Mason. "Have you done anything with him?"

"I've done lots with him. That girl has turned him inside out. He's going to be a bad man for you to handle, but he tells the girl that he's trying to protect Frances Celane, or that he *was* trying to protect her until the District Attorney brought pressure to bear on him."

"Look here," Mason said, "my theory of this case is that Norton *gave* Fran Celane that money before Crinston called. Now, Graves must have some information that'll support that theory."

"That," said Drake, "is the worst part of his testimony. He says he could hear every word of the conversation; that Norton took out his wallet and showed the girl forty thousand dollars, telling her he had originally gotten the money to give her, but that he wasn't going to give her anything except a small amount for current expenses. Then he took out two one thousand dollar bills and handed them to her.

"Don Graves has the idea the girl took the one thousand dollar bills, and that she and Gleason planted *those* one thousand dollar bills in the pocket of Devoe, the chauffeur, while Crinston was talking with Norton; that the girl and Gleason came back afterwards and killed Norton, taking the balance of the money from his wallet to use for the purpose of bribing the housekeeper to silence and paying you a sufficient cash retainer so you would interest yourself in the case. That's the theory Graves has.

196

"The District Attorney had things planned so that most of this would come out on cross-examination. He was going to slap you in the face with it. The fact that you've restricted your cross-examination so much has got Drumm worried. He's going to try and bring out all of this stuff on redirect examination now, asking permission to recall the witnesses."

Perry Mason stretched his long arms, stared at the detective, and laughed.

"Paul," he said, "there are times when caution is a vice."

"What do you mean by that?" Paul Drake asked.

"I mean," said Perry Mason, "that at times it is wise to stake everything on one dramatic blow, one crashing knockout punch. I've only got one string to my bow in this case. If it breaks, I'm finished. But if it doesn't break, I'm going to shoot an arrow right through the bull's-eye of the whole case."

Drake said: "Well, Perry, if you can figure this thing out, you can do a lot more than I can. The more I see of it, the more mixed up and confused it looks."

Perry Mason started pacing the floor back and forth.

"The thing that I'm afraid of," he said, "is that I'm not keeping my real objective sufficiently concealed."

"How do you mean?" the detective inquired.

"I'm stalking a bunch of geese behind a horse," said Perry Mason, "and I'm afraid the horse may not be big enough to give me the concealment I want."

Paul Drake started for the door.

"Listen," he said, as he paused, with a hand on the knob of the door, "don't worry about that. I've seen a lot of murder cases in my time, and I've talked with a lot of lawyers who thought they had a point when they didn't have. If you think you're going to be able to save either one of your clients in this case, you've got more optimism than I have. I just bet half of Della Street's salary for this month, that your clients were going to be convicted, and, after talking with you, I'm going out and try and get a bet for the other half. That shows how much confidence I've got."

As he closed the door, Perry Mason was standing in the

center of the office, with his feet spread wide apart, his jaw thrust forward, heavy shoulders squared, staring in steady concentration at the closing door.

Chapter 23

Headlines streamed across the front page of the *STAR*.

   "WITNESS TO MILLIONAIRE'S MURDER RE-
FUSES TO MAKE TEST."

Perry Mason, with the paper propped up in front of him
on the table, cracked his three-minute eggs and smiled with
satisfaction. Down below the large headlines were smaller
headlines:

   "DISPUTE OVER VISION OF STATE'S STAR WIT-
NESS. DEFENSE CHALLENGES TO MAKE TEST
AND PROSECUTION REFUSES."

Perry Mason salted and peppered his eggs, dropped in a
square of butter, reached for a slice of crisp toast, and chuckled.

He read the verbatim account of the trial, noticed that the
challenge which he had hurled at the prosecution was printed
in black-faced type, finished his breakfast, folded the newspaper, and went to his office.

"Any news?" he asked Della Street.

She regarded him with a wistful, half-maternal smile on
her lips.

"You've got it in your pocket," she said.

He grinned at her.

"If the District Attorney refuses to accept the challenge
now, I've got the case won in front of the jury," he said.

"What will you do if he *accepts* the challenge?" she
wanted to know.

Perry Mason walked to the window and stared thoughtfully out at the morning sunshine.

"Now that," he remarked, "calls for another question. Did you double your bet with Paul Drake?"

"Yes."

"Good girl!" he said.

"You think the D. A.'ll consent to the test?" she asked.

"Yes."

"How are you going to determine that it's a fair test?"

"I can't," he told her, "but there's no harm in trying."

"Well," she told him, "you've got some good advertisement in this case, anyway. Every morning newspaper is speculating what it is you've got up your sleeve. You're referred to a dozen times as 'The Old Fox of the Courtroom,' and most of the reporters state that the chief trial deputy was plainly worried at the manner in which the case was expedited."

"You mean," he told her, "the newspapers figure I couldn't possibly be as dumb as I seem."

She laughed. "I'm betting on you," she said.

"The D. A.'s got a couple of surprise witnesses," Perry Mason said.

"Surprise to whom?" she inquired.

"That's the question," grinned Perry Mason, and walked to his inside office.

He had no sooner closed the door than the telephone rang.

"This is Drumm on the line now," said the voice of Della Street.

"Hello," said Perry Mason.

"Good morning, counsellor. This is Drumm speaking. I have been thinking over your demand for a test of the vision of Don Graves, and have decided to consent to making a test under exactly identical circumstances. I shall ask the court for an adjournment over the week end to enable the test to be completed and thought I would let you know."

"Nice of you," said Mason.

"Not at all," snapped Drumm.

Mason chuckled.

"I meant letting me know," he said.

"Oh," said Drumm.

"Have you any plans worked out for making the test?"

"I will announce that in court," said Drumm. "Goodby."

Perry Mason was still chuckling as he slipped the receiver back on its hook.

Perry Mason pressed the button which called Frank Everly to his office.

"Everly," he said, "there's going to be a continuance granted in that trial this morning, so that arrangements can be completed for a test which is to be made. I'm not going up to court, but am going to send you up, to be there and arrange for the continuance. There will be nothing except the formality of getting the case continued over the week end. Drumm will undoubtedly have some scheme worked out under which he'll want the test made and he'll try to rush you into a consent to that scheme, while you are there in court in front of the jury.

"Simply tell him that you were sent up to represent me for the purpose of consenting to the continuance, and that you have no authority to conclude the terms under which the test is to be made. That will necessitate his getting in touch with me when we are *not* in front of a jury."

Frank Everly nodded his approval, and there was a look of admiration in his eyes.

"You forced him into it, eh?"

"I don't know. He's consenting to the test. That's all I want. I don't care *why* he's doing it."

"And by this means,' said Everly, "you keep from having to quibble over the details in front of the jury?"

"Exactly," smiled Perry Mason. "Tell him that I'll be in my office this afternoon to arrange the details of the test with him, or that I'll meet him at any mutually satisfactory place. Be sure when you make the statement that you do it with an air of the utmost candor and frankness. The jury will be watching you closely and there's been a little too much talk in the newspapers about my being an old fox."

"Okay, Chief," said Everly, and swung out of the office, his face flushed with enthusiasm.

Perry Mason got Harry Nevers on the telephone.

"Just wanted to let you know," said Mason, "that the Deputy District Attorney just called up and told me he was going to consent to a continuance over the week end this morning, so that a test could be made."

The voice of Harry Nevers sounded in a husky, bored monotone over the telephone.

"I can go you one better on that," he said. "I was just going to call you and give you a tip. The D. A.'s office has a scheme framed up for that test. They're going to put it up to you in front of the jury. You won't like it, but you won't dare to argue with it in front of the jury."

"All right," Perry Mason said, "I can raise you one on that. I'm not even going to be in court. I've sent my assistant up to consent to a continuance. He hasn't any authority to stipulate in regard to the conditions of the test."

Harry Nevers laughed. "That sounds a little more like it," he said. "Will the court order the test?"

"No," Mason said. "I don't think the court will want to have anything to do with it. It's something that will have to be handled by stipulation. We'll make the test and then let the witnesses testify Monday morning."

"When are you going to figure on the details of the test?" asked the reporter.

"Probably right after the court adjourns," Mason told him. "Drumm will get in touch with me. I thought I'd give you a ring and let you know that I can't control the publicity that comes out of the D. A.'s office, but as far as I'm concerned you're going to have an exclusive on the details just as soon as I reach an agreement with the District Attorney's office."

Harry Nevers gave a dry chuckle.

"I guess," he said, "it's a good thing that I had the photographer get a couple of pictures of you when he was over in the office. Something seems to tell me we will be running them about Tuesday morning, or in the evening editions Monday night."

"There's one other thing I want you to do for me," Mason said.

"Gee, you're full of those suggestions," the reporter told him.

"That's all right. This is a simple thing."

"All right, shoot."

"When that test is arranged, I'm going to have things fixed so that Drumm and I will be downstairs in the automobile, and Graves will be upstairs. We'll summon him by some kind of a signal. When we give that signal, I want you to detain Graves up there in that room."

"For how long?" asked Nevers.

"As long as you can."

"What's the idea of that?"

"I want to get him rattled."

"You can't rattle that bird. He's a foxy guy, if I ever saw one."

"He may think he's foxy, but he can be rattled just the same. I want you to put up some proposition to him that will hold him behind until he has to appeal to the District Attorney."

"Now," said the reporter, "you're asking something that's making me suspicious."

"It doesn't need to," Mason told him. "If you'll do that, I'll give you a break afterwards so that you can claim you participated in the final result."

"Maybe I don't want to participate in the final result," said Nevers. "Those final results sometimes ain't so hot."

"You won't have to unless you want to," Mason pointed out. "I'll take *all* the responsibility. You can share in the credit."

"I think," Nevers told him, "I'd better come over and talk this thing over with you a little bit."

Mason chuckled.

"I knew you wouldn't forget it," he said.

"Forget what?" asked the reporter suspiciously.

"That bottle of whiskey in my desk," said the attorney, and slipped the receiver back on the hook.

Chapter 24

The Norton mansion blazed with light, every window in the place was illuminated. More than a dozen automobiles were parked along the curb, or crowded into the driveway. Men came and went through the open door, and four or five police officers strutted importantly about the premises.

Up in the study where Edward Norton had been murdered, Claude Drumm stared speculatively at Perry Mason.

"I don't know what you could ask for that is more fair than this," he said.

"Well," Perry Mason told him, "it doesn't seem particularly complete to me as a test. Don Graves has only a fifty percent chance of guessing wrong even if he were blindfolded."

"I don't see what you're getting at," said Claude Drumm with purposeful stupidity.

"You've got two women here," said Perry Mason, "one in a black dress and one in a pink dress. You've got three men, all of whom are known to Graves. Now the idea is, as I understand it, that Judge Purley will drive his car up the roadway at exactly the same rate of speed, as nearly as he can remember, that he drove it on the night of the murder. When the car reaches a certain position in the roadway, Judge Purley is to shout: 'Look!' And at that time Graves is to turn and look.

"After we have started up the roadway, the figures will arrange a pantomime. One of the three will stand with a club in his hand, and one of the women will stand so that her head, shoulder and arm are visible to a person going up the roadway."

"That is correct," said Drumm.

"Very well," said Perry Mason. "Now the point that I

am making is this: As far as the men are concerned, if Graves simply guessed, he would stand one chance in three of being right. As far as the women are concerned, if he simply guessed, he would stand an even chance of being right.''

''Well,'' said Drumm, ''you can't ask to have conditions any more favorable to your side of the case than they were at the time of the murder. Now there were only two women in the house at that time. There was Mrs. Mayfield, the housekeeper, and Frances Celane, your client. Now, it's conceded that there was a woman in the room at the time of the murder . . .''

''No it isn't,'' snapped Perry Mason.

''Well, according to my theory of the case, and according to the testimony of Don Graves, a disinterested witness, there was,'' said Drumm, ''and, if the test is going through, that has got to stand. Now that woman who was in the room either had to be Mrs. Mayfield or Miss Celane. Similarly, there were three men who might have committed the murder. There was Pete Devoe, the chauffeur, who was drunk when we found him, but who, nevertheless, was under suspicion; there was Rob Gleason, the defendant in the action, and Purkett, the butler. One of those three men must have been the one to swing the club.''

''That,'' said Mason, ''is taking for granted that the evidence of the footprints under the window, and the window that had been jimmied open, is evidence that was planted.''

''Of course it is,'' said Drumm. ''You wouldn't want us to have the whole city standing here in the room because there might have been someone in the city who had broken into the house. You can't have this thing all *your* way.''

''I should have it enough my way so that we can tell whether Graves uses his eyes, or whether it's just a lucky guess.''

Claude Drumm showed a glint of triumph in his eyes.

''I have arranged this test,'' he said, ''under circumstances which are identical to those which surrounded the commission of the crime. This test is made as the result of a challenge by you. Now, if you are afraid to have Graves go ahead with it, all you have got to do is to say so, and we'll call the test off, because you didn't dare to let the witness go through with it."

Mason shrugged his shoulders.

"Very well," he said, "if you're going to put it on that ground, go ahead."

The glint of triumph which had been in Drumm's eyes became a light of victory, and he grinned with blatant assurance.

"All right," he said to the compact group that had gathered about the two men, "I think you two gentlemen understand the situation perfectly. We are to go up the hill in the car. I will be seated in the back seat with Mr. Graves. Mr. Mason, the attorney for the defendants, will be seated in the front seat beside Judge Purley.

"After the car has started up the hill, you gentlemen of the press will select one of these women, who will stand so that her head, neck, shoulder and arm will be visible through the window, to anyone standing on the curve in the road at the point where Graves looks back. You will also select one of the three men, each of whom is attired in a distinctly different suit of clothes, to stand with a club in his hand, leaning over the chair in which Edward Norton was sitting when he was killed.

"I think that covers the situation. The reputation and integrity of Judge Purley will be sufficient to guarantee that whatever may happen in the automobile will not subsequently be distorted by either party."

Perry Mason said: "Just a minute. Before Don Graves leaves this room I want to have a confidential word with Judge Purley."

Drumm looked at him suspiciously.

"Not unless I am along," he said. "This is a test, and if you are going to have any confidential words with anyone, I'm going to hear what they are."

"I have no objection to your listening," said Perry Mason, "but naturally, inasmuch as this is a test, I *don't* want Don Graves to hear it."

"Very well," said Drumm. "You can wait here, Graves, until we call you."

"We'll blow the horn on the automobile," said Perry Mason, "when we are ready."

In frigidly dignified silence, the two opposing attorneys walked down the broad stairs, through the front door, and to the automobile where Judge Purley sat in ponderous dignity, surrounded by flashlight photographers, his face wearing an expression of satisfaction which he endeavored to conceal beneath the cloak of a judicial and ponderous dignity.

"Are you ready, gentlemen?" he asked.

"It is understood," said Perry Mason, "that I am to sit in the front seat with Judge Purley; that you, Mr. Drumm, are to sit in the rear seat with Don Graves?"

"That is so understood," said Drumm.

"Under those circumstances," said Perry Mason, "I am going to ask that you remove your glasses."

"That I what?" snapped the Deputy District Attorney.

"That you remove your glasses," Perry Mason said. "You will readily understand that if you are wearing your glasses so that your vision is fully corrected, and you should turn at the same time that Don Graves turns, it *might* be that by some involuntary exclamation or motion, you would signal Don Graves which one of the three men you thought was holding the club. In which case I should be having a test made with two pairs of eyes instead of one."

"That sir," said Claude Drumm, "is an insult to my veracity."

"No," said Perry Mason, "it is no such thing. It is merely a matter of precaution against an involuntary betrayal."

"I refuse to consent to it," said Drumm.

"Very well," said Perry Mason. "I shall not insist. I have merely mentioned the matter. One other thing is that I am going to ask Judge Purley to keep his eyes straight ahead on the road."

"No," said Drumm, "I am not going to consent to that condition, because when Judge Purley was driving the car on the night the murder was committed, and Don Graves gave his exclamation, it was only natural that Judge Purley should have looked back to see what it was that had caused the exclamation, and in doing this, he naturally slowed down the car, which gave Graves opportunity for a much longer and steadier look."

Perry Mason sighed wearily, after the manner of one who has been out-generaled.

"Very well," he said, "summon Graves."

Judge Purley pressed the button of the horn on the automobile.

They waited a few minutes, and Perry Mason reached over and again pressed the button of the horn.

There was still no Graves, and Judge Purley pushed his left palm imperatively against the button on the steering post of the car, looking expectantly up at the window.

There was a commotion for a moment, and then Don Graves stood in the window and shouted: "One of these newspaper reporters wants to change the conditions of the test."

Claude Drumm gave an exclamation, slammed open the door of the car, strode across the street, and stood under the window. "The conditions of that test were fully arranged when we left the room," he said. "Don't discuss the matter with any of the newspaper reporters. If they can't coöperate in this thing they'll be excluded. Come down here at once!"

"Very well, sir," Don Graves said, and left the window.

Almost at once Harry Nevers thrust out his head and called: "This test isn't fair. We should have the right to have one of the men stand where Graves claims the woman was standing, if we want to. That would determine whether Graves could actually see that the other occupant of the room was a woman. It might have been a man."

"In a pink negligee, eh?" sneered Drumm. "Now listen, the only function that you gentlemen have is to pick which one of the three men, and which one of the two women, will stand in that position. That was definitely understood, and that is the condition of the test. If an attempt is to be made to change it, I will call off the test."

"Oh, very well," said Nevers, "have it your own way. But it doesn't seem fair to me."

Don Graves came down the stairs, left the front door, and said in a low voice to Claude Drumm: "The man is drunk.

He made a nuisance of himself up there, but I didn't want to offend him because I didn't want his newspaper to roast me.''

"All right," snapped Drumm, "leave him to me. Are we ready?''

"All ready," said Perry Mason.

They took their positions in the automobile for the last time. Flashlights boomed up in puffs of dazzling flame as newspaper photographers took action pictures of the car pulling away from the curb.

Judge Purley snapped it through the gears and drove up the winding roadway at a fair rate of speed.

"It is understood," said Perry Mason, "that Don Graves will not look back until Judge Purley indicates the place on the road where Graves first gave his exclamation."

"So understood," snapped Drumm.

The car purred up the roadway, swinging around the curves.

"Now!" said Judge Purley.

Don Graves pushed his face up against the rear window of the automobile and cupped his hands around his eyes.

Perry Mason flashed a glance at the study window of the house.

The figures could be seen for a single brief glimpse, standing in position.

The car swept around the curve in the roadway, and the house vanished from view.

"I got it, sir," said Don Graves.

"Who was it?" asked Judge Purley, braking the car to a stop.

"The man in the blue serge suit with the dark hair, and the woman in the pink dress," said Don Graves.

Claude Drumm heaved a sigh.

"There, counsellor," he said to Perry Mason, "goes your defense in this case—blown to smithereens!"

Perry Mason said nothing.

Judge Purley sighed ponderously.

"I will now turn around and go back," he said. "I presume the newspaper people will want to make some more photographs."

"Very well," Drumm told him.

Perry Mason said nothing. His rugged face was expressionless. The patient, thoughtful eyes stared meditatively at the face of Judge Purley.

Chapter 25

The courtroom was jammed with spectators as Judge Markham marched in from the chambers in the rear of the bench.

"Stand up," shouted the bailiff.

The spectators arose and remained standing while Judge Markham strode to the judicial chair and the bailiff intoned the formula which convened the session of court.

Judge Markham sat down, and banged the gavel, and spectators, attorneys, jurors and defendants dropped into their seats.

The atmosphere of the courtroom was electric, but sympathies were all with the prosecution.

In man there is implanted a sporting instinct to side with the underdog, but this is in man, the individual. Mob psychology is different from individual psychology, and the psychology of the pack is to tear down the weaker and devour the wounded. Man may sympathize with the underdog, but he wants to side with the winner.

And the results of the test had been spread to the public through the pages of every newspaper in the city. It had been dramatic and spectacular. There had been about it something of the element of a gambling proposition. The defense had staked much on the happening of a certain event, on the turn of a single card, and it is human nature to crowd breathlessly forward as spectators when men are risking high stakes on a single card.

Therefore the reading public eagerly devoured the newspaper accounts of that which had happened. The outcome of the case was now a foregone conclusion. Don Graves had vindicated his ability to identify the occupants of the room from the exact point where he had seen the murder committed, and under exactly similar circumstances.

The gaze of the spectators in the courtroom had shifted now from the witnesses, and was fastened upon the defendants, particularly upon the shapely and slender figure of Frances Celane.

Old campaigners who have participated in hard fought legal battles will agree that this is the most ominous sign which a courtroom can give. When a case first starts, the attention of the spectators is fastened upon the defendants. They strain their necks with curiosity, watch the faces of the defendants for some flicker of expression which will convey a hint of their feelings. The average spectator likes to look at a defendant, try to visualize the defendant in the midst of the circumstances surrounding the crime, and reach an opinion as to the guilt or innocence of the prisoner, to the extent that he or she seems visually to fit into that picture.

Then, after the trial is under way, the auditors become interested in the unfolding of the story of the crime itself, in the battle over testimony. Their attention is centered upon the witnesses, upon the judge, upon the dramatic personalities of the attorneys as they match wits in legal arguments.

So long as the issue is in doubt, so long as the interest remains centered upon the outcome of the case, so long will the spectators continue to fasten their eyes upon the witnesses; upon the actors in the drama that is being unfurled. But let some event crash the testimony to a climax, remove the element of uncertainty, convince the spectators of the guilt of the defendant, and the eyes of the spectators will automatically shift to the defendant; not trying now to visualize how the defendant looked in the commission of the crime, but staring at the prisoner with that morbid curiosity which comes to men who look at one who is about to die. They like to terrify themselves by thinking of the morning when the inevitable hands will drag the protesting prisoner from the cell and march the lagging footsteps along that last grim walk.

It is the sign which lawyers dread, the verdict of these masses, the thumbs-down signal which shows the turning point has been passed, and that the prisoner is condemned.

Never a veteran trial lawyer who has fought his way through

the intricate web of many cases, but has learned to appreciate the dread portent of that shifting attention. Defendants do not know its fatal significance, often they smirk with satisfaction as they see themselves the sudden cynosure of the eyes of the spectators; but not so the attorney who sits at the counsellors' table, his law books piled in front of him, his face calm and serene, but his soul shrinking from the portent of that silent verdict.

In this case the silent verdict had been rendered. It was guilty of murder in the first degree for both defendants, and there was no recommendation of mercy.

Judge Markham's level tones cut the tense silence of the courtroom.

"Mr. Don Graves was on the witness stand," he said, "and was being cross-examined. The case was continued from last week, pursuant to a stipulation by counsel that a test was to be made with this witness—a test that had been suggested by the defense, and stipulated to by the prosecution.

"Gentlemen, do I understand that the results of that test were to be received in evidence?"

Claude Drumm rose to his feet and said sneeringly: "It was a test which was conducted with every possible degree of fairness to the defense, at the challenge of the defense, and pursuant to stipulation. It was participated in by this witness under conditions identical to those which surrounded the commission of the crime, and I asked that it be received in evidence."

Judge Markham looked at Perry Mason.

Perry Mason rose to his feet.

"If the court please," he said, "there is no objection to that. It is, however, not a part of my cross-examination. That is, it must come in as a part of the redirect examination of this witness, and the question is therefore not properly before the court at the present time. But, when the question does come before the court, if the District Attorney desires to examine this witness as to the test, *I shall make no objection*, subject, however, to the fact that I shall have the right to

213

cross-examine the various witnesses to that test, as to the actual circumstances surrounding it.''

It had been said of Judge Markham that the lawyer did not live who had ever brought an expression of surprise to the face of the magistrate when he was sitting in a court of law. Now Judge Markham stared at Perry Mason as though he would try to read what might be in the mind of the counsel for the defense, and his eyes were wide and thoughtful.

Perry Mason met his gaze calmly and placidly.

''Shall I proceed with the cross-examination of the witness?'' he asked.

''Proceed,'' snapped Judge Markham.

''You are familiar with the business affairs of Edward Norton?'' asked Perry Mason in an even monotone of passionless inquiry.

''I am fully familiar with all of those affairs,'' said Don Graves.

''You are then familiar with the expiration date of the insurance policy which lay upon the desk of Edward Norton?'' asked Perry Mason.

''I am.''

''What was the expiration date of that insurance policy?''

''The twenty-sixth of October of the present year.''

''Ah! Then the insurance policy expired but three days after the murder of Edward Norton?''

''That is correct.''

''Is it a fact, Mr. Graves, that you have some animus, some prejudice against the defendant, Frances Celane, in this case, due to the fact that she is married to Robert Gleason?''

The question came as a surprise, and there was that suppressed rustle of motion from the courtroom which indicates a sudden snapping to attention on the part of the spectators, a craning of necks, a pushing forward to the extreme edges of the seats.

''That is not true!'' protested Don Graves, with a show of feeling. ''I did everything I could to keep the name of Frances Celane out of this. I am testifying in this matter only because I was forced to court under a subpoena.''

"And you have no bias against Frances Celane for any other reason?"

"None."

"Or against Robert Gleason?"

"No. I hold no feeling of friendship for Robert Gleason because I know him but slightly; but for Miss Celane, my feelings are entirely different. I would not say a word in this courtroom which would connect her in any way with the murder of Edward Norton unless I knew absolutely and beyond all reasonable doubt that what I said was true and correct."

"No further questions," said Perry Mason, with the air of a man who has been defeated.

Claude Drumm got to his feet, and said with just a trace of a sneer in his air of triumph: "I have a few questions to ask upon redirect examination. You were asked upon cross-examination, Mr. Graves, whether you had ever made a test, under circumstances identical with the circumstances surrounding the murder of Edward Norton, to determine if you could recognize persons in the room where Edward Norton was murdered."

"Yes," said Don Graves, "I was asked that question."

"Since that question was asked you," persisted Claude Drumm, "have you made such a test under exactly identical circumstances?"

"I have," said Don Graves.

"Describe the circumstances under which that test was conducted, and the result of it," said Claude Drumm.

"The test was made at night," said Don Graves slowly, and in a low tone of voice, while spectators held their breath. "There were three men in Edward Norton's study and two women. One of the women was dressed in black, and one in pink. One of the men had on a blue serge suit, one had on a tweed suit, and one had on a plaid suit. I knew each one of the men, but had never seen the women before. There were present representatives of the press, and there were present Mr. Drumm, the Deputy District Attorney, also Perry Mason, the attorney for the defense."

"Then what happened?" asked Claude Drumm.

"Then," said Graves, still speaking in that low, strained voice, "we got in the automobile and went up the winding road which goes over the hills toward the main boulevard. When Judge Purley had the car at the place where it had been the night of the murder, when I gave the exclamation, he told me to look back. I looked back, and continued to look until the car had swung around the curve, and out of sight."

"What did you see?" asked Claude Drumm.

"I saw a woman, the one who had the pink dress on, standing in about the same position that Frances Celane was standing when Mr. Norton was killed, and I saw the man who wore the blue serge suit holding a club over the chair where Mr. Norton had sat on the night of the murder."

"Cross-examine the witness," said Claude Drumm triumphantly.

Perry Mason's voice was almost drawling.

"You haven't told *all* that happened there during the test, have you, Mr. Graves?"

"Yes sir, all of the important points."

"Wasn't there a newspaper reporter there who annoyed you and delayed you somewhat?" asked Perry Mason.

"Yes sir. There was a chap named Nevers, I believe, who kept insisting upon certain changes in the way the test was being made. I had no authority to make any change in the conditions of the test. Those were agreed upon between Mr. Drumm and yourself, and I told this reporter so. But he kept hanging on to me, even hooking his finger in the buttonhole of my coat, and holding me."

"Where were we at that time?" asked Perry Mason.

"You were down in the automobile."

"How did you finally get free from him?" Mason inquired.

"I called down to Mr. Drumm, and he told me definitely that there were to be no changes in the conditions under which the test was to be conducted. When this reporter heard Mr. Drumm make that statement, he seemed to realize that he was out of order, and let me go."

Spectators who had been straining their necks to listen, now glanced curiously at one another.

"That is all," said Perry Mason.

"Call your next witness, Mr. Drumm," said Judge Markham.

"Just a moment, Your Honor," interrupted Perry Mason. "Before the prosecution goes on, I would like to recall Arthur Crinston for further cross-examination."

"Very well," said Judge Markham. "The proceeding has been slightly irregular, but, under the circumstances, the matter being entirely in the discretion and control of the court, I will permit you to cross-examine any of the other witnesses that you may care to call. The court is not unmindful of the fact that various new conditions have entered into the case since your *very brief* cross-examination of the other witnesses."

Judge Markham could not resist a slight emphasis upon the words describing the brevity of the cross-examination; an emphasis which was in the nature of a very faint judicial rebuke to counsel who would so lightly dispose of the cross-examination of important witnesses in a murder case.

Arthur Crinston came forward, his face grave, his eyes solemn.

"You have already been sworn," said Perry Mason. "Just take your position in the witness chair, if you please, Mr. Crinston."

Mr. Crinston sat down, crossed his legs and turned to look at the jury.

"Mr. Crinston," said Perry Mason, "you were in conference with Mr. Norton on the night of the murder?"

"Yes, sir, I have already testified to that effect."

"Yes. You arrived there, I believe, at seven minutes past eleven, and left at about eleven thirty?"

"Yes," said Mr. Crinston, and went on to volunteer a statement: "I can fix the time of my arrival with certainty because Mr. Norton was a stickler for keeping appointments on time. I was seven minutes late for my appointment, and he pointed that matter out to me rather sarcastically."

"Yes," said Perry Mason. "And from seven minutes past eleven until eleven thirty you were in conference with Mr. Norton?"

"That is correct, yes sir."

"As a matter of fact, Mr. Crinston, wasn't that conference in the nature of a quarrel?"

"No sir, I don't think I can add anything to the statement that I made before, as to what was said at that time."

"Mr. Crinston, the partnership has an indebtedness at the Wheeler's Trust & Savings Bank of some nine hundred thousand dollars?"

"Yes sir."

"With deposits in that bank of only seventy-five thousand dollars."

"Yes sir, approximately that amount."

"Yet it has deposits of eight hundred and seventy-six odd thousand dollars at the Seaboard Second National Trust Company, and deposits of approximately two hundred and ninety-three thousand dollars at the Farmers & Merchants National Bank?"

"Yes sir."

"Now, Mr. Crinston, isn't it a fact that the indebtedness of nine hundred thousand dollars which was incurred at the Wheeler's Trust & Savings Bank on a promissory note which bears only your signature, was money that was borrowed without the knowledge of Mr. Norton, and was money that was not used for partnership purposes, but was used solely for your own individual speculations in the stock market?"

"No sir!" snapped Arthur Crinston. "That is not the case."

"Why was it necessary for the partnership to borrow nine hundred thousand dollars from one bank, when it had over a million in liquid assets in other banks?"

"That was because of certain business policies. We had some large purchases we were intending to make, and we desired to keep cash assets to that amount on deposit in those banks. We didn't wish to borrow from that particular bank or those particular banks, because we wanted to keep our cash there readily available. If we had made a large note at those banks and checked out all of our cash, there would have been some explanation required. Therefore, inasmuch as the Wheeler's Trust & Savings Bank had been very anxious to get our account, and had intimated that we could have an unlimited amount of short term credit, we executed the notes there."

"It is a fact, Mr. Crinston, is it not, that those notes at the Wheeler's Trust & Savings Bank came due some two days prior to Mr. Norton's death?"

"I believe so, yes sir."

"And the bank sent out notices through the mail, did it not?"

"I believe so, yes sir."

"And isn't it a fact that Mr. Norton received one of those notices on the day that he was killed?"

"I'm sure I can't tell you, sir."

"Isn't it a fact that on that day Mr. Norton knew for the first time of the indebtedness at this bank?"

"No sir."

"Isn't it a fact that Mr. Norton called you into conference that evening in order to tell you that he had given you a certain limited time to make restitution to the partnership, and, you having failed to make such restitution, Mr. Norton was going to notify the police?"

The spectators could see that Mr. Crinston was visibly worried. His face had turned a few shades whiter, and his knuckles showed white as his hand clenched tightly, but his voice remained even and steady.

"Absolutely not," he snapped.

"And," persisted Perry Mason in the same even, imperturbable tone, "isn't it a fact that when you advised Mr. Norton that you had been unable to make restitution, and could not do so, he took down the telephone receiver, called police headquarters and said: 'This is Edward Norton speaking. I have a criminal matter to report to you,' or words to that effect?"

"No sir," snapped Arthur Crinston, and his voice now, for the first time, showed the strain under which he was laboring.

"And," said Perry Mason, slowly rising to his feet, "isn't it a fact that when he had made that statement, you crashed a club down on his head and caved in his skull?"

219

"I object!" shouted Claude Drumm, getting to his feet. "This examination has gone too far afield. There is absolutely no ground for . . ."

"The objection is overruled," snapped Judge Markham. "Answer the question, Mr. Crinston."

"No, I did nothing of the kind!" shouted Arthur Crinston.

Perry Mason stood on his feet, staring at Arthur Crinston until the courtroom had grasped the full significance of the question, and all that it implied, until the spectators, leaning breathlessly forward, had made of the courtroom a vault of silence.

"And," said Perry Mason, "isn't it a fact that you then placed the receiver back on the hook, stared tremblingly about you, and suddenly realized that Edward Norton had given his name to police headquarters when he made his call and stated that he had a criminal matter to report—didn't you know then that when the body of Edward Norton was discovered, the police would check back and find a record of that call, knowing then the exact time that Mr. Norton had been killed, and being able to surmise something of the motive for his murder?"

"No sir," gulped Arthur Crinston, but his forehead was glistening in the light which came from the high windows of the courtroom, as the beads of perspiration oozed through his skin.

"And isn't it a fact that with the consciousness of guilt upon you, you knew that it was necessary to explain that call to the police in some way; that you saw the insurance policy lying on his desk; that you knew this insurance policy lay there because Mr. Norton, who was very methodical, had intended to make certain that the insurance had been renewed before the expiration date. Isn't it a fact that this insurance policy gave you an inspiration, and that you immediately called back the Police Headquarters and stated to the desk sergeant that you were Mr. Norton, who had just called; that you had been cut off, and that you desired to report the theft of an automobile, and that you then and there read the description of the Buick automobile from the insurance policy which lay upon Mr. Norton's desk?"

"No sir," said Arthur Crinston in a tone of mechanical defiance.

"And isn't it a fact that then the door opened, and Don Graves came into the room; that Don Graves had been your accomplice and assistant in connection with the embezzlement of the nine hundred thousand odd dollars which you had lost in speculations upon the stock market, using partnership funds to cover your individual losses? And isn't it a fact that you and Don Graves then and there fixed up a plan by which the murder of Mr. Norton would be blamed upon others?"

"No sir," came the same mechanical denial.

"Isn't it a fact that you knew that Judge Purley did not know Edward Norton personally, and therefore would not recognize his voice from the voice of any other man? Isn't it a fact that you and your accomplice, Don Graves, sneaked down to the room of Pete Devoe, the chauffeur, and planted evidence in that room which would have a tendency to connect Devoe with the murder? Isn't it a fact that you jimmied a window and left footprints in the loam on the soil outside of the window so that it would appear that Mr. Devoe had made a clumsy attempt to divert suspicion from himself?

"Isn't it a fact that you then went back to the study where the dead man was slumped across his desk, and that you arranged with Mr. Graves so that you were to go down the stairs and start for Judge Purley's automobile; that Mr. Graves was to raise the window in Mr. Norton's study, keeping the desk light well to his back, so that Judge Purley would see nothing but the blurred outline of a human form, and that Mr. Graves, pretending to be Edward Norton, would call down and ask you to take Don Graves in the automobile to your home, and that you then and there arranged that you would go to ask Judge Purley for his permission, and that Don Graves would then move away from the window, rush downstairs, and be standing by your side, while you pretended to call up to Mr. Norton, whom you pretended that you could see in the window, saying that it was all right, and Judge Purley had given his permission?"

"No sir," said Arthur Crinston.

"That," said Perry Mason, in tones that rang through the courtroom until they seemed to make the rafters in the ceiling vibrate, "is all the cross-examination I have of this witness."

Judge Markham glanced at Claude Drumm.

"Is there any redirect examination, counsellor?" he asked.

Claude Drumm made a sweeping gesture. "None, Your Honor. A very pretty theory has been advanced, but there has been no evidence to support it. The witness has denied . . ."

Judge Markham banged his gavel on the desk.

"Counsellor," he said, "you will make your argument to the jury at the proper time. The question of the court was whether there was any additional redirect examination. Your answer was in the negative, and the witness will stand aside."

"Recall Judge Purley for further cross-examination," said Perry Mason.

Judge Purley came to the witness stand. Gone was the judicial assurance which had clothed his manner earlier in the trial. His face was drawn and strained, and there was a haunting doubt in his eyes.

"You also have been sworn in this case, so there is no necessity for you to be sworn again," said Perry Mason. "Take your place on the witness stand."

Judge Purley heaved his big bulk into the witness chair.

"When this test was being made over the week end," said Perry Mason, in the tone of voice of one who is pronouncing a final and solemn judgment, "you sat in your automobile under the window of Edward Norton's study, in exactly the same place and position as that you occupied on the night of the murder, did you not?"

"I did, sir, yes, sir."

"And from that position, by craning your neck, you could see the study windows in Edward Norton's house?"

"Yes, sir."

"But because the top of the automobile was so low as to interfere with your vision, you could only see those windows by craning your neck, is that right?"

"Yes, sir."

"And isn't it a fact, Judge Purley, that while you were

222

seated there in that automobile, in exactly the same position that it occupied on the night of the murder, Don Graves came to the window of the study and called down to you, or to Claude Drumm, who was with you in the car?''

"Yes, sir,'' said Judge Purley, taking a deep breath.

"And isn't it a fact,'' thundered Perry Mason, extending his rigid forefinger, so that it pointed directly at Judge Purley, "that now the matter has been called to your attention, and your recollection has had an opportunity to check over the circumstances of what happened upon that fateful night of the murder, that you *now* realize that the voice which called down to you from that second story window on the night of the test, was the same voice which had called down from that window on the night of the murder?''

Tense, dramatic silence gripped the courtroom.

Judge Purley's hands tugged at the arm of the witness chair, and his face writhed in agony.

"My God!'' he said. "I don't know! I have been asking myself that question for the last ten minutes, and I cannot answer it satisfactorily to my conscience. All I know is that *it may have been*!''

Perry Mason turned half around and faced the jury. His steady, unwavering eyes surveyed the faces of the nine men and the three women.

"That,'' he said, in a tone of finality, "is all.''

For a long moment the courtroom remained silent, then there were rustlings, whispering, half-gasps. Somewhere in the background a woman tittered hysterically.

Judge Markham banged his gavel down on the desk.

"Order!'' he said.

Claude Drumm bit his lip in an agony of indecision. Dare he go into the matter on redirect examination, or dare he wait until he could talk privately with the Municipal Judge?

And, in that moment of indecision, in that moment when the attention of every human being in the courtroom was fastened upon him, Claude Drumm hesitated for one second too long.

The attention of the crowd shifted.

Perry Mason, leaning back in his chair, his eyes placidly

surveying the sea of faces, saw it shift. Judge Markham, sitting on the bench, wise in the ways of the courtroom, veteran of a hundred murder trials, saw it shift.

As with one motion, as though actuated by some subtle, psychic command, the eyes of the jurors, the eyes of the spectators, turned away from Claude Drumm, and fastened themselves upon the agonized face of Arthur Crinston.

It was the silent verdict of the courtroom, and that verdict exonerated the two defendants, and fixed the guilt of Edward Norton's murder squarely upon Arthur Crinston and his accomplice.

Chapter 26

Perry Mason sat in his office. The light from the window streaming in upon his rugged, virile features made him seem somehow older, brought out the strong lines of his face.

Frances Celane sat in the big black leather chair, her forefinger poking and twisting as she slid it along the smooth arm of the chair. Her eyes were dark and filled with emotion.

Robert Gleason stood leaning against the book case, his heavy, dark face twisted into that agony of silence which comes to those inarticulate men who have much to say, yet cannot find a means of expression.

Through the open windows, from the street below, came the cries of the newsboys, shouting their extra edition of the *STAR*.

Perry Mason tapped the newspaper on his desk; a paper which was still damp from the presses.

"That," he said, "is clever journalism. Nevers had that paper on the street before you had gone from the courthouse to my office. He had the thing all figured out and blocked out. All he needed to do was to add a brief summary of the testimony of Judge Purley, and the headlines."

He slid his forefinger along the headlines which streamed blackly across the top of the newspaper : "MURDER CASE DISMISSED."

Frances Celane said softly: "It wasn't the journalism in this case that was so remarkable, Mr. Mason; it was your wonderful analysis of what must have happened, and the steps you took to reconstruct the scene so that Judge Purley would be convinced. I watched him when he was on the witness stand the first time, and I could see the problem that you had with him."

Perry Mason smiled.

225

"Judge Purley," he said, "is rather opinionated, and he would very much have disliked having to confess himself in error. In fact, if I had asked him that question the first time he was on the witness stand, he would have indignantly denied that such could have been the case, and the denial would have so impressed itself upon his own mind, that no amount of subsequent testimony could ever have caused him even to entertain the faintest notion that he might have been mistaken.

"But the fact that I managed to duplicate the conditions in such a manner that his mind was totally unprepared for what was taking place, gave me the opportunity to approach him on a blind side, so to speak.

"Of course," went on Perry Mason, "I had all of the facts in hand at the moment that Arthur Crinston, in telling me about the murder, discussed the telephone call to the police as though he had no knowledge of it, except what he had learned through the police.

"That was the slip that Crinston made, and the fatal slip; that, and failing to report that telephone conversation in his testimony to the jury.

"You see, he was so obsessed with the idea that he must keep the authorities from knowing what had transpired in that room when Norton was murdered, that he made up a story out of whole cloth, and stuck to it.

"That is not skillful lying. It is not the proper way to commit perjury. The skillful perjurer is he who sticks to so much of the truth as is possible, and only departs from it when it becomes absolutely necessary. These men who make up stories out of whole cloth usually leave a few loose threads somewhere.

"Yet it is a strange thing about the human mind: It has many facts constantly thrust upon it, and it doesn't properly correlate those facts. I had the facts at my command for some time before I knew what must have happened.

"You see, Crinston had borrowed heavily on the partnership credit. The partnership was, of course, solvent, but Crinston's credit as an individual was all shot to pieces. He had made Graves an accomplice, and, together, they were

226

deceiving your uncle; but when the bank sent the notice to your uncle, then Edward Norton learned for the first time what had happened.

"We can imagine what happened next. He gave Mr. Crinston a definite deadline, at which time Crinston was to have returned the money, or else be reported to the police. When Crinston failed to make the payment, your uncle, acting with that cold-blooded efficiency which is so absolutely merciless, picked up the telephone and called Police Headquarters.

"Crinston sat there behind him, watching dumbly, knowing that the words which Norton was to say next would lead to his confinement in a penal institution. He heard Norton say: 'Police Headquarters, I have a criminal matter to report,' and then Crinston acted upon a blind, murderous impulse. He struck Norton down without warning and probably without any great amount of premeditation.

"When he had done that and hung up the receiver, he suddenly realized that the police must have a record of that call which Norton had sent in, and that this would lead to his detection. So he did a very clever thing. He called Police Headquarters right back and pretended that he was Norton. He had to have something to report in the nature of a criminal matter, because your uncle had already said that he had such a report to make.

"The policy of automobile insurance was lying on the desk, and Arthur Crinston plunged blindly into that lead. Then, when you heard of your uncle's murder, and knowing that Rob Gleason had been in the house with you, and that there might be some possibility you would either be implicated, or have to explain what Gleason was doing there, you seized at what seemed to be the best opportunity to establish an alibi for yourself, by stating that you had been driving the Buick automobile at the time that your uncle reported it lost.

"On the face of it, it was almost mathematical. In other words, a man with a trained mind, sitting down and concentrating upon the evidence, should have been able to point his finger to the murderer at once. Yet I confess that the circumstances were so dramatic and so unusual that I was confused

227

for some little time, and failed to realize what must have happened.

"When I did realize it, I knew that I was up against a most serious problem. I felt certain that I could explain my theory well enough to raise a reasonable doubt in the minds of the jury, and get either an acquittal or a hung jury, but I realized also that unless I could trap the murderers into betraying themselves, I could never entirely remove the stigma of doubt from your names.

"I recognized at once that Judge Purley was the key witness, and knew that the man's conceit and love of posture, would render any ordinary cross-examination futile. Therefore, I had to devise some means by which a doubt would be raised in his own mind before he knew that the doubt was there, and then crash it home to him with dramatic force."

Fran Celane got to her feet with tears showing in her eyes.

"I can't begin to tell you," she said, "what it has meant to me. It's been an experience that will always leave its imprint."

Perry Mason's eyes narrowed. "You're lucky," he said, in a tone of tolerant patience, "to have escaped with nothing but an unpleasant experience."

Frances Celane smiled and blinked tears back as she smiled. "I didn't mean it that way, Mr. Mason. I meant that it has been an experience I wouldn't have missed for anything!"

He stared at her.

"I mean it," she said. "Not the murder trial, but the being in jail, getting a glimpse of the sufferings of other people. It gave me a chance to see things in a different light. I think it's helped cure my fiendish temper.

"And then it brought out the loyalty in Rob. He knew that I couldn't be guilty, but he knew that the evidence was against me, and that I stood a chance of being convicted. In those dark hours when you didn't take us into your confidence and things seemed to be stacking up so much against us, he came forward and was willing to give his life to save mine."

"Yes," said Perry Mason, looking thoughtfully at Rob Gleason, "it was a noble and magnanimous thing to do, but

228

if I hadn't been sure of my theory of the case, he would have thrown me entirely off my stride. His confession was most convincing, save for the fact that he claimed he had taken the thousand dollar bills from the body. I knew that he couldn't have done that, because you had given me ten of those bills the next morning. And then you, Miss Celane, weren't frank with me. You kept certain things back, trying to protect yourself.''

''I know it,'' she told him. ''It was all on account of that first lie about the Buick automobile. I couldn't tell the truth after that. I grabbed at the story about being out in the automobile as the best way to prove an alibi, and then I found I was trapped. I couldn't even tell you about getting the money from my uncle, because I was supposed to have been out in the automobile at that time.''

There was a knock at the door, and Della Street entered the room.

She looked at Perry Mason with eyes that were starry with pride. When she spoke, her voice had something of caressing tenderness in it.

''There is a telegram for you,'' she said.

Frances Celane walked quickly across to Perry Mason and extended her hand.

''Rob and I will be going,'' she said, ''and there's no use trying to tell you how much we appreciate what you've done. We can compensate you financially, but in addition to that we want you to know . . .''

Her voice shook, and there were tears in her eyes.

Perry Mason gripped her hand, then nodded. ''I know,'' he said.

When the door leading from his private office to the corridor had closed on them, he turned to Della Street.

''Here,'' she said, ''is the telegram. If you can make sense from it, you can do more than I can.''

He took the telegram and read:

''SENDING YOU SPECIAL DELIVERY AIR MAIL PHOTOGRAPH
OF UTMOST IMPORTANCE IN CASE I AM ABOUT TO PRESENT.

229

KEEP PHOTOGRAPH AND AWAIT ME IN YOUR OFFICE WITH-
OUT FAIL.

(Signed) EVA LAMONT."

Perry Mason stared at the telegram curiously.

"Did the photograph come?" he asked.

"Yes," she said, "a few minutes ago." She opened a drawer in her desk and took out a photograph. It was the photograph of a young woman, generously displaying a beautiful pair of legs. Below the photograph was a typewritten caption which had been pasted to it. The caption said, simply: "THE GIRL WITH THE LUCKY LEGS."

The photograph did not show the woman's face, merely her shoulders, hips, arms, hands, which held the skirts very, very high, and the legs. They were slim, straight legs, perfectly formed, stockinged and gartered.

"Now," said Perry Mason, his curiosity aroused, "what the devil does *that* mean?"

"I don't know," said Della Street, "but I'm going to make a file—*The Case of the Girl With the Lucky Legs.*"

Perry Mason looked at his watch. The weariness had dropped from his face, and his eyes were sparkling.

"I wonder," he said, "just what time Eva Lamont is due here."

About the Author

Erle Stanley Gardner is the king of American mystery fiction. A criminal lawyer, he filled his mystery masterpieces with intricate, fascinating, ever-twisting plots. Challenging, clever, and full of surprises, these are whodunits in the best tradition. During his lifetime, Erle Stanley Gardner wrote 146 books, 85 of which feature Perry Mason.

Also by
ERLE STANLEY GARDNER